SAY

YOU

WANT

ME

SAY

YOU

WANT

ME

RICHARD
COHEN

SOHO

Library of Congress Cataloging-in-Publication Data

Cohen, Richard, 1952–
Say you want me.
I. Title
PS 3553.0462S28   1988   813-'54
ISBN 0-939149-12-5   88-4492

Design and composition by The Sarabande Press

To John and Christopher

Special thanks to Ann Althouse, Susan Bergholz, Peter Clagnaz, Jay Clayton, Diana Finch, Laura Hruska, Juris Jurjevics, and Alice Sohn.

SAY

YOU

WANT

ME

1

We lived in Brooklyn, just a block from Prospect Park. From the park to the East River a long hill of well-kept townhouses descended, and on a sunny day the sky gleaming in the row of clean windows looked like a staircase of blue glass. If you woke up in the middle of the night and looked across the street through the slats of your cherrywood shutters, your palm cold from the glass of milk you were drinking to help you back to sleep, you wouldn't see a light on in any other house.

In the mornings I took Jeff to the playground. There was a great playground near the Third Street entrance to the park. As you curved down the cobbled path between two hills, you heard time-honored cries like, "Watch out with that water gun!" or "Come get your juice!" Jeff was eighteen months old: being able to walk was the thrill of the season, and while he only knew how to say about ten words, he asked the name of every piece of litter on the ground.

"Dat?"

"That's half a pair of sunglasses."

"Dat?"

"That's a surgical glove."

"Dat?"

"Those are styrofoam S's that someone has thoughtfully strewn around the garbage can. See? S. This is the letter S."

"S!" he said, and swaggered down the ramp into the playground, in the pride of new knowledge.

The day that I'm thinking of was a sunny October morning after a night of rainshowers. There were only a few other people in the place, which made it feel roomy and intimate. There were puddles on the cement, and black tire-tracks of bicycles leading away from the puddles. The metal swings were rain-gleaming and empty. The sand was damp and clumpy, the kind that sticks to the stitches of your jeans and somehow ends up in your cuffs, heavy as acorns. It was a texture Jeff particularly liked, because he could pack it into his red pail in big, clayey handfuls that wouldn't collapse when he overturned it.

A pyramid of unstained redwood overlooked the sand. I sat on its steps, watching Jeff and the sky and the trees, and trying to clear my mind so I could think about the composition of a picture I was having trouble with. I'm a commercial illustrator by trade, and I was also a full-time, all-day father. I was proud of how I was bringing up Jeff. It was only my own life I wasn't sure about.

I was still trying to get established in my field, and I didn't know whether my career problems had come from devoting myself so much to Jeff, or whether I was devoting myself to Jeff because of my career problems. When I told myself that raising Jeff was as important as other men's office work, or as my own art, I was never certain I'd convinced myself. But I did know that this kid, whom I loved more than anyone, was going to become gradually more distant from me, year by year, if his upbringing was any good. There would only be a few months out of his life when we would be an inseparable pair, true companions, when he would gravitate toward me with a smile of first love and without the acquired pulling-away of a son from his father. And they would be these months, in this place I complained about so much, when we took fifteen minutes walking two blocks to the playground every goddamn morning.

I heard him crying.

4

"Hilary, give the boy back his pail," said a woman's voice from behind the pyramid.

Jeff was moaning, looking around at me for help. Too young to know about hitting people, he thrashed his arms in the air as if they were hot.

As I stood up to go to him, I saw a good-looking, small, skinny brunette walk into view from the other side of the redwood pyramid. I'd never seen her in the playground before.

She knelt down and did a smooth job of taking Jeff's red pail away from her daughter without making her cry. That was my professional appraisal—I admired people who did this job well. She gave Jeff his pail back, tousled his wavy, light brown hair, and walked away, up the pyramid, two steps at a time, leaving him smiling after her in wonder. A looming maternal creature had restored his pail! I watched her skinny, quick legs, in straight blue jeans, as she went up.

"Hilary!" I said, by way of pleased comment. "I like the name Hilary. It was one of the names we were thinking of if we'd had a girl."

"What name did you use when you had a boy?"

"Jeff."

Jeff looked up, hearing his name spoken, and the woman waved to him animatedly, as if she really had called him. He waved back, laughing. He liked her.

"We were thinking of Jeff if we had a boy," she said. "Amazing!"

"I guess it is amazing," I said, and what I really meant was, it was amazing how a stranger was making me glow about a silly, meaningless coincidence that would scarcely be worth telling Lila about. Lila and I, wineglasses poised over the dinner table, would have smiled ironically about anyone who placed importance on such a coincidence. But now I was thinking: It does mean something that we chose the same names for our kids. It means we have similar minds.

Hilary's mother had urgent, pale gray eyes, and black lashes that made them look very bright. She had black hair that turned

5

under at her shoulders. She was in her early twenties, five feet tall, and thin enough to fit on the children's slide without squeezing. She was the kind of modern woman who excites you with the wings of her pelvis, the knobs of her wrists. Now she sat at the top of the shiny, damp slide, rocking back and forth as if she wanted to leap off and fly straight over the playground fence and past the whole neighborhood. She was wearing a blue satin baseball jacket with "Brooklyn" on it: a replica of an old Brooklyn Dodgers jacket, still available in local stores a generation after the team moved west. She had a Brooklyn accent, too, unlike those of us who moved here recently because we couldn't afford to stay in Manhattan.

"Look how nice they're playing together," she said.

"Well, of course—they're great kids. We made them."

We laughed. And when our eyes met, I didn't obey the usual polite reflex and break contact after a couple of seconds. Her gray running shoes, on the aluminum slide, tapped each other as if unaware of me, but our glances locked. Her look was telling me, not that she liked me personally—we didn't know each other well enough for that—but that our being of different sexes was a happy difference. It was a look that a single man gives and receives all the time; but in this place, where we were supposed to be overridingly devoted to our kids—where the most admired human quality was marital stamina—it was unusual. It reminded me of what I used to be.

Jeff was climbing up the redwood pyramid to try to get to the top of the slide. He kept his head raised to keep his eyes on Hilary's mother, his goal. I followed behind him, as I always did, to catch him if he slipped.

"Hey, Mr. Big!" she said when he reached the top step. And as a matter of fact he *was* Mr. Big, in my eyes. His birth weight was more than mine had been; he was a potentially larger person. He had my broad face and wavy hair, but he would get height from Lila's side of the family. With his red sweater on, his torso looked burly; with his hands on the top step and his rear end sticking out, he looked like a football player to me.

6

"Mr. Big, get over here!" She stretched out her arms to him. And to my surprise—for he was sometimes hesitant with strangers—he rushed forward to let her grab him and put him in her lap. They slid down the slide together, the woman's blue denim soaking up the beads of water, and landed with an explosion of clumps of sand that made Hilary, who was tunneling her hand and sulking, turn around.

That was when I felt it. It wasn't just that in the midst of laughing and playing together, I felt a sexual impulse and wondered what her body felt like, what she looked like naked. I could wonder in that way about any young mother in the playground, and not think about it twice. But I wanted to kiss this woman so bad, I wondered how I would stay alive without it. A sweet, hungry, crying, public kiss, this minute, in front of three or four other mothers and their children. I wanted to say to her, as part of normal playground conversation: "If I could taste your mouth it would save my life." I felt unsteady on my legs; the breeze at the top of the slide felt dangerous, and for a second or two, as if in harmony with my penis, my head swelled as large and tall as a cloud, and I could stretch my arm out from the top of the slide to the sand below and pull her up to me and we would stand fused at the top of the pyramid . . .

Then it began to subside.

I looked away from her, at the sky above the road where a jogger jogged. I felt as if I were landing after dropping through the air a long way: landing on strange ground, short of breath, and looking at everything from a distance. I glanced down at Jeff. My son! I thought, and was rather surprised he was still the way I remembered him.

Hilary's mother knelt down to retie Hilary's shoelace. When she stood again, she coughed, and rubbed the tip of her nose with two fingers, making a face.

She's just an average nice-looking woman, I told myself.

Is she just an average nice-looking woman or someone who can send waves of desire over me?

I'll tell Lila about this, I thought. Sophisticated, ironic: "Listen

7

to what happened to me in the playground today. I think the isolation is turning me into a schoolboy again."

I'd been coming to this place for almost a year, and had never been affected like this before. I was used to being the only man among women, and my survival strategy was: smile politely and don't get too close. Whatever sexual fantasies I had about them were just to keep my mind occupied during the time when I had nothing to do except watch Jeff and make sure he didn't hurt himself. I assumed that the mothers had some sexual fantasies about me in return, but it didn't make me think seriously of carrying anything out. It was just a way of making parenthood easier for each other, like borrowing diapers when we were caught short.

The mothers and I usually limited our conversations to pleasantries about whose toy was whose. Even when we talked more lengthily about the local nursery schools or pediatricians, or the stages of development our children were at, we rarely gave any information about our own selves. If I knew some of their names, it was from overhearing them talk to each other. I heard them making plans to join health clubs together, arranging to meet for lunch in each other's apartments, trading elliptical jokes about their husbands. None of them ever even asked me my name or what I did for a living. It used to anger me to hear them forging these close, sisterly bonds while they acted like I wasn't even there.

But when other fathers showed up, we tended to be reserved with each other; we didn't know quite how to act. Man-talk would be out of place and we didn't want to start doing woman-talk. The less accustomed fathers, who came only when they had a day off, tended to sit on the blue and orange benches on the side, uncomfortably reading the newspaper and shouting instructions to their children from afar. On weekends, of course, there were quite a few fathers, and if Lila and I came here together, we would give each other elbow nudges when we thought we spotted some Divorced Dad cruising the sandbox in search of Single Moms. But on weekdays, the playground was heavily into marriage, and everyone was careful and knew their obligations, and desire was kept out just as dogs were kept out.

But I kept sneaking looks at Hilary's mother, asking myself: "Do you still feel it?"

I wanted to go up to one of the other women and point her out. I wanted to ask: "Who is that woman? Have you seen her here before? Do you think she's pretty? Do you think that this fragile-looking, skin-and-nerves type of woman is a type that appeals to me without my having known it before, or do you think that I was just ready, today, for someone?"

Then, as had to happen, we drifted to different areas of the playground. The movements of parents within this fence were dictated by the movements of their children, and children didn't stay in one place very long. Hilary wanted to push a tire swing; Jeff wanted to chase a brown and white pigeon that was separated from him by an obstacle course of puddles. I followed him halfway around the playground: we stopped to look at the water droplets traveling down the links of the fence, and at the concrete tables with chessboards built into their tops. By the time we got back to the redwood pyramid, Hilary and her mother were sitting at the other end of the sand, playing with an abandoned blue dump truck, their backs to us.

"What do you want to do now?" I asked Jeff.

"Doh."

"Yes, 'Go.' Yes, you're right." I gave a loud clap of my hands, so Hilary's mother would hear me. "You're absolutely right, Old Bean, it's time to go."

Hilary's mother didn't turn around. She was making the blue dump truck hop along the wall of the sand pit. I stood lingering.

"Doh! Doh!"

"Okay, okay. We're going now," I announced.

I looked at the folds of light blue satin on her back, and the faded darker blue denim on her ass. Well, what did I expect her to do, turn around and plead with me not to leave?

I went over to where Jeff's stroller was parked, and kicked the brake levers to release them. Then I turned the stroller over to him. He didn't ride in it much anymore, he mostly liked to push it, imitating his Daddy. He pushed it up the exit ramp, and when the incline got too steep, I got behind him and gave a helping push, his faithful father again.

We started on the cobbled path. But when we had gone a little way up the hill, Jeff stopped and turned around.

"Dound! Dound!" He pointed, looking at me for verification.

"Yes, that's the playground, that's where we just were."

The shiny-fenced place where he spent so many of his mornings was fixed in view. He laughed as if his world had been put in order.

"Yes, the swings, the slide, the sand. We played there with Hilary and her mother . . . Come on, don't you want to eat lunch?"

I walked forward in a rush. But Jeff, with the stroller, dawdled behind. Every few yards, he stopped to kick a pile of brown leaves, or watch a gray squirrel cling upside down to the bark of an oak, or just to see what it was like to bang his wheels into the wooden curb. He looked for his friends—the half-pair of sunglasses, the surgical glove, and the styrofoam S's; but it was basically a well-maintained park, and a sanitation crew had already taken them away.

Every time he stopped, I had to look downhill, through the playground fence, to find that blue baseball jacket and that head of black hair. And the last time, before the curve of the hill blocked our view, from a hundred yards away, Hilary's mother was looking right at me.

2

"It's Mommy!" I said when the wrought iron gate in the front yard swung open and Lila's legs stopped in front of our ground-level windows. Jeff and I rushed to the apartment door together, but as soon as Lila turned the knob, Jeff had the wit to march away and start rolling a foam soccer ball against the side of the sofa. I, on the other hand, stood at the threshold, thrilled by the sight of her and needing a kiss.

"What a greeting," she called to Jeff over my shoulder. "Don't you even come to see Mommy?"

She gave me my kiss and walked by in her brown business suit. She knelt beside Jeff and set down her briefcase. Laughing in apprehension of kisses, Jeff clutched his soccer ball tight.

"You hang around with Daddy all day and you forget about me? Does Daddy coach you to run away from me?"

"As a matter of fact," I said, "I just got through our daily session of telling him how horrible you are."

She stuck out her tongue at me; we laughed. But Lila was the kind whose eyes watered even at a play insult. She looked, not exactly stung, but afraid that I had intended to sting.

"Your Daddy is hostile," she told Jeff.

She gave me a pat on the ass on her way to the bedroom closet to change clothes. I sat on the living room sofa, drumming my fingers, feeling that strange mixture of joy and restlessness I always felt when my wife came home. Craning my head, I could see, through two doorways, Lila getting down to bra and slip, then taking off slip and stockings, and her reflection in the closet mirror doing the same things. I'd seen her perform the same actions hundreds of times, day after day, but I still liked to watch her. In the five minutes between the time the wrought iron gate swung open and the time she got her sweatshirt and jeans and socks on, I was so flushed with conflicting emotions I could feel my skin get warmer, as if I too had put on sweatclothes.

"Day?" I asked when she re-entered the living room.

"Medium. It was quiet at the office, but we're going to have a *working dinner* when he gets back from Houston Friday."

I groaned. "Well, maybe I can do some drawing Friday evening. If he goes to bed on time." There were two "he's" who ran our schedules: Lila's boss and Jeff.

Lila was an operations manager for a very oily oil company. We rarely reminisced anymore about the summer when she used to come home from work in a sweaty-underarmed waitress's uniform and change into maybe a daffodil yellow T-shirt, maybe into an aster purple T-shirt—a T-shirt with no bra underneath!—and we walked barefoot toward ice cream down the sidewalks of a Vermont college town. That was when we were just falling in love. My hands got motor oil stains on the cone, and vanilla and peach dripped over my dirty fingers. I was on vacation from art school, and she from art history. We used to walk down a street where the town ended, step off a cracked pavement onto a field, and sit with our legs stretched toward mountains that were round-topped and green and crisscrossed with yellow ski trails. We'd lick the ice cream off each other's lips. "Uh-oh, you've got ice cream on your lips." Lick, lick. "That's better." We would watch the sun go down behind the mountain. Then we walked home holding hands in mountain shadow under blue sky, and tell ourselves the story of how we had fallen in love.

We had sat two seats apart in Italian Renaissance all term; but when spring came, the guy between us started skipping classes and changed our lives. I moved into the seat next to hers, partly to get a better view of the slides. The lights were out most of the period, and when they were on, we both had our heads in our notebooks, but soon enough I noticed that in her narrow and serious profile was the quickest and sweetest dimple I'd ever seen. It flashed not just when the professor made a joke, but when the lights came on and Lila was all fogged in smiles because a man five hundred years ago had painted well. I decided that I was going to learn how to arouse her dimples too.

Neither of us thought that we were going to end up with each other permanently. In fact it was so clearly juvenile, our college infatuation, that we used the expression, "When we grow up," to mean, "When we break up." We thought we were training each other for lives that wouldn't really begin until we were self-sufficient enough to part. A couple of years after graduation, we were such different people from how we'd started out, we didn't understand how we could still be compatible. But to our surprise, we kept being compatible, we kept staying together.

This year, she had been made second in charge of the movement of all her company's oil tanker traffic between the Persian Gulf and the Atlantic Coast. From a gangly bookworm who sucked the ends of her hair while writing term papers, she had evolved into a person who knew about foreign currency and banking, tariffs, ship specifications, admiralty law, computerized traffic control, satellite communications, accounting, the merchant marine, the politics of Arab sheikdoms, the causes and prospects of the Iran-Iraq war, and why certain people in her company were being fired and others promoted. I had gotten to know a little about those subjects too, and when she told me more about them than I really wanted to know, over the last glass of Rhone, I smiled at how worldly and capable she had become, and asked:

"Is it time for his bath?"

By the time Jeff had been bustled through his evening's round of upkeep, and Lila and I had stood by his crib singing him a song with his hand curled around my thumb, until his grip loosened and he fell asleep, the wine had burnt out inside us and it was too late to drink coffee. We sat at opposite ends of our white Haitian cotton sofa, searched the TV channels for a minute, then turned the set off. We talked about Saudi Arabia, then I took out the garbage, then we entered the bathroom together and brushed our teeth standing side by side. We went to bed early, listened to a call-in psychotherapist on the radio counseling a woman who kept falling in love with the wrong men, then turned it off. We lay in bed, face up, and I tried to think of the best way to paint the ocean.

"What's the matter?" she asked.

"Nothing. What do you mean?"

"I thought you might be in a bad mood."

"No, not at all." The lamb chops had been broiled nice and rare, the Rhone robust and complex, Jeff's bedtime smooth and successful.

"You're not mad because I'll have to work late Friday?"

"If I minded every time you worked late," I said, "we would have broken up years ago."

But suddenly, pressing her smooth, long fingers in the dark, I realized that I probably *did* get sad every time she worked late: that must be why I got so little painting done those evenings. I wanted to tell her about it—how I still missed her after all these years—but I was afraid she would say something satirical, or worse, that she would give a burdened sigh.

She said, "I wish I could be home as much as you. You know Jeff better than I do. The other women at work are always asking me about you; they envy me. Their husbands are all business-men, and if they ever have a kid at all, it'll be raised by some nanny. They all think you're the greatest, taking care of Jeff—really."

"Have them call me for a date," I said, and glided my fingers along her long, slim flank.

"We still get along, don't we?" she asked.

I stopped my hand on her pelvic bone. "Of course."

"I just like to know," she said in a voice so frail it startled me.

"You know." I encircled her wrist with one finger and thumb, as if telling her that we were so close we could communicate with the faintest touch. "But . . ."

"What?"

"Lila, don't you sometimes feel you've outgrown me?"

"No! I don't think that!"

"But don't you have to? I mean here you are, a big executive—"

"I'm not!"

"You will be. You're destined to be. You're part of this high-powered business world which I'm not part of. Those women at your work—don't they ever ask you what an upscale business-woman like yourself is doing married to an impoverished artist? Don't you ever think, 'Oh, yes. Brendan. I met him in my confused youth. Before I attained poise.'"

"I don't consider myself poised."

"I know you tell me that. Very feminine of you, I'm sure. But it's pretty clear that I'm the junior spouse."

"Oh, horrors, that a man should be the junior spouse!"

"Oh, come on. I don't mean—"

"I think you do, Brendan. But I'll let it go, in my weak and soft-hearted but somehow smothering and oppressive female way— that's the way you see us, isn't it?"

"No, it's not. You know, I'm not one of these stereotypical males you read about in your magazines, and I don't know what good it's going to do you to talk to me like one. You're talking to some stereotype in your mind instead of to me, this person, here. I can't stand that."

"I know you're an individual, Brendan. So am I. That's why we can stay together despite some superficial differences—which I don't know why you dwell on so much if you're so profound. It's also why I don't see our marriage as a hierarchy, a contest, or any other sort of competition."

"Yes, but what if it is? I mean, by its very nature? What if it has to be, in every case? Doesn't that make you kind of willfully blind? And—if my hypothesis is true, okay?—wouldn't your pretence, that it isn't, just serve your own ends in the competition?"

"I don't know. I don't want to talk about that right now. I don't know how to convince you of this, but it's true, it's my deepest conviction, and it will just hurt my feelings so much if you don't believe me—but I don't see you as the junior spouse. I wouldn't want to be married unless the man and I were truly equal. And I feel we are."

I touched the point of her shoulder with the tips of two fingers. "But don't you agree we have less in common than we used to?"

"We have a *child* in common!"

"Yes, but ourselves. Don't you feel that you've gone past me? Admit it. You have to, it's a fact. Your career is booming, you feel less and less at ease with me . . ."

"Don't tell me how I feel!" she shouted. I shushed her so we wouldn't wake Jeff, and she continued in a very soft voice. "I don't know why you say these things. Are you testing me? Trying to get me to say I still want you? Or that I don't want you? Just tell me which answer you want, and I'll give it to you. Will that satisfy you?"

"I want you to give me your own answer," I whispered. "Say you do, or admit you don't. One or the other, at least make it clear!"

"I thought it was clear."

I fell silent. When it grew unbearable, I stroked her shoulder, and ran my fingers down to the hollow of her elbow, up and down her beautiful arm. We moved closer. Our feet touched.

"I'm sorry," I said. "I just feel agitated, I feel belligerent for some reason. It's not you. Okay?" I waited for her to answer. "Okay?"

"I remember things you used to say. You used to say, 'People don't get along any better than we do. We know each other, we like to be with each other, we have intimate talks.' I guess this is one of our wonderful intimate talks?"

"I guess so," I said quietly. "And we'll probably be doing it for decades. Do other people have more than that?"

It seemed to me that every couple was living in its own burrow and didn't know what the others were doing. You burrowed forward, in faith or doubt. For decades.

"We're doing great for first-time parents," I said, feeling obliged to add a piece of positive evidence.

Under the blanket, she grasped my hand. "It's good to keep that in mind."

My hand got all kinds of memories from hers. I remembered when even under a blanket, her skin would be cool from the winter air coming through the window cracks in our Vermont bungalow. We stayed there a couple of years after college: I had this idea about wanting to paint in rural poverty, and Lila—God, she was young then!—stayed with me. She worked as a waitress in a country inn. I pumped gas, and posted signs in the local stores to advertise art lessons. We sat home in the wintertime a lot more than we skied, and we drove a rattly old van that seemed to take half an hour to warm up.

Then came her inspiration to move to New York and get a business degree. The night she decided on it, we hug-danced all around the living room and shouted good-bye to maple sugar, ski traffic, foliage traffic, and everything else we could think of to scorn in that little paradise. It was the best inspiration either of us had ever had. It solved all our problems in one stroke. At last we'd make money. We'd be able to afford a family: afford Jeff, whom we'd talked about for years before we ever had him. I'd be able to buy Winsor-Newton paints and linen canvas. I'd be living in the capital of art, and would have barroom conversations with strangers who would turn out to be the owners of West Broadway galleries . . .

The thing I admired most about Lila was her ability to remake herself. All her childhood, she told me, she'd been gawky and too tall, with dumb eyeglasses, and stringy brown hair she couldn't stop twirling and sucking. She'd been the kind of girl who giggled too much when boys came near, and who not only read books but tried to tell other children about them as a way of opening conversations. But in high school, when it was too late to spoil her, she saw that she was becoming beautiful. Reading fashion magazines, she saw pages full of women who were just as tall and lanky as she, who were considered highly desirable. Here was one, a famous, wealthy one, who had the same kind of narrow, oval face as Lila, except that the model was a blonde.

After high school graduation, when she was sure the people in her home town would never mean anything to her again, she did some very easy things. She bleached her hair. She got contact lenses. And she developed her uniform of tight black jeans, pastel sweatshirts with the sleeves pushed up, and brightly colored socks. She went to college as a freshly self-made beauty.

It wasn't a frivolous thing. It was something she did to give her the confidence she needed in order to do serious work. It was really her first step toward becoming a great businesswoman.

And tonight, with our bedroom overheated like all middle class apartments, I remembered the good winter drafts in our Vermont house, and wondered why, when Lila came home from work these days, I was thrilled for a few minutes but then felt as if she, or I, or something, needed another makeover.

"It seems like we're always in bed," she said suddenly. "We're alive, but we're lying here, just a shade away from total darkness."

"From death," I said melodramatically, and she laughed. I knew from experience that Lila preferred to set her anxieties on the cosmic plane. She was unnerved by the fact that her body wore down and had to mimic death every night, and that no one knew why. She scared herself obsessively by wondering whether time was linear or circular, whether there was anything outside the universe or not, whether matter was real or only a probability. She was spooked by having to live in a universe where there were anti-protons and black holes; she showed me magazine articles boasting that the appearance of life had been nothing but an advanced form of crystal formation, or claiming that everything in existence was a kind of sculpted empty space. I would stroke her hand. I couldn't refute her fears; she was very smart. But I stroked her hand and teased her.

"Here we are, going through the woods together," I said. It was one of our phrases.

"What did you two do today?" she asked. "Did you go to the playground?"

"Yeah."

"Did anything interesting happen?"

"No."

"I wish I'd been there. It sounds so nice."

Then I remembered that something interesting *had* happened that morning, and that our evening's conversation was supposed to have gone like this:

"This is so funny: I was talking to some woman, some mother with a kid, and suddenly a *flood* of sexual desire . . ."

But I didn't tell her.

3

I saw Hilary's mother again in November. At that time of year
the playground was starting to be deserted on chilly days, so
Jeff and I strolled through Prospect Park proper—the big
green place that made this part of Brooklyn livable. It was what
all the well-dressed young couples who moved to our neighborhood bragged about most: prettier and quieter than Central
Park, with meadows for ball-playing and kite-flying, and a lot of
short round hills great for picnicking. In the back half there were
woods where you could get robbed and beaten, but you avoided
that half; and there was an ice skating rink, a lake where children
fished, a small zoo, and a bridle path on which people born in
slums learned to ride English saddle.

We plowed through brown leaves piled as high as Jeff's chest.
Half the trees were already bare.

"See, when it's cool and gray out it's most beautiful," I told
him, to awaken his visual sense. "The clouds make everything
look soft—look at those blackbirds flying out of that tree!"

There was one isolated maple, standing next to a street light
and a path, that had stayed fire-orange for weeks. Now, long-
tailed blackbirds with iridescent purple feathers flew straight up

out of its branches, two and three at a time, making a dozen that raced over our heads for the hilltop groves.

"Da!" he said, and I congratulated myself as he charged up the hill after them. But at the top of the hill, under a big brown oak were two human figures: a child taking an acorn from the hand of a woman. Parked further in the shade was a child's blue stroller. Jeff had spotted Hilary and her mother even before I had. She wore the same Brooklyn Dodgers jacket I had first seen her in, but with a silver-gray silk scarf tucked down the front. Her black hair streamed out from under a silver-gray beret.

I felt as if I was blazing orange in full view like the maple across the field. My legs started going up the hill. I walked behind the running Jeff, to give the appearance of just keeping tabs on him.

All of a sudden I was standing right in front of her, on the hilltop, and she was looking up at me above Hilary's yellow-hooded head.

"Hi. It's Hilary, isn't it?" I asked.

"And Jeff?"

As if we could have forgotten the children's names that were codes for our own.

"No stroller!" she said, gesturing at Jeff with her chin. "Very brave of you."

"When he gets tired he rides on my shoulders."

"See? It's better to be a man, even for raising kids."

"That's true!" I laughed. "I can carry him for miles. I can carry him and grocery bags at the same time."

We were smiling at each other with barely enough restraint so that our smiles might conceivably be justified by the words coming out of our mouths. Hilary's mother was wearing mascara on her black lashes, and I liked it, even though I traditionally did not like mascara on Lila.

"You take care of him all the time, then?" she asked.

"In the daytime, yeah. Of course my wife comes home in the evening, and she does a lot."

She nodded approvingly at this invocation of my wife as chaperone. I looked away at the two kids crouching over the grassy slope. Hilary had the same coloring as her mother, but her hair was curly and her face round; that had come from someone else. She was picking up acorns, so many that when she stood up, they all fell out of her hands and she had to start over again. Jeff was on a search of his own: for aluminum pop-tops, his latest rage. Every minute or so he found one and held it up to me so I could be shocked.

"Yes, that's very dangerous, we have to throw it out."

I took the pop-top he offered me, and tossed it into the shade, where I knew he wouldn't go. Satisfied that I was doing my duty to protect him, he trotted downhill to look for more pop-tops.

"You know your son so well!" Hilary's mother said. "So much better than other fathers. You should come over some time and give my husband lessons. When he changes a diaper, he has to go lie down for the rest of the evening."

We laughed together at her husband.

"I mean, he works very hard," she added. "He's tired in the evenings, naturally. He's a contractor: he renovates houses, a lot of the ones in this neighborhood. He's doing our own." She shrugged.

"Well, I don't love to change diapers," I said. "It's something that has to be done so I do it." A man's got to do what a man's got to do. "I was working at home anyway, so when my wife had the baby, there I was." I paused before giving her the seductive answer to the question: What kind of work do you do? "I'm an artist."

It was such an easy shot, I almost winced at myself. An artist, how glamorous! It didn't work on all women, but on the ones it worked on, it really worked. I had suspected all along that Hilary's mother was one of those, just from the way she looked, and the introspective urgency of her quick, stray gestures, and the elusive anxiety of the way she joked. She might be thinking that I was in a whole different world from the men she knew—more spiritual, more sensitive, more understanding. My being a househusband must have made her think that already, and now it was doubly confirmed. An artist—yes—I must be one of those people who

throw out convention and live by the laws of the soul . . . I mentioned, with the greatest casualness, that I had published illustrations in *Harper's* and done a record cover. The record cover—for a
group she had heard of—made her eyes widen.

"I'll buy their album, and I don't even like their songs!"

I smiled at her.

"And you have time to work, with him around?" she asked.

"I work around him. I work when he naps."

"You sound so disciplined! When Hilary naps, all I can do is
take a nap myself. I'm trying to do something—I mean something creative—but I have trouble just meeting the average
responsibilities."

"No," I said, though I knew nothing about her. "I'm sure you
take care of the average responsibilities."

She moaned, as if I'd hurt her.

Wanting to take her mind off her self-doubts, I asked: "So have
you lived in this neighborhood long?"

She laughed. "Yeah, in my dreams. When I was little, my
father used to drive me here and show me the houses on Prospect
Park West, like we might get to live in one someday? Then, of
course, when I was thirteen, he raped me."

I stopped in the middle of writing my name with a twig on a
black boulder. "Jeff, don't wander, stay here!" I shouted, as if to
say that I wanted everything to stop, everything to listen.

"Your father?" I said. "You mean that?" I must have sounded
very stupid.

"Yeah, but I provoked him. I had the nerve to be taking a bath
when he came in drunk."

She turned away, with her arms cradled tight against her
chest. It was almost as if she'd forgotten someone was with her.
She blinked her eyes and turned to me again.

"My father was an insurance salesman," she said. "Still is, as a
matter of fact. I don't see him anymore. But I guess he still works
out of the same place."

"And you were thirteen. What did you do, did you tell your
mother? Did you call the police?" Why was her father still at

23

large, my middle class indignation wanted to know. Why wasn't he in jail?

"No, I did not call the police. I did tell my mother, I called her on the phone right after it happened, but she told me to shut up, I deserved it, he deserved it, she deserved it. That was her motto. Everybody deserves everything. She's telling me this over a pay phone with lots of people talking and a jukebox in the background. Afraid to let her companions find out about the scandal, right?" She laughed. "I knew the phone numbers of all the bars she hung out in, I could usually track her down when I needed her. I think that's why the old man went for me—her going out all the time. He was frustrated, and he sees someone in his bathtub who looks like his wife. In fact, what do I know, it probably wasn't even incest. I mean, how did he know if I was his daughter or not? He might have been a very, you know, decent individual all that time, to raise a female that wasn't his. And not go after her when she was ten, or five."

I snapped the twig in two, and let it drop to the ground. I didn't know what to say to a person to whom such things had happened. *That fucking pervert, I'd like to break his neck?* That would certainly do her a lot of good, besides showing her what a macho man I was. *Jesus, you poor kid, you must have been through hell?* Undoubtedly the kind of unworldly pity she would most like to hear. I just hoped she sensed that a person who cared about her was listening.

"Well, after it was all over," she said, "he was asleep, and I was thinking of kicking him to death but I said, No way am I gonna go to jail for his crime. So I just got dressed and ran away. There was this girl in my class, she wasn't a particular friend of mine but I knew she hung out in the East Village. She was like the tough girl in the class. So I took the subway down there and I'm asking people on the street if they knew her." She laughed again. "Lucky I stayed alive long enough to find her. But anyway I saw a wall poster for this band that I knew were her friends, and they were playing somewhere that night. I was too young to get in the club. So I stay outside, hearing the bass through the wall, you know?, till four a.m., and then when they came out I asked them to take me with them. My classmate didn't happen to be there, not that it matters. But I became like their teenage Avenue B housewife, cooking breakfast for them at sunset, shoplifting dinner under my shirt, bandaging them when they got mugged."

She had a nostalgic smile on her face. I wished I had known her in those days, and, after sampling the street life with her for a few months, had rescued her.

"Then I got caught shoplifting, and my father came to court." She laughed and shook her head. "Acting like he's been looking for me all this time. 'Judge, I can't handle her anymore, look at her for yourself, what am I supposed to do?' Judge puts me in a foster home. The foster parents are like lunatics, you wouldn't believe. I don't know how they ever passed an interview. I mean like, 'Let's all drive out to the Jersey swamps in the middle of the night because the Book of Revelation says two aliens from outer space are going to land there on March fifth and take us up to heaven.' So I got sent to two more foster homes, all very special in their own way. Then finally to a group residence till I was eighteen. I learned to set a proper table there. Among other things. Anyway, when you're eighteen you gotta leave the group residence and go out into the world at large like the mature adult which you now are, so I moved into an apartment with this girlfriend of mine from there, Bonnie. She was the straightest person I knew there. She really *was* just someone with a bad home life, not a criminal or even a runaway. We both got jobs to pay our rent. And we both started going to Brooklyn College part-time. I got forty-something credits, in English and what-ever. Anyway, I got this job in a plant store. I applied to a plant store because, at the time, I thought I was a plant. So I figured I understood the merchandise. I don't even remember why I thought I was a plant, but it shows you. Anyway . . ."

She took a big breath, and shook her head hard, as if trying to shake memories out of it. "One day after work," she said, "I came home and found Bonnie in the bathtub, with her head under water. The water was bright red."

An airplane flew overhead, screaming: though we couldn't see it through the overcast, it came loud and low over the meadows of Prospect Park, on its eastbound descent to Kennedy.

I said, "I'm sorry."

She nodded thanks. "Well, I couldn't pay the rent all by myself. And I was afraid to live alone. I still am, as a matter of fact. With all I've been through, that's one thing I've never done, lived alone. But I wasn't too optimistic about what happens when you live with other people, either."

We shared a smile of likemindedness, even though my experience of living with people had been incomparably happier than hers.

"This guy Mike, my husband, used to come to the store and talk to me. He likes plants. He used to buy all these plants and tell me what a great saleslady I was. He was the first normal, decent man I ever went out with. And when he learned about me, he wanted to give me a home." She shrugged. "So I married him."

She looked up suddenly. "Hey—you kids—come back here!" she called. Jeff and Hilary had wandered all the way down the hill, staying parallel to and at a distance from each other like a two-man reconnaissance mission for acorns and pop-tops. They were now heading south on a strip of bare soil over the flat meadow. Hilary's mother and I ran to retrieve them. Each of us scooped up our own kid under one arm, jouncing them as we carried them up the hill.

"Now stay here," she said, and we laughed together at their adventurousness. We licked our lips against the November wind. She swept her black hair off her face.

"I didn't mean to tell you all that," she said. "I'm sorry."

"Sorry? Why?"

Was she sorry she had decided to reveal herself to me? Had my reaction seemed weak to her? Had she thought, Oh well, he's just one of those rich people?

As different as we were—because she was different from the other women I'd known—I wanted to be worthy of her revelation.

"I'm sorry for upsetting you," she said. "Really. It was so hard to live through, it's hard enough just to hear it. I know that. I usually keep it a secret from people. So they can deal with me like a normal person. If you think I just go up to everybody and tell them the story of my hardships . . ."

"No." I shook my head. "And I won't tell anyone."

Usually, when a married man says that, he's exempting his wife. He won't tell anyone except his wife. Everyone understands that. But I wondered whether this woman understood that, and whether I even meant that. If I told Lila, how would she respond? Lila and I had thought that wearing eyeglasses instead of contact lenses was teenage misery. Yet this woman standing close to me, trusted me to listen and understand.

"You know how I knew I could tell you?" she said.

"No. How?"

"Well, I bring Hilary to the playground a little—not a lot. I know it's good for her but I can't really talk to those other women. They're talking about their diets, their vacations, and when should they go back to work. It's wonderful for them, I wish them all the luck. But I can't join in and talk like that. I don't want to go back to the plant store. And every time we go on a vacation, I'm afraid I'm gonna walk into the woods or something and never come out. I mean . . ." She stopped herself from saying something. "But when I saw you, I figured you didn't talk like that either."

We laughed.

"Not just because you're a man," she said. "I mean, I'm not after men." (I nodded with complete understanding. She was saying the right and good thing, and I fully supported her, and she had certainly been through enough with men, but my heart sank.) "But you have a sad expression on your face when you think no one's looking. And then, when you're watching your son play, or talking to him, you look like you're in love."

I blushed. "Only when I think no one's looking." I cleared my throat. "I think you found them all, Jeff. Why don't you look for blades of grass? That's easier." He was walking in circles on the hillside, head down, dissatisfied because he saw no more metal, only nature. Hilary had walked behind us into the rocky, grass-less, broken-glass-studded region under the trees and had climbed into her stroller, and was making sulking sounds in order to be wheeled home.

"Okay, okay," her mother said. "Well, that's how I came to be living this average lifestyle. I hope I can make it. I worry about her so much, being with me; I worry about what kind of mother I can be . . ."

"You're fine."

"Well, I'm trying. Listen, wanna hear something *really* sickening?"

"Oh no, what else?" I laughed.

"Well, I'm writing a children's book. It isn't finished yet. I've been working on it so long it's embarrassing me. I keep thinking, 'What's wrong with it?' I can't even tell. But I had to see if I could do something—anything in this world. I got an idea, I wanted to see how it worked out. That's how people do things, isn't it? They don't just forget it, they see how it works out?"

"Yes."

She nodded and bit her lip at the information, as if she had genuinely learned something.

"What's your story about?" I asked, perhaps a little condescendingly.

"Ah . . . Wanna read it?"

"Okay. When?"

She laughed. "I happen to have it right here." She unstrapped the purple canvas bag that hung from the handles of the stroller. "I've been carrying it around for weeks."

She pulled out a bunch of white pages from a three-hole looseleaf notebook, written on in blue ballpoint. Without look-ing, she handed it to me and then rushed back to the stroller, busying herself in re-strapping the bag and murmuring to Hilary. I took a couple of steps downhill and turned my back to the wind, but the top page almost blew away anyway: I was almost as nervous as she was. What would I tell her if I didn't like it?

28

I read. The story was called *Rhino Yogurt*. A couple of times Jeff tugged at my down jacket as if asking me what he could search for now. "Yes, yes, later," I mumbled.

It was about a girl named Bettina, who'd lost her mother, and whose hapless father—that's all he was in the story, just hapless—sent her off "with yucky, slurpy kisses" to a combination reform school and yogurt factory run by rhinoceroses with three-inch-thick eyeglasses. God, it was a good story! I deducted for infatuation with the author, and it was still good. The author had taken the horrible experiences of her adolescence and transformed them into something witty and colorful. She made herself triumph; and the generosity—or perhaps wishfulness—of her nature was such that her villains weren't irredeemably evil, only benighted and lost.

There was no ending yet, and perhaps there were too many animals and people and crises for a children's book, but the person who could think up such a story could certainly fix problems like that. What excited me most was that while reading it, I'd seen it so clearly that the right illustration for each scene sprang spontaneously into my mind.

Just the other night, Lila and I had discussed how I might try to break into children's book illustration. It was a very tempting, happy field to work in. It didn't pay much at first, but once you got known, you'd be in demand, book after book. Jeff would see books full of his Daddy's paintings whenever he went to the toy store or library; it would be like a free gift for his self-esteem . . .

"Okay, I know it was terrible," she said.

"No, no!" My pause after reading it must have worried her. "I like it, really."

"Tell the truth. Really?"

I like *you*, I thought. "I like it, you mind?" Maybe no one had ever praised a creative effort of hers before.

"Well, what should I do with it?" she asked.

"Send it somewhere. To a publisher. I don't know exactly how. I have an artist's representative; he must know how you go about it. He might know literary agents. He'll be involved anyway, when I do the illustrations."

"Oh, no!" she protested.

"You don't want me to do the illustrations?"

"Please. It's not that. I mean, I wasn't trying to set you up for that. I was just asking you as a friend to read my story. I know you're an illustrator and everything, but you have other work you're busy with. I just thought you might be able to give me some advice about children's books. You don't have time to do something that probably won't get anywhere."

"I've got time. I've got too much time," I said, contradicting my habitual complaint that housekeeping kept me too busy to do my real work. "Anyway, I'm inspired," I added, in a mock-Brooklyn accent. I *was* inspired, for the first time in so long, it was almost a new feeling. Yes, I thought, it's a *visual* story. I can make the setting funny-scary. I can give the rhinos subtle facial expressions within an overarching animal stolidity, and I can give the girls long, wavy, pre-Raphaelite tresses. I know how to do it. Not that the text was weak; but the pictures—my pictures—would make the book special.

"I'll do one picture, on spec," I told her. "If they like it, I can do the rest; if they want a different artist, I won't have wasted much."

"You're serious? You sound like you're serious."

"I'll tell you how serious I am. As soon as I go home, right after I make him his lunch, I'm not going to do anything else. I'm going to start drawing for you."

She bit her lip, quite hard. In her gray eyes I saw thoughts I could not decipher, and that made me want her still more: to get inside her any way I could. I wanted to know her better than anyone else did; I was jealous of anyone who knew anything about her that I didn't: jealous even of the woman herself, for possessing private memories and colorings of emotion, shadings of perception and nuances of mood, hidden thoughts, unspoken fancies—parts of herself I was eager to love, that I, being a separate person, could never gain access to. I began to feel one of my surges, in other words . . .

And what are these fucking climbs and plunges that our endocrine systems put us through, that make us not only galloping stallions in the hot-nostrilled, bulging-eyed fury of single-minded goal-storming, but simultaneously philosophers? Is a man supposed to dismiss it as a hormonal delusion when a window seems to appear in front of him with a view of his unlived other life, and the woman waving for him to step through the window happens to have dark hair instead of blonde, and say "maybe" instead of "perhaps," and be light enough to lift above his head instead of a big-boned bundle of arms and legs? It was the same kind of surge that put him in this lived life in the first place, in the dimmest history of his early adulthood. Blame hormones just as much when the surge subsides, and the window shade is drawn—blame them for his lived life, too . . .

Meanwhile, I was telling her excitedly about her story, praising the idea and the details, encouraging her to finish it, mentioning delicately the places where I thought it could be strengthened, assuring her it would all click into place with mere hours' more work.

"Yeah, yeah," she said.

"What, did I say something wrong?"

"No, not you."

I thought about that for a moment. "So what does your husband think of it?"

"Oh, he pats me on the head and says 'Very good,' like it's trivial."

I shook my head at his behavior. I sighed. "Well, listen. What do you think of colored pen and ink over a pencil underdrawing, with red washes for the warmer scenes—and blue washes for the cooler ones—like the moonlit hallway?"

She sputtered aloud. "Don't ask me, I don't know! That's what I need *you* for. Sounds great, okay? I mean, you *sound* like you know your job."

"Oh, I talk a good illustration, huh?"

"I'm kidding. Yes, please go ahead. Whatever you do with it I'll be thrilled to death, I don't have to tell you."

"Or I could try watercolors."

"Okay, watercolors—whatever. You know; I don't know. I'm sure either way would be—" She turned her head. In the stroller, Hilary was starting to cry "Mommy!" She was trying to grab her mother's leg, and the rocking of her body was moving the stroller back and forth in place.

"Okay, okay. Bring me back to reality." With one hand she pushed the stroller back and forth to pacify Hilary temporarily. "Well . . ." she said to me. "You're really gonna help me?" She seemed amazed, as if she'd never heard of such a thing before.

"If it works out it'll help me too."

"We'll force each other to get off our asses and start working."

"Exactly. Exactly." We were both smiling. "And I'll call you, or you call me—or we'll both call each other and get busy signals . . ."

I told her my telephone number, and she told me hers. We didn't even have to say that there was no need to write them down on paper.

"Oh," she said, "and my name's Maggie Ferro."

"Brendan Beame."

"Hi."

"Hi."

I started a movement of my hand, then stopped it almost before it became visible. But then she stuck out her hand, and we laughed at our hesitation and shook hands. There was no lingering touch in it, no meaningful squeeze, no invitation, no prolonging of contact for contact's sake. It was an instantaneously, but very carefully, calibrated handshake.

"We'll see each around, in the playground, wherever," she said. "And we'll know . . ."

"Something," I finished for her.

"Right. We'll know something."

I lowered my head shyly and turned around to look for Jeff. He was busy digging up dirt with a used popsicle stick; but with that sixth sense kids have for detecting parental attention, he stood up and ran to me. He ran swivel-hipped, as boy toddlers often do before the femininity is trained out of them, and his forest green windbreaker seemed to be slipping off his shoulders and riding up his chest at the same time. The energy of him, the way he anticipated my call as soon as I even glanced his way, gave me a fierce pang. He had been within earshot when Maggie told me about her past, but even if he had paid attention, he couldn't have possibly understood how it exceeded normal middle-class life. More than Maggie, *he* was in a different world from me.

"Hey, pal," I said, clapping my arms around his back, "what's happening?" He wrapped himself around my leg. Then he wriggled out of the hug and began walking through the columns of my legs in a figure eight, grabbing my pants, sometimes inadvertently pinching me, sometimes tickling. I drummed lightly and happily on the crown of his ragg wool cap as he passed under me. It was an old running hat of mine that had shrunk in the wash.

"Okay, we're going," Maggie told Hilary, who was really bawling now. And without another word to me, she was pushing the stroller bumpily over tree roots, then down onto the cobbled path that curved toward the Ninth Street exit. I kept watch on Maggie's silver-gray beret, and on Hilary's hand hanging over the side of the stroller. Apparently they lived on one of the higher-numbered streets, which were the cheaper and tougher ones in our neighborhood.

Jeff and I started walking home toward Second Street.

There won't be sex, I told myself. There should not be sex. Decide it now and stick to it. I don't want to be next in the line of people who've hurt her. We'll be friends and collaborators, that's all. No, not "that's all": friends and collaborators is a lot.

I was so happy, I took both Jeff's hands in mine and started running around him in circles, like in Ring Around the Rosie, and shouting, "Hey, who is this Daddy guy, huh? Who's this swinging you around all of a sudden? What a day! God! What a day!" and making him laugh. There was a sense of relief in his laughter, I think, as if he had been annoyed by my staying and talking so long, and hadn't been optimistic about what kind of mood I would be in afterward, and was glad to see I was in a good one.

33

We walked hand in hand a few steps, then I swung him onto my shoulders so suddenly it startled him at first. "Okay?" I asked. "You settled up there?"

"Otay."

"Good. You get a much better view this way. See the trees, the meadows, the baseball fields?"

"Yes."

"Very well pronounced! Oh, Jeffrey, you big guy. Let me tell you, it's something. I don't know what." I broke into a trot toward the stone wall which bordered the park. I imagined his view of things: how he could now see over the wall to the traffic on Prospect Park West, and the hot dog cart with the blue and orange umbrella, and an old person or two sitting on the green benches or slowly shuffling along, and how they all seemed to be bouncing. My knees hurt from running while I carried him, but I remembered how great it felt to be a small boy riding on Daddy's shoulders, taller than Daddy.

"Hey!" I called up to him when I stopped at the exit, with its twin bronze panthers, their granite bases spray-painted with I.R.A. slogans that the Parks Department had only partially obliterated. I was panting a little. "I might become quite something in the field of children's books. What do you think? I think she digs me too. But the really strong thing," I said, proud to be able to teach him so much, "is when you *could* make a conquest but you don't."

4

Winter is the lonely time for parents. You're stuck inside the house with someone who can't sustain a conversation, doesn't know which the good hockey teams are, doesn't care about the President's State of the Union Message. He only worries about the things he has no cause to worry about, like whether you're going to give him his food and whether Mommy's ever going to come home. In the warm months, Jeff and I had established a rhythm: I took him outside in the morning, and in return he napped through the afternoon and gave me time to work. In the winter, the rhythm fell apart.

It was too cold to spend all morning in the park, and even if we decided to be sturdy intrepid boys and walk through the slush and the wind, there were no other children out to play with. Some mornings, I took him on long excursions that required the stroller: around the north side of the park to the Brooklyn Museum, or through the Botanical Gardens, or southward into the working class neighborhoods where the only men visible during midday were either unloading delivery trucks or loitering in front of bars—not pushing babies. All Jeff got out of those trips was chapped cheeks. I treated them with Lila's hand lotion. He loved the smell of it, and kept asking for more.

After a few weeks, I'd used up all the excursions, and all the indoor games too. I'd drawn him pictures of every animal I could think of: he could identify the gnu, the armadillo, and the bighorn sheep. I in turn could identify every regular character on every childrens TV show, and I became, I'll bet, the best wood-block architect in all Park Slope. I had named every object in our cupboards for him dozens of times: every spice and condiment, every pot and pan. He was developing a great vocabulary for household nouns. He could tell cumin from coriander both by sight and by smell, and if I asked him, "Where's the trivet?" he would gleefully open the lower cupboard and point to the round macramé doily that Lila and I had bought in a roadside souvenir stand just days before we learned she was pregnant with him.

Children love their parents so much that sometimes they won't leave them alone. You ask your child to please stop climbing all over you while you're trying to think about what you're going to paint; and since that saddens him, it makes him need to hold onto you all the more. After a long winter of tolerating it and some-times even enjoying it, you lose your patience one day of sleet and freezing rain when both you and he are groggy and flushed with colds, and the street light outside has been vibrating like a plucked bowstring all morning, its lamp flickering a reluctant pinkish purple, and the only three pedestrians you've seen walk by have all slipped on the exact same square of buckling side-walk, and even the TV picture acts like it can hardly drag itself out of its warm studio, and there's nothing for dinner in the house and this is normally your morning to go to the supermarket with him, and the radio has announced long delays on the D, F, and RR lines, which are of course the only trains that can bring Lila home, and he climbs into your lap just as you're trying to read Kandinsky's *Concerning the Spiritual in Art*.

When he turns the page before you've even read half of it, the sight of his inconsiderate, uncultured little hand trying to press the white paper down on top of your knuckles somehow enrages you this time, rather than endearing him to you as usual; so you stand up to get him off you, and you scream, "Why are you always climbing on me? Why are you torturing me? Can't you play by yourself for ten goddamn minutes? I haven't read one page—one page, is that too much to ask?"

You throw the book onto the floor and you stamp on it, you kick it across the room, you chase it down and kick it again till its pages are shoe-printed and torn.

"There, are you happy? Now I can't read Kandinsky anymore. Satisfied? Is your goal for the day satisfied?" And the look on his face, of innocence wide-eyed in terror, infuriates you more. Its pathos is so simple you can't believe it's not a crafty ruse. You suspect him of deliberately goading you to anger for his own curiosity's sake, and you decide to give him what he asked for. "Anything else I shouldn't be allowed to read?" You bound over to the living room bookshelves, and start pulling books so that they fall to the floor. "Albers's *Interaction of Color*? Van Gogh's letters?" And you squat down to the tall bottom shelf where your most precious possessions are kept: the art reproduction books. "Georgia O'Keeffe? Saul Steinberg? *The Book of Kells*?"

The books are shelved so tightly that it takes a conscientious effort with two hands to get the first one out; but after that, it's easy. One at a time at first, then in bunches, you whip the books out behind you. You kick the ones that have piled together, as if to show that their unity won't save them; and you kick the ones that are lying separately, as if to show them what life does to loners. You kick books in every direction, as if they were rats attacking your feet. Picasso goes spinning under the coffee table, Braque parting from him at right angles. You lift up Goya in your hands, in all his earth-colored heaviness, and hurl him down again. Your chest is heaving. Your breath is the rhythmic gasp of someone having a nightmare.

You tell yourself: Okay, stop. Stop acting. *Now* stop. But every rational bit of advice you give yourself seems like a self-suppression, and you have to rage against that as well as against him. And in his pale, puffy face and wet eyes, you see that he is not only filled with fear and dread, but observing you with minute interest. He is learning something. He is learning how to have a temper tantrum.

"That's right!" you scream. "This is how. Any further questions? Anything else you want to know?" He shakes his head like a scared recruit with a sergeant screaming in his face. You can see his complexion drain by the second. In the midst of all this, you remember that you've seen a book in the children's section of the library, called *Daddy is a Monster—Sometimes.* You make a mental note to check it out. It will reassure you that this sort of behavior is common among fathers. You shout at him: "No? Think maybe you should have let me read in peace? Well, how about this?" And you run to the front door and punch it, punch it, until your knuckles are skinned and swollen and there are red spots on the white paint.

Standing there, panting, picking the top skin and the flecks of white paint off your knuckles, with dots of blood rising to the surface as if from an underground spring, you see the child watching you. He is trembling in place. He is alone with you, with no way to get help if he needed it. He doesn't understand why you got mad this time, when so many previous times you didn't get mad.

When you rush up to him, he gives a cry of fear, until he sees that you are bending down on your knees with your arms open. You hug him. He is amazingly willing to hug you in return. He lets his emotions burst forth in loud sobs, his lower lip shaking. You kiss the tears on his face. "I'm sorry, sweetheart, you didn't do anything wrong. It was my fault, I shouldn't have gotten mad at you . . ."

Three minutes later, when he has helped you put the books back on their shelves and you're laughing together and playing horsie, you thank God you've never stepped over the border between hurting the books and hurting the child, and that you've done enough good things to make him resilient; and you swear you're already wiser than you were three minutes before. So when Lila comes home that evening, haggard and soaked and hours late and starving, and groans, "Well, how was *your* day?"

it's both honest and compassionate to say, "Oh, pretty good. Nothing special."

Almost all the adults I knew worked in offices, and even if I called every one of them up, not one of them would be able to tell me how to keep a small child, and myself, cheerful through three months of cold weather. Lila would know the most, of course, but I didn't want to worry her with my momentary household blues. She had given me responsibility for the well being of her child, and at bottom I felt I could handle things.

What I did was, I called Maggie. We spoke on the phone almost every afternoon, the time when our kids were usually napping. Even on days when we had run into each other on the street or the Prospect Park promenade, we would call each other up to add something we had forgotten to say in person.

We had the same job, that was why. We understood the stresses first-hand, and we took turns reassuring each other and boosting each other's confidence. Our kids were at the same stage of development, too. We could compete jokingly about Jeff's and Hilary's progress in speaking, in playing with toys, in being sociable. More than once we discovered that we were simultaneously diapering the two children, in separate apartments, phone receivers tucked against our shoulders. Often I drew or painted under the necessity of keeping the telephone cord out of the way of my brush. The phone had one advantage over a physical meeting: no other adult could see us. If it hadn't been impractical, I suppose we would have walked around all day with our phones in our hands, the line open to each other.

So far we had never visited each other's homes. I think we both understood, without talking about it, that such a visit would be a step beyond meeting on the neutral territory of the playground. We found the pretext one winter day when I was describing my career to her over the phone. I was telling her what an artist's rep does, and was describing my rep, Rawley Johnson, and complaining that taking care of a child made it more difficult for me to go into town and see him. A rep, it's true, takes over much of the burden of making the rounds and pursuing assignments, so in theory the artist can live halfway around the world and still have quite a successful New York career. But in practice, especially at the beginning of your career, close personal rapport with your rep is a big advantage if he's going to make the rounds enthusiastically for you in the first place. And after he lands an assignment for you, there are still art directors to be met and lunched and cultivated, specifications to be clarified and esthetic matters to be debated.

"Sometimes I take Jeff into town with me," I said, "but it limits how much time I can spend, what restaurants I can go to—*you* know. If I could only get into town more often by myself . . ."

"I'll babysit for him!" she said.

"Oh, I can't impose him on you."

"Impose? Come on, we want our kids to play together, don't we?"

"Okay, well . . ." I tried to give it the appearance of a normal business arrangement. "We usually pay babysitters three dollars an hour . . ."

"Get outta here! You're not paying me! I'll kill you, Brendan, you mention paying me for babysitting! I'm doing this as a friend."

The next morning she and Hilary came over to stay with Jeff.

We were only together in the apartment for a couple of minutes, while I showed her where things were and went over Jeff's schedule. But after I left, I felt as if I were venturing forth into the big city to bring back wonderful things for Maggie. (I did buy a jar of Sarabeth's Kitchen pear preserves for her, and forced it on her as a gift.) At my meeting with Rawley I was especially charming and forthright, and came off as a dynamic but highly dependable professional, determined to seize the rising curve of my career; by the time we shook hands good-bye, I felt that I had raised my status a notch or two on his roster of clients.

On the subway ride home, I closed my eyes, and reveries of Maggie, rushing to the door and hugging me, rocked me over the tracks.

On Brooklyn's Seventh Avenue it was already dark. The trendy new shops and the old-line Mom-and-Pop stores—the Italian bakery that sold hamentaschen for its Jewish customers, the shoe repair shop, fragrant with leather and polish, that had been bought by a Rastafarian family—were lit up, waiting for the returning rush-hour crowd. I turned onto Second Street, an uphill climb under bare plane trees.

The lights were on in our ground-floor windows. I could see Maggie sitting crosslegged and barefoot on the floor of the apartment. She wore stonewashed blue jeans and an oversized plaid flannel shirt with the tails hanging out—one of her husband's, but I didn't want to think about that. While I was gone she had put her hair in a ponytail, which I had never seen her do before. I lingered in front of the window just so I could look at her from that angle, in the amber light of our teardrop chandelier, and imagine stroking that ponytail, and also fantasize about painting her. She looked like she belonged there, in my home.

She met me at the door, with a finger at her lips. "Hi, they're both asleep, you should see."

I took off my snow-wet boots and set them to dry next to hers in the outer hall. We walked into Jeff's bedroom together, conspiring at quietness. The white pull curtains had been lowered. I looked into the crib in the night-deep darkness. Jeff and Hilary were sleeping side by side, crosswise, so that their stockinged feet stuck out through the bars. One plaid wool blanket covered them both. Jeff's arm was draped over Hilary's shoulder.

"They're beautiful!" I whispered, leaning my head toward Maggie so she could hear better.

"Yes."

Our hands were on the cool, laminated pine railing of the crib, a few inches apart. Our shoulders touched.

"There's some coffee left over," she said in a slightly raspy, strained whisper. "Want some?"

I nodded. Had she made extra coffee precisely because she'd wanted to share it with me? We tiptoed into the kitchen with exaggerated, bobbing steps, as if to show that we understood the need not to wake the kids; and walking behind her, I deliberately walked faster in order to put my hand gently on the small of her back.

I watched her pour coffee into the mugs Lila's money had bought. Maggie had an impressive diamond engagement ring and a thick, braided gold wedding band on her finger, but her nails were polished red like a teenager's. I wanted to take those fingers into my mouth and taste the polish and the skin and nail and sweat-dampness, and nip my way from her fingertips to her arm and to her mouth.

"What do you want in this stuff?" she asked, which I thought was a funny way of putting it—as if coffee were something new to her, though in fact she made Mike's breakfast and dinner every day.

I whispered: "Milk and two sugars."

I took my first sip of Maggie's coffee. It was sweeter and lighter than Lila would have made it, or than I would have made for myself, but that was fine. One way was as good as another. We carried our full mugs past Jeff's door, into the living room, gasping—in virtuous whispers—when we spilled hot drops of coffee on our fingers.

There was that special kind of quiet that settles over a house where children are sleeping. The adults are gentle with doors and chairs; when they laugh, it's civilized and not raucous; no matter what the subject, their voices are subdued as if in serious discussion; and the tinkle of glass or china is as sharp and light as if it came from the air above. Every once in a while, in one of those random moments when all the little speeches have ended and no one has started another yet, you think you can hear the softest snore from rooms away, or a stuffed animal falling over on its side, or an unconsciously moaned syllable that might be your name.

I told Maggie all about my trip to the city, in the same way you'd tell a spouse about it, but she was more interested than a spouse because she hadn't heard it all before. Also, her own work was riding with mine: we'd sent Rawley her completed manuscript of *Rhino Yogurt,* along with my pen and ink drawing for it, and had asked him if he would handle it for us along with whatever literary agent he might feel he ought to bring in.

Maggie, in turn, told me how cute Jeff had been all day. He had kept batting his eyes at her so that she had no choice but to bat hers back.

I laughed. "He does the same thing with waitresses—you should see. He picks out some woman and decides she's his. I don't know where he gets it from."

"Yeah, I don't know," she laughed along with me.

This was one of those times when I wished I could tell Maggie not just about my work, or my child-rearing frustrations, but about conflicts between Lila and me; but some inner barrier blocked me from opening up the subject. It just seemed shabby to complain to my woman friend about my wife. Also, I was happy to be with Maggie and didn't want to include Lila in our idyll even by hearsay. Far from spilling my discontents, I found myself compulsively reciting the legend of Lila: how great she was, how destined for wealth, how wide in her aptitudes; how Lila's business studies had enabled us to escape picturesque squalor and have the child we'd talked about for years, under various names and descriptions, before his actual appearance. I told her how Lila always left time to play with Jeff and teach him to laugh and dance and make faces, and how this actually aided her career, kept her spirit alive for the birthing of ideas that were beyond the reach of workaholic males.

We heard the creak of the wrought iron gate, and footsteps coming to the outer door.

"Oh, good, now you can meet her," I said, quaking inside.

Maggie put on a pleased expression and set it tight.

I heard Lila toss off her shoes outside, in the hall. From the way she paused out there, I could tell she was looking at Maggie's boots and wondering whose they were. She only delayed a few seconds before entering, but she couldn't have sent me a more excruciating message if she'd thrown a dart at me.

I knew her messages, she knew my messages—could that have been the real trouble? We knew each other too well.

She unlocked the door, came in, and stopped. Her Burberry trenchcoat was open over a taupe Paul Stuart wool suit. She was in stockings, but she still must have been a good eight inches taller than Maggie. Her cheeks were apple red from the cold. A few blond hairs were sticking out at the sides of her head, from the static electricity when she'd taken off her chocolate-brown bush hat. She tucked her head down, rubbed the back of her hair with her hands, stood up straight again, and shook out her hair so she had a mane like the palamino mare that all the stallions are kicking each other's goddamn teeth out over.

She reshaped her discomposure into a politely, satirically questioning, "Hi!"

"Hi, this is Maggie. Maggie, my wife Lila. Maggie's that children's book writer I told you about. She's been here this afternoon babysitting. I happened to mention I wanted to go into town today and she very kindly offered . . ." As if testing alibis, I tried to start over. "I went into town today. I saw Rawley; he has some interesting—"

"You saw Rawley and you didn't tell me?" she said, as if that were what hurt her. It was awful to see her emotionally stranded in the middle of her own living room, and it made Maggie look like an outsider again, someone who should just get out of there. But, for that very reason, it made me feel a backlash of sympathy for Maggie too. Why was Lila assuming ill of Maggie, making Maggie the enemy? Maggie hadn't done anything wrong—it wasn't as if we'd committed adultery, after all. In fact Maggie had helped Lila by aiding me in my business duties.

Lila was making a show out of opening her purse. "How much do we owe you?"

Maggie looked down and mumbled that it was okay, and she had to be going anyway. She didn't want to look at Lila, I could tell, but kept stealing glances at her, nonetheless, the way you would if your friend had a Rolls-Royce and you didn't want to show how curious and intimidated you were. It wasn't fair.

Then Lila threw her arms around me and kissed me. She kissed my cheeks and neck and ears, and kissed my lips hard but with closed mouth. She pressed her body against mine and stroked my toes with her stockinged foot as if she hadn't seen me for weeks. "Brendan, I'm starving, did you make me something wonderful for dinner? Like your famous lasagna or moussaka, because I just want to eat and eat and eat . . ."

I blushed at Maggie. "She only loves me for my cooking." I'd never seen Lila act this way in front of other people. I felt guiltily responsible and thought I'd better calm her down, and calm myself down too. I was in orbit from having the two women in my life in the same room. "I haven't started dinner yet, I just got home."

"You don't have to make dinner tonight!" Lila said. "Let's go out and celebrate!" I supposed she meant celebrate the new prospects I'd raised during my day in town. "We'll take Jeff out and teach him how to eat spaghetti, and I think I'll have three pieces of cheesecake! I think I'm thin enough to afford it, don't you?" This last question she directed at Maggie, as if genuinely seeking her opinion, and spread open her trenchcoat and did a half-turn to display her fashion-model figure. "Let me change my clothes!" she told me, and dashed away, tossing over her shoulder, at Maggie, the sentence, "It was nice meeting you!"

Maggie looked crestfallen. "She seems very nice," she murmured bravely. I knew Lila *was* very nice, but I thought she'd shown something else just now.

She's jealous. I mouthed those words silently and very distinctly.

Maggie's head went back a fraction of an inch, as if someone had lightly slapped her. *Of what?*

I pushed currents of air back and forth between us.

"Gimme a break, that's so unfair!" she burst out. Then, as if to prevent Lila from hearing, she took a step closer to me. "You think she's really? What's she think we're doing?"

"I don't know. It's one of those human emotions."

"She doesn't want me here?"

"I don't know. She's really a nice person, I think you would both like each other if—"

"Shit!" She was no longer listening to me; her defenses were up. "I can't have a friend because he's a man? That's so unfair, Brendan. That sucks so bad. If that's what you're telling me, it disappoints me. I can talk to my husband's friends because they're *his* friends. But I can't talk to you, because you're *my* friend. Thanks a lot. That makes a lot of sense."

"I'm not saying that's what I believe. I'm saying people—wives," I added, with an attempt at a smile, "do sometimes get jealous."

She still wasn't listening.

"Your hotshot wife comes up to you, she says, 'You can talk to me or to all the other women in the world—which is it?' And you accept that? Okay. I should leave," she said. "We should never talk to each other again. If that's the way the normal people play it. Then everyone's nice and married, nice and pure. You'll know whose corpse your corpse is gonna rot next to. That's the important thing, right, Brendan?"

"I don't want you to leave," I said quietly. I think that if Lila had emerged and tried to send Maggie away at that moment, I would have told her off and gone away too. But Lila had probably heard her through the bedroom door, and wisely chosen not to confront her. Maggie and I were left alone, facing each other. "I want to be able to talk to you," I said. "But maybe she's right."

"*Right?*"

"I mean, we do like each other, and we're of opposite sexes—if you happened to notice." I gave another attempt at a laugh. "Haven't you ever thought about it?"

"No!"

I didn't believe her, of course, and I doubt if she wanted me to.

"You wouldn't settle for me anyway," she said more softly. "She's better looking."

"You're good looking."

46

"No," she said.

"Cut it out. You are. And don't talk about yourself in terms of 'settle for.'" I looked at her in a way, and for a length of time, that felt to me like a declaration. We said nothing. We looked at each other. We could hear Lila opening and closing drawers. In half a minute or so the kids woke up and started to cry and that finally got us moving.

Lila came out of our bedroom, wearing a shocking pink sweatshirt and electric blue socks. She *was* better-looking than Maggie, but that fact was somehow having little effect on me. I was just senselessly disappointed to see her.

"Gotta go! Nice meeting you!" Lila repeated, and dashed off to Jeff's room. But Maggie had to go there too, to get Hilary, and I hustled after them.

The two kids were awake and crying in outrage to find each other in the same crib. Hilary had grabbed Jeff by the front of his alligator shirt and was shaking him. Jeff, for all his strength and occasional temper tantrums, was not a hitter. Each mother lifted her own child out of the crib. Hilary snatched at Jeff, who was now out of range. Jeff turned away tearfully and tried to climb over his mother's shoulder.

"Be friends!" I said. No one responded.

"She's cute," Lila said, at the neighborhood Italian restaurant.

"Who?" I said. She gave me a look that said she wasn't going to accept *that* move. I tried again: "She's someone I may work with, if they like that first drawing I did."

"They *will* like it. It's a good drawing. I can tell you were inspired when the Little Bored Housewife sidled up to you with her masterpiece."

"Come on. She's a very interesting person who's had a very hard life, and she's very insecure about the whole idea of—"

"I meant no disrespect."

I smilingly gave her the finger, and she replied the same way; it was our traditional way of declaring a truce.

47

"*I* could write children's books for you, you know," she said. "Don't you think I could do it as well as she does?"

"Yes, I do." She had spent her whole childhood reading, she knew all the fairy tales, and she had begun to make up stories for Jeff at bedtime—good ones. For one of the most important facts about Lila, quite visible to those who knew her well, was that she had a creative urge but had not found an adequate medium of expression for it in her life so far. She was a generator of ideas and an enthusiast, but while the idea of a brilliant business career excited her, she couldn't quite hide the fact that she found the substance of her job a little dry. She also knew a lot about art—I don't mean just art history; she had an instinctive feeling for the way a picture works. She would purse her lips at a new illustration of mine for half a minute and come up with some tremendous off-the-cuff analysis like, "The composition is made up of nine squares, actually, and if you'll notice, the three diagonally this way are the weak ones," and she would be right, and I would bear down on reworking those three ninths of the picture, and it would become better. But in the studio courses she had taken in college—life drawing, ceramics, photography—she'd been wildly impatient with her own efforts: she let herself be thwarted by the fact that they didn't turn out right the first time. She would insist that they *had*. When a teacher or fellow student—or I—tried to suggest improvements, she would go red in the face and either do the opposite of what we recommended or throw the work in her closet in a fit of pique. They were idiots, she would say; their taste was warped by their need to justify their own feeble styles. If I tried to get her to calm down and discuss it open-mindedly, she would utter her famous phrase, "I don't want to talk about it." Yet since she did eventually calm down, and sometimes became more than usually subdued in the aftermath, I got the feeling that she sometimes grasped what her critics had meant, but her vanity wouldn't let her admit it.

"We could become a great children's book team," she said. "We'd dedicate all our books to our kids,"—both of us smiled at the plural—"and we could retire to a farm in New England.

Wouldn't that be nice?" She stretched out her hand and caught mine. "But please, Brendan. I've told you before. If I ever find out that you've been sleeping with another woman, I'll have to leave you. Not that I think it's immoral or anything. It's just something I know about my own personality. If you did something like that and I found out, I would think about only that whenever I saw you. Just thinking about it now is starting to make me nauseous. I don't even know if I can finish my calamari. I'm not saying I'm right to be that way. Maybe I'm very wrong, prudish, immature, whatever you decide to say I am. And, I admit, I would probably suffer too, if I threw you out. Or left you. Whichever. I mean, I don't have a plan, I would probably just shriek and rant and be overcome by the anger of the moment, until one of us left. But I warn you not to take this as an idle threat. Okay?"

I gave her hand a squeeze.

5

During the winter, Maggie babysat several more times while I traveled to Manhattan, but I never told Lila about it. She, I think, must have known that I was still friends with Maggie, because she never asked. She couldn't really have objected. Lila herself sometimes went for drinks or working dinners with male colleagues, and we had agreed from the start that it would be uncouth—and impossible—for me to prohibit her. Maggie and I were actually in the apartment together for only a short time, with the kids always present. So I could have discussed the issue with Lila some calm day and we might have negotiated fair limits to fraternization. But it had become important to me *not* to seek her approval. The truth was, I wanted a secret life.

That spring there were record-breaking rains in New York, and they always came on the weekends. Seven or eight weekends in a row, everyone's plans were washed out. Politicians on TV sounded embarrassed when they said that people should still conserve water to avoid a summer drought. Lila and I stayed home a lot and watched college basketball and exhibition baseball. In the park, there were ponds where bike paths used to be.

A male and a female duck from Prospect Park Lake had flown over to swim at these temporary resorts. They tested each pond for an hour, or a morning; swam, dunked for grass, and, shaking their feathers, walked out onto the mud toward any humans who had that indefinable look of possibly being about to throw bread. They were the only married couple whose life was widened by the rain.

When playground weather finally came again, people must have noticed that Maggie and I always sat close together, always talked together, that we even crossed and uncrossed our legs at the same time. They must have seen the way our hands lingered, on the grayish redwood of the slide-pyramid, a millimeter away from touching. When newcomers asked us which children were ours, they asked us both with one question—they thought we were husband and wife. Yet Maggie and I had never articulated our feelings for each other, even though we had often agreed that we could tell each other anything.

Every day we took each other's emotional temperature.

I'd say, "You look unhappy."

"Oh yeah, what makes you think that?" she'd say sarcastically. Bitterness was her mode of being. We were comrades in melancholy. Anxiety lit up her gray eyes and paled her olive skin into beauty.

"What is it?" I'd ask. And my arm would practically ache from the desire to put itself around her. But a tormented conscience was my way of equaling her misery.

"I'm a shit, Brendan," she said. "I'm an evil person."

"No! What's wrong?" I said indignantly. I always suspected that her husband did not go out of his way to boost her self-esteem.

"I always thought," she said, "that I was made out of basically good material, you know? But my environment messed me up? So I thought, if I had a daughter, she would be like what I would have been if I'd 've come from a better home. Me, but with advantages. I don't know, Brendan. I mean, there's nothing wrong with her, but—it's still me, it's me, I can't do it, I can't handle it. I'm afraid I'm gonna mess her up just to mess her up—just so she won't pass me. I'm scared I'm a hereditary bad mother."

"No, you're a wonderful mother. I watch you; I can tell. The first time I ever saw you in the playground, I commented to myself on what a skillful parent you seemed like."

As usual, she only sneered, distrusting any praise.

A good deal of my time was devoted to thinking of ways to make Maggie feel better, because it made me feel better. She was so defensive, so vigilant for slights, that it was a delicate skill for me to acquire. Often I made mistakes. As when I happened to mention the irony that, because Jeff was too young to understand birthdays, I would be taking him with me when I shopped for his present.

"Oh, when's his birthday?"

"Tomorrow."

She gaped in astonishment. "You didn't invite us? You weren't going to tell me!"

"We're not having a real party." I told this truth with as much edgy calculation as if it had been a lie. "Two is too young for that. None of our parents wanted to fly in, anyway. It'll just be me, Lila, and a cake."

"Yeah, it's good you have so many excuses, 'cause I wouldn't be invited anyway."

"Look, it's not her—" I said, starting to defend Lila.

But that was one thing Maggie didn't want to hear. "It's okay, I'm not criticizing," she said bitterly. "I'm sure you and her know more than me. Wish him a happy birthday for us, okay?"

We pouted in unison, and turned toward our kids, who were walking this way and that over the sand, watching their own small shadows stretch and contract under the spring sun. It was a perfect, bleached blue day up in the sky, with clean rags of clouds, but down here below, just try to find a swatch of clean cloth! Children's pants were always dirty from sand and food; their blankets were grimy and drooly from being clutched and sucked and dragged around outdoors; parents' jackets inevitably

52

had cheesy stains on the shoulders and backs. Homemakers don't put on their good clothes till late afternoon, for their spouses' arrival.

"Come after lunch tomorrow," I said. "You don't have to bring a present."

She brought helium balloons, green and blue and orange, and we sent them bouncing across the ceiling by tugging their strings. She brought a big chocolate cake with chocolate frosting; I helped Jeff blow out his candles while he sat on my lap and went, "Phuh, phuh." The four of us ate the entire cake. Full as geese, Maggie and I sat on the living room rug in our bare feet, our legs extended side by side. Maggie was looking at the kids through a green balloon.

I said, "I think this is the least hurt I've ever seen you."

We watched them. Like all kids that age, Jeff and Hilary played parallel to each other, but didn't say anything to each other, so it often seemed as if neither of them was aware of having a playmate. Hilary would grab the toy from Jeff the way you'd grab an umbrella from an umbrella stand; Jeff would burst instantaneously into a bewildered, disillusioned sob, which vanished as soon as I put a different toy in his hands. He wouldn't grab a toy from Hilary, even if it was the same one she had just stolen from him; he was braver than she about jumping and climbing, and wouldn't cry if he fell and scraped his knee, but I had probably trained him a little too well in being considerate of others—considerate of me, that is, when I was painting.

Once in a while, like seeing the first crocus of spring, you'd see one of them hand an interesting object to the other: a felt frog, a stick of chalk from a new box, a wrapped bar of hotel soap. They might even make a game of handing it back and forth, saying, "Here . . . Here . . ." Two minutes later they would lapse back into selfishness, but they couldn't fool you: you had seen it.

I pulled the blue balloon down from the ceiling and held it in front of my face. I looked at the living room through blue rubber.

The kids looked peaceful. I held the balloon between Maggie's face and mine, and we smiled at each other through the blue. I vibrated the balloon against both our foreheads, making a rubber sound.

Without either of us, I think, knowing the exact point when it happened, we shifted slightly so that our extended legs were pressing together.

A serious look came over our faces. We listened. We didn't hear Jeff banging his toy piano or Hilary pounding on Jeff's workbench; we heard ourselves breathing.

It was the moment when you haven't admitted it out loud yet, and you can still separate without comment, as if the touch were accidental. Then we passed that moment, and with a visible movement, pressed closer together. We pressed together all along our sides, shoulder to shoulder, hip to hip.

Where our legs touched, it was as if all my cells were jumping, as if each thread of my blue jeans was carrying a current. My fingers were sweating on the balloon. When they moved, the rubber groaned from my pressure.

I batted the balloon out of the way, up to the ceiling, and we joined hands, palm to palm. We slowly rotated our palms in opposite directions, turned them straight up. With my index finger I traced the whole outline of her hand, and interlocked our fingers tight, then brought our hands down to rest in the crevice between my leg and hers.

I could smell the skin of Maggie's neck, as different from Lila's as olive oil is from cinnamon. I had never smelled Maggie's neck before, I never wanted to stop. Even though I would doubtless soon have to stop, I would have been a fool never to have gotten to smell it at all.

"I like you, Maggie," I said.

"Shh . . ."

"Oh, they're okay." Three feet away, the kids were in another world. "And we're careful." My nose hovered along her jawline. "They can't tell anyone yet. In a few months they'll be able to tell. So I don't know how much we'll be able to do. But I just *like* you."

Which I considered a mere approach to the truth; but I hesitated to say the more ominous word. "I like to rest my legs against yours."

"I know." She rubbed her cheek against my hair.

Jeff gave his alarm. "Di'per, di'per!"

I stood up at once. "Dirty, or just wet?"

"Doorty."

I uttered the appropriate sigh. "Okay, we'll fix it with all celerity, my man." And I picked him up and carried him to his room, giving him a couple of kisses on the way.

It was odd: I felt relieved to be away from the intensity of the living room, touching instead a skin that did not make me sweat with fever and apprehension. This was a breather. It was a chance for me to practice my simple domesticity—about which I was already getting nostalgic—and to think about desires, possibilities, values, costs, and benefits. Not that I actually did any thinking. I did stare into space for quite a while, however, forcing Jeff to stage a vocal protest that snapped me back into the present.

"Yes, yes, thank you for reminding me. We're here to change a diaper . . . So what's new?" I asked him, once he was smiling up at me from his changing table, his bottom naked and clean. "What's new with you and Hilary out there? Playing nicely?" Then I risked: "Notice anything?"

He just laughed, glad to be wiped.

"Well, you should feel my heart, Jeff," I said as I taped the new diaper in place. "Feel it, then maybe you'll understand." I placed his hand to the left of my breastbone. He gave a gurgly laugh, and pressed harder because, I think, he liked to touch me. "Feel that? What'll you do when you're my age and you feel like this?"

I placed my hand on his chest in return. His heart was beating even faster than mine: he was a kid, and they run around all day at that pulse rate, without immoral stimulation and without worrying. Then he decided it was time for a vocabulary lesson.

"Dat?" he said, pointing at my blue jeans.

"That's my belt loop. Belt loop."

He moved his finger to the right and pointed. "Dat?"

"That's my rivet. Rivet."

Well, I taught him "change pocket" and "stitching" and "waistband," on the theory that some outlandish word heard at this stage of his life might resurface as if from nowhere and give him an extra point or two on the SAT's. He asked each word with the robust confidence that teaching him was the one thing in the whole world I most wanted to do.

"Come on, my pal," I said, and lifted him to his feet to pull his jeans up, swung him over my shoulder, and took us back to the living room. I placed him next to Hilary, stood watch over them until I was sure they were absorbed in their toys, then sat down beside Maggie in the exact same position as before.

"Hello," I said.

"Hello."

We kissed—more a brushing than a kiss. Our lips were dry from tension. I had to move my head to the side to look over her shoulder to see what the kids were doing.

Then we had our first long kiss, tongue kiss.

This too, had to be broken off, to make sure the kids weren't on to us. Then we bounced our lips together, one, two, three, four times, congratulating ourselves. Finally we looked up, scared.

"Hey kids, what's up?" I asked.

They weren't paying any attention to us at all. It was eerie. Even at two, there were so many times when children seemed to be declaring that they didn't need their parents. What would they be like at twelve, at fifteen? Would we be totally superfluous, hanging around them like fools, waiting to be needed?

We stopped nuzzling, just to look at them. Perhaps on some level we even wished for signs that we were having a bad impact on them, rather than no impact. Every couple of minutes Jeff glanced our way and gave us his broad-faced smile, satisfied that we were still there, and apparently not noticing, or seeing anything untoward about Maggie's foot riding on my foot. Hilary never looked at us at all.

Then a fight broke out between them, under our very noses

and without our being able to tell exactly what had caused it: some trespass upon territory, a botched trade of toys, a sudden surge of possessiveness because developmental progress seemed too much to ask. While Maggie and I were still shifting around and grumbling and wondering whether it warranted intervention, Hilary was suddenly pulling Jeff's hair and Jeff was screaming. Then Jeff did something I had never seen him do to another person before: he socked her. It was a good straight punch to the chest, and it made him stop screaming, and her start. The punch rocked them both back with surprise, it seemed to me. A look of rapid thought crossed over Jeff's face, and he socked her again.

He turned around and looked at me, his hand at his side as if he had forgotten he was fighting, yet still closed in a fist because, I think, he had simply forgotten to open it. I gave him a proud little nod.

His second punch had actually made Hilary *stop* crying, because she apparently realized that his punches had not affected her in any functional way. She leaned forward and squeezed his arm till it made him flail and sob, and made her turn red.

Maggie and I stepped in and separated them, each picking up our own offspring and carrying him/her to a remote corner of the living room, and there delivered a brief, sober lecture of dismay. We apologized to each other, and of course we both said it was okay, forget about it, they were probably just tired.

With that touching way toddlers have of giving their parents evidence on cue, Jeff began rubbing his eyes.

"Aha, time for his nap," I said.

Jeff, understanding the word "nap," cried.

Maggie clutched my hand. "Should we put them in for a nap together? We've done it before."

Jeff was trying to hammer on the workbench, but he kept having to rub his eyes, and the hammer got in his way. I went over and tousled his hair. He let me lift the blue plastic hammer out of his hand with only the least resistance.

"Gotta go in, Birthday Man."

·   ·   ·

Quieting his last-minute squawl, I walked up and down the length of Jeff's rug, with Jeff in my arms, my eyes closed, smiling. It reminded me of when he was a very new baby: all those nights I'd had to walk him to sleep after a middle-of-the-night feeding. Sometimes I had to do it for half an hour or more, and I was so tired, and it was so dark, that I could only gauge my turns by the feel of the fringes of his rug. Sometimes I closed my eyes as I walked him, and sometimes I even fell asleep walking. I had dreams. That walking sleep was light, extra calm, extra happy, because I was proving I possessed the skills of caring for him even at the unconscious level. I was testing my capacities.

Maggie leaned in the doorway of his room to watch me put him to bed. Her thumb was pulling down the waistband of her beltless blue jeans. The lines of her legs and arms in the doorway space, and the shadow of her body on the foyer wall, were so different from Lila's.

Soon Jeff was asleep in his inevitable position: head wedged into the corner of the crib, knees tucked under his chest, blanket underneath him. Maggie came up and kissed me.

I was beginning to know the bony places and the soft places on her body, and I liked them all. I lifted her up, my arms a sling under her ass, and we kissed while her legs were wrapped around me.

"What do we do next?" I said.

"It doesn't matter. Just being able to call you up and talk to you—it's so much more than I ever had." She pressed her face against my chest. She made little sounds.

"Hey, I thought you were a tough guy," I said.

"No, I'm not. You're the first person I ever liked."

I was the first person she had ever *liked*.

"What about Bonnie?" I reminded her.

"First man."

I assumed there was some hyperbole in that. Nevertheless, I thought about the implications. Maggie kissed me deep and hard; we concentrated everything on our mouths rather than ranging all over face and neck with little love-tokens, as Lila and I did. My fingers reached up around her ass toward the front, and stroked the denim.

Something grabbed my right leg. Miniature arms wrapped themselves around my knee; a head pressed itself to the seam of my jeans. I opened my eyes and looked down.

I let go of Maggie, the sling opening beneath her. For a moment she hung on to my neck, but then she too looked down, and dropped to the floor. Hilary embraced me, eyes closed.

"Oh, Jesus," Maggie said. She knelt down, gently pried Hilary off my leg, and hugged her. "Get me out of here. I'll take you out of here, Baby."

I slumped against the wall and sank all the way to a sitting position, knees up.

Hilary peeked around her mother in mid-hug, and looked at me with curiosity, rather than hostility or the juvenile neediness I had sensed in the way she attached herself to my leg. Her mother picked her up and kissed her.

"We can't do this ever again," Maggie said to me. "I can't bring her here to play, either. I'm sorry. I'm not mad at you. Where are our jackets?" She turned. "I guess I should stick to the Ninth Street playground."

"Yeah," I said.

I rose and led them to the hall closet, my hand feeling unwelcome on Maggie's back even though she allowed me to keep it there. Hilary looked at me over her mother's shoulder. I tried to smile at her. She made a very typical bashful-kid grimace and hid her eyes against Maggie's face; under other circumstances it would have seemed completely normal and not at all a cause for worried interpretations.

At the wrought iron outer door, Maggie had to try five or six times before she could get Hilary's pink windbreaker zipped. Then she stood up.

"Mad at me?" she asked.

"Of course not. I'm glad this happened. It stopped us before we did something really stupid."

Anyway, I had just decided, then and there, that she was The

59

Person I Would Never Get Angry At. I needed such a person. I needed to be able to treat people with more forbearance and forgiveness, and she was my chance to start learning how. I got angry at Lila when I was frustrated with my career, and at Jeff when I was frustrated with Lila, but I was going to learn infinite sweetness with Maggie.

"We don't have to feel guilty," I called out as she headed across the short, cement front yard to the wrought iron gate. "It was inevitable. We had to try it out, the way things were going— getting along so well and everything. We tried it out, it didn't work, so that's fine. It's a good sign about our marriages." She opened the iron gate, and set Hilary down on the sidewalk. "We can still call each other up and talk to each other and see each other, can't we?"

She gave me a sad smile. It was a warm, breezy April day, and white-bloused Catholic school girls walked by with gum in their mouths and their blazers on their arms, talking at full speed and volume, and not paying the slightest attention to us.

6

"Where is he?" Lila called when she came home that afternoon. "Where is the boy of the hour?"

With her wind-blushed face and angel-blond hair, and all charcoal gray from neck to knees, she looked like a Christmas card you'd see in a museum gift shop, and you'd stop and say, "*This* is my Christmas card." She rushed up to Jeff, sliding on her stockinged knees.

"Excuse me, sir, are you the boy of the hour? Are you the famous boy everyone is talking about? Are you the famous boy who is *two*? Oh, sir, sir, I'm so delighted to meet you, one so rarely has the privilege these days, oh let me shake your hand sir, please please let me shake the hand of someone who is two."

She pumped his hand so fast I could see its afterimages in the air. He was lurched forward and back in a state of complete giggles, the only motionless part of his body being his eyes, fixed on his mother.

"Why, look on the coffee table!" she said. "A box has suddenly appeared!" And they both gasped in wonder at the red-stringed white bakery box which she had unobtrusively brought out from behind her back. The legitimate birthday cake.

She smiled at me. "Day?" she asked.

"Medium."

Medium, what a way to describe my day! Couldn't she hear my voice shaking? Couldn't she tell anymore when I was lying? Wasn't she going to ask me, *Well, was she a good kisser?* Then I would confess everything to her, and if I did it wholeheartedly and freely, the wise and compassionate Lila, not the jealous Lila, would answer, and we would hug, and renew our love, and we'd really have something to celebrate tonight, and I'd never have to see Maggie again. There would only be a simple family in this room, enjoying a simple birthday, instead of a family plus all the apparitions that were crowding us out.

"How was yours?" I said.

"Medium too. Water main break on the D train, I thought I wasn't going to get home in time, but they cleared it up for"—she lunged at him and tickled his ribs—"Jeff's birthday! The day of all days! They declared a special birthday time limit which all water mains had to strictly observe! Oh," she chanted, "Your Birthdayhood, we celebrate you in all your birthday magnificence, you won't even remember it because you're too young, but your parents will always remember, we are so proud of you for attaining the remarkable and extremely enviable age of two! Two! *Two!* TWO! *TWO!*"

I smiled and scratched my nose, and sat on the arm of the sofa. I knew how bad Lila felt for having to be away from him for most of his birthday; that was why she had greeted him so effusively. It wasn't far from his bedtime; he would be getting tired, his responses slower and less alert; she was trying to crank him back up.

I'll tell her what happened, I thought. Telling my feelings to Lila was something I'd depended on for years and hadn't been able to do for months. These months of not being able to express my feelings about Maggie—to either woman—hadn't made me any saner or happier. While both of them could probably guess those feelings, or at least a milder approximation of them, the real strength of my feelings might have surprised them both. I'll tell her, I thought. But what is there to tell her? Maggie and I kissed. Is that a crime a grown man has to feel guilty about?

Lila came over to me. "Happy birthday." She stretched her arms out and moved in between my legs.

"Happy birthday." I kissed her lips and cheek and earlobes, and nuzzled her hair and sniffed her cologne all up and down her neck.

"Feel like celebrating?" she asked, cheek to cheek.

"Yes."

"I'll go change my clothes. Put the candles on the cake, will you? They're in the top kitchen cupboard. Wait till you see the butter cream on the cake I got . . . We should have bought balloons!" she said suddenly, and I practically jumped. Thank God I had released the balloons into the sky after Maggie had left.

"Oh, it's okay," I said. "You've done plenty."

But she was sailing on a gust of self-flagellation. "Jeff, Mommy forgot balloons! How can we have a birthday without them? Oh, I'm such an idiot! Should I run down to the toy store and buy some?"

"Maggie 'loons!" Jeff said, trying to console her.

That brought her down to earth fast. "What?"

"Maggie balloons," I interpreted unnecessarily. I cleared my throat. "We saw Maggie on the street the other day and she had balloons, coincidentally."

"Oh," Lila said.

"Maggie t'ake!" Jeff said.

"What?"

I knew that it was not a matter of her not understanding his accent. She understood perfectly well.

"Maggie cake?" she said. She turned to me. I thought I saw something in her eyes that pleaded with me to lie to her, but it vanished very quickly. "Birthday cake?"

My muteness was an answer.

"She got him a birthday cake and balloons?"

"She insisted. I tried to tell her tactfully not to do it."

"Oh, so I wouldn't find out."

"Come on. She's his friend's mother, and she's rather pushy. I happened to let slip that it was his birthday, and all of a sudden she's coming over with balloons and cake. What was I supposed to do, throw her out? Anyway, is it so terrible if he has two parties in one day? I think it's nice, actually."

"It could be nice, Brendan."

I exhaled in exasperation. "What do you think we did? We slept together? Give me a break. The kids are under our noses all the time; even if we wanted to do something we couldn't. I mean, yes, of course, we're attracted to each other, but so what? It can't possibly develop into anything. So it stimulates a friendship. I honestly don't see what's wrong with that."

She seemed to sag in disappointment. "I guess it's not wrong."

"Maggie and I have talked about it; we know we're attracted to each other. And we've agreed to keep it nonsexual. Frankly I think that's a fine, upright way to act, and I ought to resent your trying to make me feel guilty about it."

"I'm sorry," she said quietly.

I went over and patted her on the back. Enervated, she put one arm around me and gave me an I-need-a-hug look. We hugged gently, silently. It was good to feel my vitality infusing her, restoring her.

"Do you want to have the cake now?" she asked.

I nodded.

We lit candles, sang Happy Birthday, blew the candles out as a threesome, and applauded for Jeff, who was delighted to go through the ceremony a second time. Lila sliced the cake and gave each of us a piece, along with a glass of milk. It was a hazelnut cake with mocha cream and apricot jam between the layers, iced with a mocha butter cream, with rosettes of the same cream spaced at intervals on top, and a candied violet in the center.

We looked at it. "Well, what do you think?" Lila said.

I took a small forkful. "Fantastic."

Jeff sat there.

"Jeff, eat some birthday cake," she said.

He shook his head.

"Why not? Daddy says it's fantastic, that means delicious."

He shook his head, and looked at me for support. "All gone."

"No, it's not all gone, it's right here on your plate. We have a whole big cake I bought . . . All gone, you mean you're not hungry?"

First he shook his head no, then nodded yes.

"Yes, you're not hungry?" she asked. "Is that it? You're not hungry because you already had cake?" She turned to me.

"I think that's probably what he means," I said.

"Well, just how much of her wonderful, superior cake did he have?"

"I don't know. A couple of pieces."

"And how much did you have?"

"I guess three. I ate Hilary's piece."

We both looked at the slice of hazelnut cake on my plate, with one small bite taken out of it, and the fork lying empty except for a vestige of mocha cream.

"And when was this orgy of pastry-eating? This morning?"

"This afternoon. I don't know. Two to four."

Lila brought her fist up to her mouth and blew through it. I had an intuition then, that she was waiting for me to put some cake on my fork and eat it, just as a token, which she would accept as a gesture of concilation. But I felt as if I'd already gained a pound that afternoon; I felt swollen and leaden, spine-sweat sticking my shirt to the back of my chair, the world pulsating and too bright. And for some other reason too, I couldn't bring myself to give her that token.

She stood up, gathered all three plates onto her right arm, and pinched all three milk glasses together in her left hand. She used to be a waitress, after all.

I stood up. "What are you doing?"

She took the plates and glasses out to the kitchen counter and came back for the remainder of the cake in its box. I followed her out to the kitchen. Jeff trotted after us, with the excited, inquisitive silence of a child trying to keep up with his parents.

Lila opened the door under the sink, where the garbage pail was.

"Hey, save the cake for tomorrow," I said.

She forked the three slices into the garbage. I peered at them lying there in the white plastic bag: beautiful creations, amid crumpled tissues and crusts of toast and eggshells and an empty tomato sauce can and coffee grounds and—hunks and crumbs of chocolate cake. Those Lila noticed too.

She picked up the cake box, which she had haphazardly re-closed, its red and white string coiled on top.

"Hey, wait, wait! What are you doing? That's most of a per-fectly good cake. We can eat it tomorrow. Come on, Lila. Put it in the refrigerator." I placed my hands lightly on the cake box. "You're spiting him and yourself 'cause you're mad at me."

She jerked the box away from me, and gave me a look which she had given me only a few times in our life together, mostly recently.

"You forgot to say I'm wasting nineteen dollars," she said.

She dropped the box into the garbage and slammed the cup-board door.

7

I decided that I was going to rise above both Maggie and Lila. I would walk my own path, not detour for anyone else, and let whoever turned out to join me, join me. Of course, there was someone who *had* to join me: Jeff.

My first item of business was to visit Rawley with my latest pictures and my keenest enthusiasm, and show him I was ready to get serious. I wouldn't ask Maggie to babysit, either; perhaps the role of Person I Never Got Angry At would be best played, after all, by a memory.

I took Jeff with me on the subway into town. Let me tell you, we had quite a time. The station was seven blocks from our apartment, and I carried him the whole way so he wouldn't be exhausted before we even got there. In one arm was Jeff, in the other was my portfolio, and on my back was a blue nylon pack full of diapers, wipes, and graham crackers. At the station, we almost missed our train because he wanted to keep walking back and forth under the turnstile. I had to drag him the width of the platform, with his arm almost coming out of his socket, pull him through the doorway at the last moment so the doors wouldn't shut on him, and then wedge out my portfolio, on which the doors *had* shut. The light in the subway car flickered, a piece of newspaper blew under Jeff's feet and caused him to slip just as the train lurched violently forward, and I had to pull him off his feet just to keep him from falling to the floor.

"I had to!" I said, as he cried out in anger; but that true statement sounded wrong even to me.

As a way of apologizing for my rough handling, I didn't hold him next to me after we sat down. A grave tactical error. He immediately jumped up and ran to another empty seat across the aisle, stood up again and ran, bouncing with the sway of the car off the knees of other riders, into a seat way at the other end. It happened to be vacant because it was next to a vagrant who was sleeping stretched out, in a black raincoat, torn black pants, and toeless black shoes. This cheered Jeff up immensely. I reached him and grabbed his wrist just in the nick of time before he began twirling the man's matted, scabrous hair.

"You really should pick one seat and stay—" I began as the train slowed, but he was off, to the seats I had originally picked out for him. Which by now were occupied.

While he was running, the train stopped, and inertia made Jeff fall. No sooner did he get up, than a wave of adults began charging through the doorway. Startled and scared, he looked around for me, and I was there, holding him against my shins, shielding him with my portfolio, and somehow keeping our balance when the train started up. With the train in motion, I shuffled us over, inch by inch, to the standees' pole. Jeff sang to himself, fell down occasionally, and tried his old trick of rapidly blinking at strangers in order to get them to respond. Fortunately no one did.

We arrived at Washington Square, the train had stayed in service, and we hadn't gotten hurt: it had been a good subway ride.

We were in the Village: every time a male pedestrian made eye contact with me, I gave him a hostile glare, not knowing whether he was a boy-stealer, or whether he thought *I* was. Jeff stopped to look in the window of every cookie store, greeting card shop, and Middle Eastern restaurant on Greenwich Avenue. And at the corner of Greenwich and Perry, grasping the elementary school fence with both hands, he stopped, period, and went into the routine of gassy grimaces that meant he was moving his bowels: a totally unselfconscious curl of the mouth that, by coincidence, looked like a chagrined smile.

The problem was, Jeff had a kind of principle of personal honor: whenever he moved his bowels outdoors, he refused to walk any further until his diaper was changed. But I, from a principle of my own, refused to change his diaper on the street. So I carried him with his full load the next two blocks to Rawley's office. When we got there, the first thing I had to do was ask permission to change the diaper; which Rawley graciously gave, of course. I changed him on the oriental rug, which Rawley had me protect with telex paper; then I had to carry the soiled diaper out past the receptionist and another waiting client, leading Jeff by the hand because he wouldn't stay in the office without me.

I had exhibited the feces of a close relative in the office of someone with whom I wanted to do business.

"Sorry," I told Rawley when I got back.

"That's all right, I used to wear diapers myself."

It struck me as odd that he didn't say, "That's all right, I'm a father myself," because I knew he had one child, a grown up son. Rawley was an unusual person and I'd never been sure I understood him, but I always knew there was something in him worth understanding. He was a small, strong, quiet man with razor-cut gray hair, and a square jawline beginning to go to jowls under a good tan. He always wore a tweed or camel's-hair jacket, oxford shirt, wool tie, cashmere sweater-vest, and loafers, and he kept his hands in his pockets most of the time and rarely changed his facial expression. He seemed too reserved to be an agent, but was in fact an extremely good and successful one, working out of his own apartment in a high-rise on Jane Street. His walls were covered with his clients' work, but none of his own was on display and yet I knew he was an artist of surpassing talent. He'd started out, in his twenties, at the tail end of Abstract Expressionism, and his acrylics, while making the cleverest use of the spontaneous, paint-slapping energy of that style, were done in a light palette as calm as watercolor. I had seen his work once in a museum retrospective of the Abstract Expressionists, and it seemed to me that his two small paintings outshone the larger canvases of several more famous artists. In his clear strokes of aqua or lilac or coral or lemon, I felt as if he had dipped his brush into a lake of ideal color which lay tranquilly at the bottom of his heart.

But at the beginning of the Sixties, at the same time the fashions changed, his personal life apparently went to hell on him, his marriage broke up, he rarely saw his son anymore, and he collapsed, I gathered, into a depression which made it impossible even to work in his old style, much less develop a new one in tune with the times. He could have been a great color field painter—or something else, something which, because he did not do it, we do not have a label for in the art of the Sixties. But when he glued himself back together, he virtually stopped painting. He bought the shrinking client list of an elderly artists' representative, went around to Yale and RISD and Pratt and picked up some talented kids before they even graduated, and became an agent in the field of commercial art. The only artwork he did nowadays was in the form of cards to friends (my small collection of Christmas cards from him was one of my treasures) and posters for charities. As for his sex life, I had heard two conflicting rumors. His receptionist, Sharyn, had once whispered to me that he entertained in his apartment literally every kind of person there was: priests, male and female students and faculty from NYU, teenage runaways, doormen, garbagemen, cabbies, policewomen, jazz musicians, white-haired society couples, actors and actresses and dancers, homeless men and soup kitchen volunteers, street peddlers, nurses from St. Vincent's, librarians from the Jefferson Market Library, Korean grocers, indicted hit men, aging Beat poets. Everyone, Sharyn implied, except her. But a fellow client, with whom I once had a chat in the living room/waiting room, assured me that Rawley worked from the time he woke up in the morning to the time he fell asleep at night, his only venture into sexuality being a telescope aimed at neighbors' windows, his sightings recorded in a notebook the guy swore he had discovered in Rawley's desk drawer one day.

Rawley had confidence in me—had been touting my work to art directors without my even knowing it. He wanted me to go to lunch with this one, whose quirk he alerted me to cater to, and a meeting with that one, whose tic he alerted me to overlook. He had lined up a wildlife assignment and an excellent shot at some lucrative advertising work. Above all, he ordered me to work, work, work: that was the only thing I lacked for a truly prosperous career.

"You're *lucky* you have Jeff keeping you at home," he said. "That's where your paintbrushes are. You're the only artist I know who isn't wearing out his talent being a politician."

"I know you're right. It's just that . . ."

"What?"

"I mean, coming here with him today—"

"I assure you, I don't mind in the slightest."

"Yes, but just doing my daily work in an atmosphere where I have to interrupt it at any moment to wipe his ass or answer his next ten questions. It's like carrying around an extra weight. It's like being handicapped—like walking around on crutches."

"I have a client who walks around on crutches." He mentioned the name; I was surprised, I'd never known that artist was disabled.

I nodded with a chastened smile. Rawley was wiser than I; that, not his business skill, was why I treasured knowing him. I treasured Lila for her wisdom, and Rawley for his—and that was why I often wished I was talking to Maggie instead. To Maggie, *I* was one of the wiser ones.

Jeff had been drawing squiggles on the floor on some big sheets of plain bond paper Rawley had given him. Now he began to show fatigue in a way children often do: by regressing. He was crawling on the rug and trying to burrow under the pieces of drawing paper.

"I think I'm going to have to go," I said, pointing my chin at him. "Come on, Pal."

I went over to Jeff and held out my hand for him to grab. It precipitated violent resistance, head-shaking, crying; pleas on my parts, thrashing on his. Yes, a temper tantrum in the midst of business.

"Don't worry about it, some of my *clients* do that," Rawley said.

I tried the tactic of picking Jeff up decisively—and it worked. He stopped crying and took to gazing around curiously and rubbing his eyes. I shook Rawley's hand and thanked him, he handed me my portfolio, and I left.

In the subway, Jeff was extremely fussy. I tried to get him to lean against me so he could rest, but he hollered, "No!" and kicked my portfolio off its precarious position on my metatarsals, and onto the dirty floor of the train. Repeatedly he tried to climb over my shoulder to look at his reflection in the dark window; when I tried to pull him down and maneuver him into a sitting position, he actually bit me on the shoulder. Public place or not, I felt biting deserved swift punishment, so I gave him a single slap on his hand. At that very moment, the lights went out in the car and the train stopped. Jeff began to cry, and clung to me.

We were stuck under the East River for half an hour. Jeff's crying subsided into whimpers, then into silence. He climbed over my leg and into my lap, and stayed there, his body going slack against mine. I murmured to him: "It's okay, the train just stopped for a while. We'll just rest here until it starts again." Meanwhile I was planning what to do if I smelled smoke.

The cars on our left and right were lit; only ours was dark. Human silhouettes passed in front of us, walking through the car, but I decided it was best to stay here: the darkness was pacifying. A match glowed, then a red ember. I smelled marijuana.

Jeff began another round of crying. "Go home now!" he sobbed. "Go home now!" He kicked the bench, kicked my legs. I started planning what to do if some subway denizen with a handgun in his pocket came up to me and said, "Shut that kid up." I knew I wouldn't be able to get Jeff to shut up on command.

The train lurched forward again and the lights came on. Jeff was now frantic from exhaustion, and for the rest of the trip he writhed and twisted in my lap, sometimes succeeding in slinking down to the floor, making me struggle over and over to get him to sit up, or lie down peacefully.

Thirty seconds before we arrived at our stop, he fell asleep.

I had to rush as fast as I could to lift him and my portfolio and get us off the train in time. I carried him over my shoulder up the stairs, onto the sidewalk, and seven blocks home. He didn't wake up until I put him in his crib. Then he woke up and bawled for twenty minutes. I tried giving him a cup of milk—he dropped it on the floor. After wiping up the spill, I stood next to his crib—he was standing too—and I stroked his damp hair and gray cheek until he sank to his mattress. I was afraid he might be getting sick, but he was only overtired; his color came back in his sleep.

I made myself a turkey sandwich and a cup of coffee, and took a nap myself.

8

One day in August, a publisher called Maggie on the phone and told her that he loved *Rhino Yogurt,* wanted to publish it, and was eager to see anything else she might be working on. He liked my illustration, too, and was ready to give me the assignment for the book.

In two separate apartments half a mile apart, our two small children wondered why their parents jumped in the air and yelled with delirious joy, and kissed them without their having done anything cute.

"So we're allowed to work together?" she asked. "I mean as far as any *other parties* are concerned?"

I laughed, and rolled back and forth on the bed with happiness, wrapping and unwrapping myself in the telephone cord.

I completed the whole set of illustrations in less than seventy-two hours. That first feeling I'd had about the project wasn't a delusion: I'd been able to zip through those pictures as if they already shimmered in the air in front of me and all I had to do was copy them.

"They're beautiful!" Maggie said when I brought them over to her apartment. Vindication! Lila had found judicious, constructively critical things to say about every one of them. But I hadn't reworked them in line with her sound and penetrating specifications; I had rushed them to Maggie, fresh from the oven, and Maggie loved them.

We were sitting in her living room, the kids playing on the floor in front of us as guarantors of chastity. It was a surprising, expensive room, with a thirteen-foot ceiling, track lighting aimed at some pretty bad Miro-like prints undoubtedly bought at a frame shop, a couple of very tall, big-leaved, flourishing potted trees, a wall unit full of every possible audio and video component, and two currant-pink sofas that looked as if they had been plucked directly from the showroom at Bloomingdale's. It was as if Mike, doing well in his renovation business, had decided to leap out of the working class and into the upper middle in one week. Lila and I, in contrast, lived on a much better street, but our apartment was furnished mostly in butcher block and we still had some studenty old bookcases and dressers we'd been replacing one at a time for years, at estate sales, and with a nostalgic hug over each piece we discarded. And where we paid rent for our floor-through apartment, Mike owned this house and collected rent from a downstairs tenant.

"He fixed it up himself, him and his workers," Maggie said. "His subcontractors did the plumbing, the electric. You know— they all do each other's houses. Here. Here's a picture of him."

She went over to a maple secretary with brass handles, and brought back a silver-framed wedding portrait. Maggie was in a white gown, smiling with one corner of her mouth as she looked at something off to one side. A good-looking man in his late thirties had his arm around her. He had curly hair, long sideburns, and a black mustache, and wore a ruffled shirt, a tight white tuxedo, and a smile that might have come either from being mystified by his good fortune, or from having gotten away with playing a joke on someone. Automatically I tried to determine whether he was bigger than I was. Judging from how he looked next to Maggie, he was probably a bit shorter and broader than me.

I silently handed the photo back to her, and silently she

75

returned it to the furniture. Our mouths crunched some cookies with colored sprinkles, which she had set out on a plain white plate before I arrived.

"What did Mike say when you told him the news?" I asked.

"I didn't tell him yet."

I looked at her in amazement.

She shrugged.

"Tell him!" I said. "You have to. I mean, if he found out you hadn't . . ."

"I'll tell him," she said, with cookie in her mouth. She glared at me as she swallowed. "What are you, his spokesperson?"

"No, I just thought he's your husband—"

"Then I'll take care of the matter. All right? You give a shit about him?"

"No," I said. "Do you?"

She looked at me, and her long pause told me enough.

I felt a little guilty for prying. Or was it not guilt at all, but merely worry that she was angry at me?

I went over to my portfolio of *Rhino Yogurt* illustrations on the coffee table, and leafed through them with an unfocused stare.

"They're not bad," I said, as if to myself.

"They're great, Brendan." She came over beside me. "What do you call this stuff, I mean the material—the medium—you used for them?"

"Colored inks. I thought watercolor would be too washed-out looking, and gouache would be too thick, and colored pencil would be—you know . . ." It was hard to describe these things precisely, especially when standing so that every little shift of weight made our clothes touch. I made little explanatory circles with my hands: "Too fussy."

"What's that other one you mentioned?" she asked. "Not watercolors—the other."

"Gouache?"

"Yeah."

"Gouache. That's also a water-based paint, but it's thicker . . ."

I knew, then, why people like to teach. You go on and on,

sounding competent and knowledgeable, and all the while your head is swarming with desire and fantasy, and you can hardly hear the words coming out of your own mouth.

She smiled. "And Baby Bear said, 'These colored inks are just right.'"

I laughed. "Yeah. That's me. Baby Bear."

"*Orsachiotto.*"

"Really? Hey, that's good. But don't make that my nickname, it's too hard to say."

"*Orso bambino,* I think. *Orsachiotto:* bear cub. So what name do you want? Come on," she said, waiting. "Gotta have a nickname."

I wanted: Darling. Lover. Honey. Sweetheart. She could read it in my eyes.

I shook my head. "Just say my name."

"Brendan," she said.

Standing beside her, I could smell the herbs of her shampoo and her slightly mint-scented mouth. (Had she used mouthwash, knowing I was about to visit?)

"I like the way you said that."

We were absolutely still. The air conditioner hummed. The kids babbled over their plastic blocks. I thought I heard a faint sound of distress from Maggie's throat, and she moved away from me, the least fraction of a step.

9

Jeff was changing from a baby into a person. Though he was still broad-faced, there was no infant roundness now in his cheeks or under his chin. In his hazel eyes we imagined we could see experience being shaped into conclusions, opinions being formed and sometimes even being withheld from us. Babyhood's discovery feast—the joy of looking at a pencil sharpener, a grocery bag, a cat, and an oil delivery man, and finding them all equally exciting—was over. Now he seemed mostly interested in how to do things to his parents.

He knew how to make us angry, and the way he tested it over and over, you would have thought he enjoyed being yelled at and made to cry; but probably what he enjoyed was learning that he could survive it. He knew how to make us bring him anything he wanted, with an entreating, reasoning tone that convinced us that having Daddy's beach thongs in his bath was absolutely crucial to his emotional development. He sometimes knew how to pick up his toys, too, when it would keep him up later at night or when he simply needed to be praised for something—or even when he realized, as he fleetingly seemed to for the first time in his life one June evening, that having all the pieces of your ranch together in the same toybox was a heartwarming thing, while having the plastic horses and cowboys and fences strewn into all corners of the room was irritating and somehow morally unsatisfying. That was an exceptional evening, though: one of those glimpses a child sometimes gives you of potentialities that won't fully emerge till months or years later. The next day he reverted to being as messy as ever.

He would be starting nursery school in the fall, but for the rest of the summer he was still my sidekick, my parodist. When I painted or drew, he studied my work with furrowed brow, then went off and drew squiggles in crayon on a pad of newsprint. When I ate a sandwich, he stood by my chair, elbow resting on my leg, and stretched on tiptoe with an air of the most urbane curiosity, until I gave in: "Okay, want half?"

He'd give me a week of strife—bickering over bedtime, cutting into my sleep with crying fits—but the bad spell seemed necessary, for it ended with him standing cheerfully on a new plateau of maturity. The next day, he might lead *me* to the post office instead of me leading him. And he also learned to speak. That is, he had said words before, one or two at a time, and he still wasn't ready to tackle any of Shakespeare's longer soliloquies, but at some point he had crossed a threshold between being a nonlinguistic creature and a linguistic one. He spoke sentences of three or four words, and he was always speaking. The verb endings weren't always right, but he was a diligent grammarian in his own way, and when he made a mistake, it was often in the direction of fastidiousness: "Give it to I," he'd say, and grab Lila's chocolate chip ice cream cone.

He was for us what golf or the stock market is for some people: he was the topic of our friendship. When he went to bed for the night and left us alone, Lila and I filled the uncomfortable silence by recounting his day's adventures. Even the ones that had worn us down or irritated us while they were happening seemed cute when we narrated them. We took roll after roll of photos and passed them back and forth with misty smiles and gushing comments, though when he had been in the room in the flesh a few minutes earlier, he had had to repeat his request two or three times before we heard him asking for animal crackers.

We probed thorny issues: Should we start a campaign to toilet-train him before nursery school, or accept the fact that we might have to send him there in diapers? Should we try to become less overinvolved with him, to avoid burdening him with a firstborn's excessive self-conscious? We exchanged shocking tales of the errors of other parents. The mother of a timid boy had publicly scolded him for not wanting to share his toys! An affluent father had bribed his son with videotapes in order to get him to stop crying!

"This isn't a marriage," I said, "it's a seminar on parenting."

"Brendan, I can't guarantee that in my current state I'll respond to your ironies the way you want me to."

"Who's being ironic?"

"I have to go to bed. I wish I could ask you to join me, but my nose is so stuffed I think I could suffocate from kissing. Also I have to try to revise as much of that report as I can stand. I hope you know this is as frustrating for me as for you."

"My fucking hat is off to you," I smiled, and she padded away to fall asleep in her sweatshirt.

It was eight-thirty.

She had been going to bed earlier and earlier. She had caught a cold going from sweltering subway platforms to the overchilled office and back every day in sweaty business suits; the cold had turned into a sinus infection, which had resisted antibiotics. She came home every night with a headache and a low-grade fever. Some nights, her bedtime followed Jeff's by only a few minutes; then she woke up in the middle of the night—waking me up in the process—and turned on the light in the kitchen to make a cup of herb tea, and stayed awake till dawn, on the sofa, reading *Fortune* or *Barron's* or doing paperwork. She would get dressed quietly and go to work at seven o'clock, explaining later that it allowed her to beat the rush hour. Having gotten up so early, it would be even harder for her to last till a reasonable hour the next night.

I went to bed at midnight and awoke, with Jeff as my alarm clock, shortly after Lila left for work.

10

Our marriage had gone through troughs before. There were still plenty of days now when we were friendly and hoped that the bad phase was over. Even in the middle of an argument I would remind myself that the list of things I admired about her was much longer than the list of things I didn't, and that I liked looking at her and being chosen by her above all other men, and liked being where she was.

One evening, having just made myself a Campari and soda in the kitchen, I ambled back to the living room with my drink, and leaned against the wall, ankles crossed, to watch Lila give Jeff a horsie ride. I was mildly surprised, because at dinner she had worried aloud about being too tired to do the report she had brought home.

"Give her the spurs, Jeff," I said.

"Watch out, the horse understands Engl . . . aghh!" she said, and reared back with a choking laugh, for Jeff was pulling too hard at the collar of her pastel orange sweatshirt. "Hey, don't strangle your Mom, you need her to pay for nursery school."

Then, still on all fours, she turned and gave me a defiant look. "Well?" she asked.

I was confused. "Well what?"

"Nothing." And she galloped away, with Jeff, on her back, laughing so hard he forgot to hold on.

"Watch out!" I shouted, as he teetered. Lila's hips swung as she reached back and groped for him, tipping him further back; he fell off, and the side of his head hit the wall. I rushed up to where he lay crying.

"Watch what you're doing!" I barked without looking at her. I rubbed Jeff's head, checked for lumps — there was a small one on the right side, I kissed it — asked him questions. "Are you okay?"

"Otay," he said.

"What's your name?"

"Jeff."

"Who am I?"

"Daddy."

"Who is this?"

"Mommy."

"How many fingers is this?"

He made a careful observation and calculation. "Free."

"Okay, Pal." I patted him and glared at Lila. I gave him a couple of extra kisses to make my point.

"He's not badly hurt," she said.

"Luckily."

"Come on, Brendan, you're the one who's always saying not to coddle him for every little scratch."

She was right, but I was angry. "You were going quite fast and you weren't careful enough about whether he was holding on. In your charming vivacity."

"Well, from now on I'll make sure not to play with him vivaciously, unless you're there to shout warnings from the side."

"All I said was 'Watch out.' I could see he wasn't holding on, and you couldn't."

"It was when you shouted at me," she said, "that I shifted position and he lost his balance."

"So it's my fault?" I looked down at Jeff. He was completely recovered; even the tears on his face had already dried. He pulled the hem of Lila's sweatshirt and said, "More horsie!"

"It's bedtime," I told him in my tone of gentle no-nonsense.

"I'm not saying it was your fault," Lila said to me. "I'm saying that, believe it or not, I know how to play with him."

"Well, isn't it odd, then, that I don't go around knocking his head into walls and you do?"

"I do not!"

"You just did. And somehow I've learned not to hurt him."

"Except when you try to bully me in front of him. Come on, Jeff, let's keep riding. You might be five minutes late for bed but sometimes we just have to throw caution to the winds."

I went back through the foyer and kitchen to the little back-yard, which came with our rental but which we seldom used. It was a wood-fenced plot the size of a bedroom, paved with flagstone except for a couple of patches of soil, on one of which grew a cherry tree that spattered the walk with white petals and bruised red fruit. I could smell charcoal smoke from nearby balconies, and hear the roar of the exhaust fan and the laughter of the cooks and the clatter of pots and pans from the natural foods restaurant on the corner. Far off, from one of the Italian or Spanish neighborhoods, came a burst of firecrackers.

I bent a cool flake of cherry tree bark, broke it off, threw it down. I wrapped one arm around the skinny tree and leaned my face against it.

When I got back to the living room, Jeff had already been put to bed, and on Lila's face was a dimpled little smirk, as if she saw through me and saw both a rage of insecurity and a subsequent sheepish embarrassment. It exasperated me no end. Because it seemed to me that the things I felt—and what the fuck, *I* was the one who felt them—were not necessarily so consummately pinned down by Lila's smirks. I was sure that despite her self-satisfied reading of my character, I was the one who really understood how things were. You look at your spouse's face, the same face you've been grateful for when you've found it waiting for you on checkout lines and outside theater restrooms and on the pillow next to you, and you think you see that all the harmony of the past years was the result of shared inertia, that you have no use for each other except as conveniences, and that nothing you've done together during the entire marriage has been what you would have wanted to do if you'd had your own way. You want to smash that beloved face just for being so necessary to you.

This feeling recurs many times in all good marriages and always passes.

"If you go out for a walk," Lila said, slumped into the sofa with her knees up and her fingers interlocked on her breastbone, "will you bring me back some ice cream?"

"What?" I said in a tone of amazement, though I knew exactly what she meant.

"If you go for a *walk,* will you get me some *ice cream*?"

"Thank you, I understood the words. What makes you think I'm going for a walk?"

"You usually go for a walk to calm down after we've had a fight."

"Oh. From now on I won't have to feel my own feelings anymore; I can just ask you what they are."

"I was just—"

"What a relief, not to have to feel my own feelings."

"I was just asking whether you were going out." She let her feet slip down off the coffee table to the floor. "Because I feel like having some ice cream."

"Oh. Well, did we have a fight?"

"I thought we did."

"Good, because then I can get you ice cream, since, as you're so aware, I only go for walks after we have fights."

In fact, my bringing home ice cream for her was one of our rituals for any occasion. I had gotten into the habit when she was pregnant. I'd enjoyed performing that courtly service. She looked so wonderful and grateful when I came back with the cold brown bag warming up in my hand to temper it: her belly was big and round, her legs stuck out thick and stiff under a tent dress as she rocked in the rocking chair—it was as if I were having a few months' fling with a woman of a different physical type. Lila herself basked in the luxury of being fat and lazy, being waited on and wearing huge flowing dresses, as long as it was temporary. I used to walk for miles thinking about the forthcoming baby, and go from grocery to grocery to find vanilla Swiss almond, her favorite flavor. After Jeff was born, she wanted to keep her weight down, so she resolved never to buy ice cream for herself; she could only get the precious stuff by hinting, coaxing, joking, or pleading with me.

But this time she said: "Forget it, Brendan. You don't have to get me any ice cream. You don't have to do anything."

"Okay, I'm sorry. I'll get you some Swiss almond, okay? Or do you want to astound the world and try butter pecan?"

But she responded with only a wan fraction of a smile. She stood up, her pastel orange sweatshirt hanging lankily and her blond hair swaying above her collar. Her whole body looked splendidly long and lean. She turned to the shuttered windows and stared at them for quite some time.

"You don't even have to be here if you don't want to," she said.

"What!"

"If you want to live in some other way, with some other person . . ."

"Come on, will you please? There's no such other person. You're acting like I slept with somebody else, when nothing remotely like that ever happened. I don't know, Lila. If that's your interpretation of my motives, you must be slipping."

"Then you've turned against me just because I'm so repugnant," she said.

"You're not repugnant. And I haven't turned against you."

"You have. You have, it's so obvious!" Suddenly there was a catch in her throat. "Is it that you resent me for being the breadwinner? Because that's so unfair: I not only have to do it, but I'm resented for it."

"I don't resent it. In fact, I get the very strong feeling that *you* resent making more money than me. I mean, I can understand that you sometimes wish you were home with your child . . ."

"Brendan, don't cast doubt on my career commitment, I get enough of that from the men in my company. If I wanted to stay home with Jeff rather than work, I would do it. We'd get by with a less expensive lifestyle, or perhaps it would give you an incentive to earn up to your potential."

I felt my face turn red. "Right. Now we're getting down to it."

"I don't mention it very often."

"Then how come I've heard *that* very often?"

"I do not mention it all that very much. You know I believe a married couple is a unit, and it shouldn't matter which part of the unit brings in money and which part raises the children. I do my best not to bring up the disparity in our incomes."

"Your magnanimity is astounding!"

"Oh, you bastard!" she said in cold anger.

This was a point we reached two or three times a year, over various issues. At the beginning of our marriage, Lila had disliked arguing. She had been raised in a family where people gave themselves cancer of the stomach and cirrhosis of the liver trying not to make a scene—and didn't even make a scene over the cancer and the cirrhosis. When I started to bluster and rant and accuse, back in our college days, she would lie on the bed curled up, until I drove her to silent tears and then apologized. I would keep going until I saw those tears—like the finish line—even when a big part of me wanted to quit sooner. But gradually, by browbeating her for her so-called repressed nature, I, who came from a family where arguing was thought of as a healthy recreation, succeeded in teaching her how to do it, with the result that she now did it better than I. Because she was doubly angry: over the subject of the argument, and over the fact that I had made her argue at all.

I paced up and down the room, combing my hair with my hands. "I don't know, Lila. I don't know."

"You're always saying 'I don't know.' I hate that."

"I don't know, I don't know, I don't know, I don't know! What do you want me to say—say I know when I don't know? That's what you do. You're afraid to ever admit you don't know something. And I've known *that* all these years, and why I keep forgetting it, I don't know."

"*I* don't know why you're doing this to me," she said quietly.

"Doing what? Countering your attacks with my own? I realize that's unfair in your world. You like people as long as they agree with you and go along with what you want and confirm your inflated self-image. Just let them dare to counterattack, and boy, you'll make them regret it."

She lowered her head sorrowfully. "What must you think of me if you say things like that?"

"That's just it—I like you most of the time. I love you. I'm saying that right now, even when we're being so nasty to each other. I mean, we're having an argument, so I'm not particularly charmed by you at this *moment.*" We exchanged wry smirks, as if, in fact, in a hostile, sour, tacitly agreed-upon way, we *were* sort of charming each other. "But people exaggerate when they argue. That's okay. But what bothers me—" It took me some time to phrase it. "—I think you don't love me anymore."

I paused, expecting her to deny this and reassure me that she still loved me despite our recent difficulties. But she didn't do that. She said:

"It's true, I haven't been especially thrilled by the way you've been acting lately."

I felt a shock, a sudden sickness in my stomach.

"It's like you're trying to punish me," she went on. "Maybe not for making more money than you—okay, I grant you're more enlightened than that—but just for being self-confident. It's like you want me to work under a handicap, so that at the office I have to give X percent of my mind to worrying about you. Are you in a bad mood? Are you yelling at Jeff? Who are you hanging around with?"

"X percent of Lila's mind: Is the servant trustworthy?"

"Oh!" she shrieked, with her eyes shut tight and her hands pressing her ears. "If you want me to hate you so much, I will! I hate you! I don't want to talk to you. If you disappeared in front of me this very instant I wouldn't care. Is that what you want to hear? You feeling-hurter, you make me feel terrible, then you interrogate me about whether I love you? I'll say whatever will get you to stop. I hate you! I hate you, Brendan!"

"If you wake the baby with your screaming . . ."

"You'll what?"

I had no idea.

"*I'll—*" She shrieked, and rushed at me, fists raised.

"Put your hands down!" I ordered.

"Why? Afraid you'll hit me?" She laughed. "'Cause you know if you hit me you'll lose your meal ticket. Come on, darling, show me your famous left jab, or whatever it's called. It'll be the most expensive thing you ever did."

We glared at each other. We listened for Jeff's voice. He hadn't awakened.

"Just don't scream," I said, "or you'll wake him."

"Don't you threaten me about my child. Don't you dare."

"Oh, really. You're so concerned about him, you scream while he's asleep. You let him fall . . ." I turned on my heel, trying to think of other ways in which she was an unworthy, irresponsible mother. I couldn't, she was an excellent mother. "I'm the one who cares about him. I'm the one who's with him all day."

"And complains about having to be. And as soon as I walk in from a full day's work, you throw him at me, as if it's really the woman's job whenever she's physically there, and it's humiliating for a man to do it."

"That's not true. I don't mind doing it. I like doing it, a lot of the time. I like *him,* I'll fucking goddamn have you know, I fucking love our mutual son."

"And I feel sorry for him, for the kind of love you sometimes show him," she said, blinking back the beginning of a tear. She had taken quite a few theater courses in college.

Me too. "Do not," I said, "do not say that. You don't know what you're talking about. It's true I'm not his mother, I don't interact with him with the well-known infinite gentleness and unselfishness of all mothers around the world. But I am his father, I am a fucking great father, and you don't understand the way a man acts with a son, but if you just observed it in an unprejudiced way and observed the results in his personality, you might learn something. And I resent your trying to turn this, to turn this into one of your bullshit feminist clichés, with me as the hypocritical male brute."

"Yes, I know you're better than other men. You've told me so yourself."

"I don't claim to be so special."

"When I come home in the evening, you rest."

I scoffed. "I make dinner. I wash the dishes. I give him his bath half the time."

"You commune in the backyard with your thoughts about who knows what."

About Maggie. My eyes told Lila she was right.

"Oh, I went to the backyard! Forgive me, I must have spent ten minutes out there!" Now I knew Lila loved me: she was jealous of those ten minutes.

"I'm sick of your mockery," she said.

"I'm sick of—" I tried to think of what. Everything, I wanted to say. I wanted to say that, whether it was true or not. I'm sick of everything about you, and me, and especially about us. I'm sick of brandy or Drambuie on cold evenings and Campari and soda on warm ones; I'm sick of knowing what's the least crowded time on the checkout line at Key Food; I'm sick of the ammonia smell that pervades the apartment once a month when you bleach your hair; I'm sick of not being able to buy whole fish, because you'll only eat fillets; I'm sick of your long, skinny, bony feet scratching my legs when you're asleep, and I'm sick of the way you start adding extra blankets to your side of the bed in October. I'm sick of finding you waiting devotedly for me at the Sunday breakfast table and trying to keep me from sticking my head in the *Times.* I'm sick of having to walk around you to get to my barbells or my donuts, the space you take up, the time you steal from my life, the consensus required before we turn on the television or listen to a tape . . .

Her cheekbones were shiny under the light of our chandelier.

Her hands, hidden under the waistband, stretched taut her orange sweatshirt.

What I was perhaps genuinely sick of, I think, was that any objection, whether a trivial objection or an all-encompassing objection, evaporated, became insubstantial and hard to remember, any time I looked at her face. I had to look away from her face now, in order to be able to stomp toward the front door. As always when I walked out, as the crowning gesture or the half-time signal of an argument, she looked as if she was too kind to tell me she knew how little fault I could honestly find with her.

"I'm sick of it!" I shouted, and slammed the door behind me.

It was a warm, clear night, fragrant with homeowners' dogwoods and lilacs. The big, full, yellow moon was just high enough to have cleared the treetops of the park. In the other direction, downhill, there were car headlights and pink streetlights and neon store lights. I thought: She didn't even ask me to stay, she didn't even ask where I was going, how does she know I'm not going to throw myself in front of a bus?

Of course, this was our usual pattern. I would leave abruptly, Lila would pretend not to care. She would sit alone fearing my death or desertion while I stalked our neighborhood and other neighborhoods for an hour or two, walking my rage away and wondering whether she was worried enough yet, whether she regretted her rash words. Then, sooner than I had planned on, my blood pressure and pulse would subside and I would find myself turning around and heading home. I would quietly open the door with my key, humbly pad toward where she sat reading a book or watching the news, and offer the tips of my fingers in an embarrassed, self-satirizing handshake, and ask: "Friends?"

We'd gone through that our share of times. I didn't remember exactly how many. A good handful over the years. Now, as I walked, I thought the usual things. I'll leave this town. I'll take the train to the plane and charge a ticket to somewhere, somewhere I've never been before. I'll hide out in the woods and only

Rawley will know where I am; I'll mail him my pictures, and he'll mail me my checks. I'll make him promise not to tell Lila where I am. In a couple of years I'll give her a call, solely for the purpose of having Jeff visit me.

No, I'll sit in some bar till closing time, then stumble drunkenly onto the street, howling like a tomcat or a teenager, and two cops will stuff me into the back seat of their patrol car and drive me home, where Lila will be waiting, crying for me.

I'll go to the movies. What's playing around here?

I'll buy some ice cream and bring it home.

I could almost taste the chocolate-covered almonds already.

Always it ended with me returning home, unsure whether I was being smart or defeated—returning home partly because I had nowhere else to go.

It took me a few minutes, this time, to realize I had somewhere else.

11

Talk to someone who understands you. Talk to someone, that's what people do. It's what *she* would say: "That's what regular people do, isn't it? They talk?" It would cool me down. I would talk to her for an hour or so, then she would send me home the way you send home any good friend.

I dialed Maggie's number from a pay phone.

"Hi, how *are* you?" she asked, without my having to say my name.

I was glad Mike didn't answer, but the possibility hadn't worried me. I had met him once for the space of a handshake—"Hey, the artist! Good goin'!"—and had spoken to him on the phone once for the length of time it took to ask for Maggie.

"I'm in a pay phone on Seventh Avenue," I said. Seventh Avenue in Brooklyn: a troop of stag teenagers swaggering as they shouted across the street to a troop of girls; couples trudging to the subway for their Friday night in Manhattan; double-parked Camaros and Fieros waiting outside the local singles' bar. "Let me give you the number, and I'll hang up, and you call me back. I'll try to shout over the noise, actually that would suit my mood."

"Brendan, what is it? You sound so hectic."

"Yes, I'm hectic. That's a good choice of words, Maggie. I can tell you must be a writer. I had a fight with my wife."

"Oh," she said in the tone of strict control she used whenever I mentioned the existence of my wife under any circumstances. Then she brightened and said: "The call-your-friends-from-a-pay-phone kind of fight. I know. Are you drunk yet?"

"No. I was going to get drunk, maybe. Anyway, here I am, calling you . . ."

She answered that with silence.

"Listen, I better go," I said. "Just hearing your voice makes me feel better, but . . ."

"Wait, where are you rushing off to?"

"I don't know." She didn't mind when I said it. She said it sometimes herself. "I feel awkward standing here telling you my troubles through a pay phone."

"So come over and tell me your troubles in person."

It was my turn to stand silent.

"Come," she said.

"Okay."

In five minutes I crossed the neighborhood to her block. One street light was broken and the parked cars were mostly old, beat-up American sedans instead of new foreign subcompacts. Families sat on stoops drinking and chatting, as they didn't do on my block, and little kids played running games in the street after dark and their older brothers and sisters played portable radios and broke beer bottles in the groves of the park. I checked my appearance in the dark windshield of a car and tucked my fuschia T-shirt more neatly into my washed-white blue jeans. I walked more slowly, preparing myself, reading the house numbers painted in white on the top steps of the front stoops.

On her front stoop sat Maggie, outlined from behind by the yellow vestibule bulb shining through the two glass panels of the oak door. She smiled at the involuntary sound I made.

"Hi," I said, "you cut your hair!"

"A couple days ago. You like it?"

Did I like it. I ran up the steps to her, two at a time. She had gotten one of those post-punk haircuts that they were lining up for in the Village: cropped short above the ears and in back, with a forelock brushed almost into her eyes. She was wearing white shorts with suspenders, and a white T-shirt with a Mondrian design. She looked like some kind of bohemian waif. She looked phenomenal. I sat down next to her. Our knees knocked together.

"I told him," she said. She drummed on the edge of the step between her legs.

"Told who what?"

"Well, you called up, and I said to him, my friend Brendan is coming over, the guy who did the pictures?"

"Yeah, we've met."

"So he asks why you're coming over and what you want. Not suspicious or anything, just curious. I didn't have to tell him anything. I mean, I should have just told him, 'He's upset, had a fight with his wife, we'll give him a couple of beers and send him home.' Right?"

"Yeah. So what did you tell him?"

"Well, I kept thinking, 'Who is this guy that I have to explain my friends to him? What gives him the right?' He's asking me about your marriage, your problems, like he'd really like to hear that you have problems. I kept thinking, 'Don't ask me about this. Don't ask me anything and I won't have to tell you anything.' Then he starts joking—he thinks he's joking. Are you and I really good friends? How good of friends are we, this illustration business is that all there is to it? Would you like to get into my pants, and so on and so forth. Which pisses me off because he's always telling me how unjealous he is, how we're both free except we don't want anyone else except each other—all this bullshit. And it became apparent, you know. I mean I could tell he was saying all this because he expected to fuck me later. Like he has some kind of *right* to sleep with me, just because we live in the same house. So he can joke about people he thinks don't have the right. Like, he says it's great with him if you get me wet, it saves him the trouble. So finally I said to him: 'Look, Brendan can get into my pants any time he wants to.' And I told him what we've done. I told him how great it was to kiss and touch each other, and that we stopped because of the kids being around, but that we want to talk to each other all the time, and that we love each other. . . . Is that right?"

We had never actually said it.

"Yes," I said. "That's right."

She leaned her face toward me and we kissed, for a long time, in full view. Oddly, I didn't fear Mike's seeing us—I sort of assumed that. I only felt uncomfortable about exposing Maggie to stares and gossip, but she had started it, she was willing.

She's presumed upon me, I thought; she's endangered me; she's plunged me into something. No, she's told the truth for me.

My hand stroked her shorts, and the thin cotton of her tee shirt fluttered against my chest. I started thinking up Woody-Allen-type explanations that I would stammer at Mike if he came storming out—"B-b-but Mr. Ferro, it only seems that way. Actually I was showing Maggie the bonding ritual of a very interesting tribe of South American Indians." It almost made me laugh in mid-kiss. Shit, he'll come out and I'll have to fight him. How will I explain my face to Lila?

But those inner voices faded far away. "So he threw you out?" I said bitterly, ready to avenge her.

"No. He doesn't have the right. I came out here by myself. He said he wasn't gonna let you in the house, he doesn't want to see you. So I said I wanted to see you. He said it was my choice."

He's not such a bad guy, I thought. "Is he going to let you back in?"

"I have the key."

"I don't mean that. I mean—"

"You mean can we take it back, can we undo it?" There was an edge in her voice. "Well, if you want to know, I'll tell you. I know he'd let me back up. I wouldn't be in any danger, either. But I know that tomorrow he's gonna find someone with a bigger chest to take my place. Whether I'm here or not. I mean, he's popular in the neighborhood. He can get along with anyone, or without

96

anyone. This was always an experiment for both of us. When we first met in the plant store, his business was just starting to get going; he decided he needed a homemaker. And he meets this little chick who needs a home . . . Oh, by the way, he told me to warn you about myself."

"Warn me? About what?"

"That I'm a devil. You already know that, right?"

"Right." I kissed her.

"He warned me about you, too."

"What?" I was offended.

"You're destroying my chance for a normal life."

"What if I am, Maggie?"

"No, only blood relatives can do that."

We kissed our best kiss yet. I could hear children playing ball down the block, their running footsteps approaching as they chased a ball that had rolled under the parked cars.

A second-floor window opened above us. We broke apart and looked up. There was crying, and childish, sniffled words I couldn't understand. Jesus, he's beating Hilary, I thought. I gripped Maggie's leg.

A man's voice shouted down to us, a Brooklyn baritone.

"Where's her alphabet book? She wants me to read to her."

"Are you kidding?" Maggie shouted up. "It's past her bedtime, she's supposed to be asleep. She's asking for a book because she thinks you'll let her stay up that way."

"I thought you want her to learn her letters."

Maggie and I exchanged a smile of pity for him. "Well, let her learn them tomorrow. Just give her a bottle if she wants, nothing else, and tell her 'Go to sleep.'"

"Sorry to disturb you," he said, and slammed the window shut. We couldn't hear whether Hilary was still crying or not.

"Trying to prove what a good father he is," Maggie said. We looked up at the window together.

I put my arm around her and leaned her close to me to comfort her. I had a premonition that she was going to go upstairs, and if I couldn't influence her to stay with me, I would at least try to remember the feel of her body. I looked at the elderly town-houses with their cornices and garret windows and keyhole windows and turn-of-the-century eaves. An old Mercury parked across the street had a new door on the driver's side, smoother and cleaner and a deeper shade of blue than the rest of the car. Repair is the great word of life. Anything that endures, does so not by remaining pristine, but by being strengthened at precisely the point where it broke.

"Do you want to go back?" I asked. "I think he still likes you."

"He likes a lot of things. Don't worry about him."

I gave Maggie a kiss on the bared back of her neck. "I like your hair."

There are rare moments when you can feel your life switch tracks. You overhear your mind plan its strategy for you in a few common words: "I'm with her now."

They sound so slight and intangible that it's hard to believe you've just altered the course of your life. But you know you have.

She looked at me, stroked my hand. "Do *you* want to go back? Did I ruin your—"

"No. Did I ruin yours?"

I was certain from the look in her eyes that she was about to say the same thing, but before she could, the upstairs window opened again. We looked up. No voice came out. No head stuck out.

Papers dropped out of the window. They were paper airplanes. They glided toward us, some hitting the brownstone wall, some spinning in loops, some diving straight down to hit the bannister or land on the garbage cans. One of them carried past the staircase and skidded under a parked car; none of them hit us or landed within reach. They were of several different designs, as if Mike in childhood had studied the various ways of folding paper airplanes, and was taking this nostalgic opportunity to compare their merits.

"Don't forget your stuff," he called out.

Maggie stood up. She ran to the top of the stoop and picked up a plane that had landed there. She unfolded the piece of paper, and read something written on it, then she turned to me in alarm.

"Help me!"

The upstairs window banged shut.

Maggie ran up and down the steps, picking up paper airplanes. She swung over the bannister, into the bay where the garbage cans were kept, and moving them aside with a clatter of aluminum she scrambled around picking up the planes that had crashed there. I retrieved one that had come to rest on the step and read it.

There were fragments of a children's story in Maggie's handwriting: some passages crossed out, others repeated several times in slightly different words. It wasn't *Rhino Yogurt*, it was one I hadn't seen before.

"It's my new story I just started this week!"

We both scurried around, picking up all the paper planes we could and unfolding them against our chests so that they became pages again. I stretched out prone next to a parked car, and reached around the front left tire to drag out the grease-blackened plane that had skidded there. When we couldn't find any more, we double- and triple-checked the area. Finally, although we couldn't be sure we hadn't overlooked one—they were unnumbered pages, rough jottings—we agreed to stop. I gave my sheaf to Maggie. She counted eighteen and said it seemed about right.

"I just started it this week. I was gonna tell you." She looked up at the window. "I'll kill him."

"Don't kill him." I took her arm. "Come on, let's go."

As if by silent agreement, we stopped at the point on the sidewalk where we could be best seen from the upstairs window. We kissed. I thought I could see the faint contour of a man's head behind the curtain; after a few seconds, it wasn't there anymore; and we ran down the street with our arms around each other's waists.

"What are we gonna do?" we said. "What are we gonna do?"

We were on Seventh Avenue, where most of the shops in Park

Slope are, but most of them were closed at this hour, with iron gates over their entrances. Only a donut shop, a liquor store, a car service, and a pizzeria were still open when we passed. But in our frame of mind, food seemed unnecessary, liquor absurd, and we couldn't spare the cash to pay the driver of a hired car.

Then there was a sound, a rumbling beneath the sidewalk, and it got louder, and a wind blew up from the metal grating at our feet. A piece of newspaper flew up into the air, and a scent of stale chewing gum and damp subterranean weeds. The sound kept getting louder, it was like a city rushing toward us and preparing to stop for us for fifteen seconds. It was the F train coming in.

At the subway station on the corner, the two green globe lights were on, showing that the entrance was open. You could hear the train's brakes screech as it began to slow down. I tugged Maggie's hand.

"Let's get on it."

"Where to?"

But she was already running with me. We raced down the station steps, jumping down the last four. I sprinted ahead of her, toward the groaning exhalation of a subway train coming to a stop. An arrow on the wall said: "To Manhattan."

I ran in that direction, through a short uphill passageway, past the token booth, just as the train doors opened. I stopped in front of the turnstile, fished in my pockets, looked around in despair. I didn't have any tokens, and we didn't have time to buy any, and who knew what doubts might arise in us if we had to wait for the next train?

"Jump it!" she called, running to catch up to me.

I vaulted over the turnstile and dashed for the train just as its doors were sliding closed.

"Hey, you!" a garbled, staticky voice said through a loud-speaker. But I didn't turn around, and the voice didn't say another word.

Turning my body sideways, I just fit through the closing doors. I pushed them open. Maggie slid under the bar of the turnstile, pages in hand, and ran forward, under my arm and across the aisle of the subway car into a seat. I let the doors close, and joined her. We were off.

The car was bright and air conditioned and fairly new, though littered with the usual debris, and it was uncrowded: most people had already got where they were going for the evening. A cluster of teenagers at the far end debated loudly about the rock concert they were going to see: "Suck my ass, man! He's the greatest fuckin' drummer!" A black woman in a flower-printed white dress and rimless eyeglasses read some sort of leather-bound book of scripture. A white woman, shifting toward us and away from the teenagers, sat very straight with her legs tight together, a shorthand textbook on her lap. A slightly built Hispanic guy with a black mustache, in a Postal Police uniform with a brown-handled revolver in a holster belt, kept tipping over, asleep, and waking up with a vigilant expression.

Maggie and I had a three-seat bench to ourselves, but Maggie didn't sit in her own seat. She sat in my lap sideways, her legs draped across me, and we drank each other's mouths as the tunnel walls flickered by faster and faster.

"You old turnstile jumper!" I said. I felt as if I were seeing Maggie the way she had been as a teenager, but happier than she had been.

We didn't say anything else during the ride, because we were making out the entire time. I've heard stories about people who've been observed having intercourse in New York City subway cars, and how we stopped ourselves from reaching that point, I don't know. We kissed and pawed through a dozen stops: through Brooklyn and under the river and into lower Manhattan. At Fourth Street I stood up and said, "Here," just on an impulse. Impulse was all we had.

We emerged in the middle of Greenwich Village. It was hotter and noisier and brighter than Brooklyn, and there were people walking all over the place: loud, laughing groups of students, and couples quiet or arguing, and solo figures weaving and slinking around them with hands in pockets or carrying small grocery bags. We joined the current, hand in hand. It was the first time we held hands without the risk of surprising anyone; like the adults we were, we could go wherever we wanted without arranging a babysitter or checking with a spouse. I held Maggie tighter.

12

We didn't really know where to go. I had a few friends in Manhattan, but they all knew Lila too, and the last thing I wanted was to have them butt in on my domestic problems. What I really would have wanted to do, if I'd had my absolute choice, was walk with Maggie to the ends of the earth and back.

We started west on Fourth Street, and got past the touristy section of greasy restaurants and sex shops, then crossed Seventh Avenue—the real Seventh Avenue!—to the quieter, more residential section of good restaurants, pastry shops, and young men dying in brownstone apartments. We kept walking almost until we were out of the Village, standing on the corner of Fourteenth Street and Eighth Avenue. Then we turned back. There was nothing open here but a donut shop standing by itself like a panhandler whom everyone is avoiding. The big old granite banks on the corner were brass-gated, and the moon, on its crosstown climb, was now small and white and hard.

We walked down every street that didn't look too dangerous, filling in the entire grid of the neighborhood, never letting go of each other, walking without plan. Coming back to Jane and

Fourth Streets, we entered the Corner Bistro for hamburgers and beer and rest. We sat on the same side of one of the wooden booths in the dark back room, feeding each other french fries and kisses.

"It's like being teenagers," I said. "We want to go to bed together but we don't know where."

"We'll find someplace. I've done this kind of thing before."

The aproned waiter-chef, a tall black man with hair white at the temples, came to relight the red candle in the netted glass bowl at our table, and I ordered coffee in case we had to stay up all night. In the candlelight we could see the names and initials of lovers carved into the bumpy oak surface of the table. I patted my pockets: I didn't even have a ballpoint pen for the purpose. I took out my old housekey: would that work?

"Wait," Maggie said, and pulled from the pocket of her suspendered white shorts a switchblade knife with a white handle.

"Hey, preparation! All right!" I said.

She handed it to me. Giving her a questioning look, I put my finger on the button: Is this how? She nodded. I pressed the button and the blade snapped out. I carved "B B + M F" and framed it in a pretty crappy-looking heart that followed the irregularities of the oak instead of being symmetrical.

Maggie closed her hand around mine, and with our forefingers extended together we traced our initials, trying to see what kind of unit they made.

"I wonder what they're doing now," Maggie said.

"I wonder if Lila's called the police."

It felt strange to say Lila's name. And suddenly a rush of panic-adrenalin: if the police came to our apartment, wouldn't it wake Jeff? Shouldn't I go back just to prevent that? He would find me there as usual the next morning and wouldn't ever know anything had happened. No, think clearly, think realistically, don't succumb to sentimental distortions. Identify your own interests and put them first. That's what everyone on earth does.

"No, she can guess who I'm with," I said, "She'll assume I'm not hurt—if she cares. Maybe she'll call your house. Then it'll be official. Or maybe she won't call anyone. Maybe she'll just go on without me, to show she didn't need me."

"She needed you," Maggie said, stroking my hand.

"At times."

"Hilary needed me," she said, in the spirit of someone sticking her hand into a flame to see if she could bear it.

"We need ourselves."

She climbed into my lap, and alternately kissed me and hid her face against me, until the waiter came with the check.

It was long after midnight and we were almost out of cash. All we had left were a few dollars and our two credit cards, which we really preferred not to use more than necessary, even though we intended to pay our spouses for anything we charged to their accounts. By the time we left the bar we could have met daylight just by walking for a couple more hours. I kept expecting to hear Rawley's voice from a window overhead: "Brendan Beame, what are you doing here? Come on up," but of course that didn't happen.

We spent another hour searching for anyplace that didn't look too horrendously unhealthy. Then, on West Street, on the Hudson River, with the old, derelict West Side Highway between us and the sky, we saw a hotel on a corner. It was a six-story building with a fading sign painted right onto the blood-red brick, and at first I thought it wouldn't be habitable. But as we were standing there, scrutinizing it from across the street, a yellow cab drove up and stopped at the entrance, and a man in a brown leather sport jacket, carrying a camera and a folded tripod and a photographer's lamp, got out. It was an artists' hotel, not a whores' or junkies'. At least it was some acceptable combination. I was a professional artist after all, and Maggie was demonstrably holding a manuscript. I took us inside.

We got a room on the fifth floor with a view of the river: one of their best rooms, still available at that time of night. I charged a week's rent in advance, so that if we woke up with second thoughts, we'd have a reason not to run back prematurely to our spouses.

Our bed sagged and squeaked, the mattress was thin, but the sheets were clean, and sitting against the headboard we could see the lights of New Jersey out the window. There was a Maxwell House coffee factory directly across the river: a huge blue neon cup was lit up, tilting out its last red drop. The western sky was changing by the minute; the east, on the other side of the building, was probably silver-yellow and palest blue. We kept the shade up; no one could see us in that location. The river was growing light with dawn. Not a car passed on the street, and on the bed, Maggie and I did what we had been fantasizing about for months.

13

I woke up before Maggie—it was three in the afternoon. A slanting bar of sunlight, coming through the western window, covered her naked legs like a warm blanket, and expanded by the minute. When it reaches her eyes, I said to myself, she'll squint and squirm and awaken, and see me—a new companion in a new place. Will she hug me? Will she rush to get her clothes on and run out of the hotel to the subway?

I sat in the chair and looked at her skinny little beautiful body, and our narrow little ugly hotel room, and considered.

I began to cry.

"I've got to get back," I said. The words were distorted by sobs, and I had the odd sensation of being unable to make out my own meaning, as if I were some onlooker, puzzled by a garbled enunciation. "Oh, Jesus. Jeff, goddamn it. I've got to get out of here."

I paced so frantically that I wondered, I seriously wondered—so unglued was my state of mind—how I would keep from crashing through the door or the window. Partly in order to stop my acceleration, and partly because of the sweet sight of her lying asleep in the sun's warmth, I zoomed over to the bed and launched myself crosswise atop her, hugging and kissing her back.

She wriggled, gave a tender moan of protest, and said: "Lemme sleep."

The sunlight was advancing to her shoulderblades and higher. Each new area of flesh it illuminated, I kissed: shoulders, neck, chin. Curling up, she inadvertently dipped her whole head into the zone of light, with a shock like ducking your head under water. The sun made her blink. She turned over, looked at me. She saw my tears, and I was ashamed.

"Tell me," she said.

"Maggie, I love you. We've got to go back. We've had a little adventure and now . . ."

She sat up. "Are you leaving me?"

I was startled. We had desired each other, dreamed romantically of each other, pined in each other's absence, and escaped together, but this was the first time either of us had asserted a claim to the other. And I would have thought I would be the one to do it. I suppose there had always been, in the back of my mind, a suspicion that Maggie was using me as an artistic contact or for a cynical fling. Well, I'm sure we had each seen the other as a source of opportunity, but she also really loved me. And the seductiveness of being pleaded with, needed, missed, began to work on me and draw me toward her.

"We have kids," I protested against my own temptations.

"We'll take them. I can get them out of there, I know how. We can—"

Then I think she saw how appalled I was at the idea of kidnapping our children. I think too, in the instant of seeing my reaction, she understood immediately the reprehensibility of her own suggestion.

"We'll figure out how to get custody for at least half the time," she said, and stroked my legs.

I began drying my eyes in the most violent way, rubbing so hard I was afraid I would actually injure them. I rubbed with my fists and gouged my closed eyes with the points of my knuckles, and saw flashes of light behind my closed, hurting lids. I punched myself over and over on the forehead, then squeezed my eyes shut and punched both of my cheekbones at once.

"Baby," she crooned at me. She caught my wrists and stopped me from hurting myself. "Baby Bear . . ."

"I have messed up, Maggie. I have totally fucked up."

"Shh. I'm with you." Her voice was more soothing, pacific. "You're still Jeff's father. You'll leave behind what you have to. You'll keep what you should."

"But maybe you should go back too. I mean, I know you love Hilary. Don't you want to go back to be her mother?"

Hilary provided me a less directly distressing version of my own troubles, and I lingered over a daydream of Hilary crying for her Mommy until I broke out in sentimental weeping.

"I'm her mother," Maggie said. "I don't know, Brendan. I don't know what I can do. He makes me feel bad. I mean he's a person who—."

She took a deep breath, trying to marshal her explanation. It was impossible for me not to concentrate on the motion of her beautiful, dark-nippled, small breasts.

"I mean, he was so nice when he was dating me, visiting me at the plant store. A fucking gentleman. Then, when he gets you in his control, he shows you how little he thinks of you. Not in a physical way—he doesn't hit me or anything. But he's like a manipulator, you know? I can't explain it, but everything I do is wrong to him. He lets me know I'm a dumb fuck-up that he rescued and he's tolerating. Meanwhile I've kept his books for his business and I've raised his daughter. I know I'm not what he makes me think I am, but it's so hard for me to believe it. How *can* I be a good mother in that atmosphere? If I had to live with him the rest of my life, I'd do like my girlfriend Bonnie—turn the bathtub red. I mean it. I'm afraid."

"No. No, sweetheart, you won't. You're stronger than that."

She sulked, as if my encouragements, by contradicting her self-image, actually made her feel worse.

I tried to weigh my alternatives. Consider who needs you

more, I told myself. Is she really a potential suicide or is she just using that to make you feel tied to her? And yet that isn't the whole problem either. What do you want to do for yourself?

Think clearly, think realistically, don't succumb to sentimental distortions. Identify your true interests and then pursue them.

Well, how the hell am I supposed to do *that*?

Maybe Lila will beg me to come back, and that will solve everything . . .

Maggie broke into my thoughts by shoving me in the chest with both hands. "Okay, go back to her. I can see it in your face. Who am I? I've got no right to you."

Trying to return things to calm reasonableness, I said: "I'm going to call her. I'll see what happens. I don't know yet. I love you. That's true."

"Yeah, yeah," she said in disgust and anguish.

When I started to edge off the bed, toward the phone, she tugged me back by the hand. She took my hand in both of hers, and placed it on her left breast. Her skin was sun-warmed and softer than Lila's—she was a good six years younger—and it quivered with the flesh-life of someone who was with me, here, present, flexing at my touch. Her gray eyes were alight.

"Fuck me first," she said.

"Hello?" Lila said.

"Hello." My voice shook. "I'm in Manhattan."

"The two of you are," she said drily.

"Yes."

"I called her husband last night. We assumed you'd gone somewhere."

"Yes, we did."

There was silence on the phone.

She'll be coldly angry for a while, I thought, but she'll see I'm sincerely repentant. Only am I? Is this what I want to happen, or is it just one scenario?

Even if she doesn't want me for myself, she'll take me back for

Jeff's sake. At first she'll make me sleep in the living room, on the sofa. I'll do it gladly, of course, as penance. On the sofa for two weeks, doing everything perfectly, making her the greatest meals—which she'll sneer at at first, but then only smirk at and finally smile at. And I'll tell her, "I see your dimples again," and she'll tell me to shut up, but I'll know she knows it's true: she's happy we're reunited. Then she'll let me into the bed again, because after all, sleeping on the sofa is too ridiculous, although it'll be understood I'm not to touch her. I'll live that way uncomplainingly for a month, two months—what's an extra month for a prize like this?—regaining her trust, never making so much as a sexual innuendo. Purity, I'll give her as much purity as she wants, I'll prove myself to her, until at last one night on the brink of sleep she'll reach out and touch my hand and say, "Brendan, you can come over here if you want."

I looked at Maggie. She was sitting up in bed, with her chest bare and one hand gathering the bedsheet below her belly button. She was anxiously smiling at me. The sunlight, coming straight in from above the Jersey hills, made her squint. All the clothes we had were lumped together on the only chair in the room. I wanted to paint her, sitting like this in the pure light in the impure hotel bed.

But I imagined, too, how Lila must look at this moment, sitting on the edge of our marital bed in a pastel sweatshirt and brightly colored socks. I hoped she was wearing her contact lenses, without which, she claimed, she not only couldn't see but couldn't hear or think. I visualized the drafting table in the alcove of our big bedroom, with my sketches, and inspirational picture postcards from art museums, taped to the wall above. Had she torn them down in a fury? Probably not, she wasn't that kind of person. She would keep my things in order, not in hopes that I would return, but out of instinctive consideration for others' property and a refusal to be anyone else's garbageman. And also out of respect for art at any level, from postcard reproductions of Henri Rousseau to my pencil sketches. Lila was the daughter of a small-town Wisconsin English teacher; she was

111

more well-bred than a sorority full of rich girls.

Was she having tea—lapsang souchong? Were there apple slices spread with peanut butter on a green glass plate on the end table, with the mug of oversweetened tea giving off thinner and thinner coils of steam while she waited for whatever I might possibly have to say for myself?

"I should have called you last night."

"Well, you had to be true to yourself," she said.

"You have a right to say nasty things to me."

"Fuck you, Brendan, don't try to weaken me by telling me what I have a right to say. I'll say what I want. If I want to curse you, I'll curse you, if I want to ignore you, I'll ignore you, and if I want to say, 'Thank you, Brendan, for removing your obnoxious presence from my life,' I'll say that. And I won't ask your permission, or consult with you about which of those things I have a right to say and which I don't. Our consulting days are over; you've found a new consultant. I hope you find her input more satisfactory, you fucked-up life-ruining bastard."

Lila always made you feel it was a sin to force her to raise her voice.

But on the other hand who was she to talk to me that way? As if she bore no responsibility for the fact that our marriage had decayed. Lila, you are so fucking haughty; that is really the problem. All your other moods—your playfulness, your plaintiveness, your superhuman concentration on your work, your devout silence when I begin to make love to you, your praise for me and your dismissals of me and even your adoration of our son, are simply the various facets of your extreme conceit. And that, that—Yes, now I've got it! Now I understand what I have been rebelling against! *That* was a regime to which I, as a man—no— as a self-respecting person, cannot be expected to submit.

But now was not the time. She wouldn't accept my side of the truth; it would only fire her up with greater defensiveness and hostility. Save the discussion for when you can do it calmly. And who knows how many of my thoughts are bullshit anyway? I'm a reasonable enough person to admit that—unlike her. Thought is the product of mood. When you're angry, you think, "Yes, this is the real truth I hide from myself most of the time." And when you're calm, you thank God you didn't blurt all that out.

"Yes," I said into the phone. "Yes."

Maggie stood up on the bed, as if to defend me, or recapture me. The sheet slid off her, and she walked off the bed toward me, naked, slight, and fine. She put her arm around my waist and leaned her head against my chest, with the bobbing black cord of the telephone wrapped around both of us. I stroked her cheek with the backs of my fingers.

I felt torn between a grateful, naked woman who was touching me—my goal achieved—and an invisible woman far away, who hated me and was telling me my faults.

But above all, I was numb with shock. I wasn't, like the night before, alertly and spontaneously taking bold action; I was feeling my way along a ledge with half-steps. I so mistrusted my own instincts at this point, that I would have considered it wisest to run full speed in the opposite direction from where they urged me, except that I mistrusted *that* instinct too.

When Lila stopped cursing, I asked her: "So did you get any sleep last night?"

"After about four-thirty."

We'd gone to bed at about the same time for once.

"Listen," I asked, "is Jeff there? Do you think he'd want to talk to me?"

"I'm not sure it's a . . . I haven't told him any—"

"It's okay, it's okay, forget it," I said hastily. "I'll talk to him later." My God, what could I have said to him, a two year old?

"You can talk to him if you want," she said suddenly.

"No, it's all—"

"No, I'm sorry. I tried to keep him from you."

"I understand. It's all right." This horrible Alphonse-and-Gaston routine. "Tell him I love him and I'll call him soon."

Then she blurted out, "Brendan, why didn't you believe me? I warned you what I'd do if you ever slept with someone else. Now I'll have to do it!" she said, as if frightened of her own resolve.

I had no answer to give her. "Well," I said after a while, "I'm trying to think of what to tell you about my plans." I paused for a long time.

The conversation ended there, and she rang off.

"Time for me to make my phone call," Maggie said, and took a deep breath. I began to step away, but she tugged me back and held the receiver so we could both put our ears to it. When Mike answered, she said, "Hi, I told you it wouldn't last."

"You told me. I thought you were kidding. My mistake."

"So how are you doing?"

"I just threw all your clothes in the garbage."

"You what?" she laughed. "Listen, you did me a favor, I'm changing my look." She smiled at me and rubbed my ass, and motioned for me to get her clothes from the chair. I handed them to her: flimsy red-and-black-printed white T-shirt, panties, wrinkled white shorts with suspenders, used white anklets. She smoothed them out on the bed but didn't put them on.

"Oh, not all my clothes?" she said into the phone. "Just one drawer? Which drawer? I don't keep any good clothes in that drawer. He never remembers where I keep anything," she said, and held out the receiver for me to listen again. "So how's my babe Hilary?"

"Fine. My mother's taking care of her."

"Your mother? Are you gonna get any help on a permanent basis, 'cause I could—"

"Maggie, don't insult my mother."

"Am I insulting? Your mother's the saint of life. I was just wondering—"

"When I find someone on a permanent basis I'll make you the first to know."

"Yeah, I know: someone with a permanently basic pair of implants, you mean."

"So? You got someone right next to you. You think I can't hear that guy breathing into the phone? Can practically hear his hardon going up. Hi, Brendan."

"Hi," I said.

"Going up?" he laughed. "You know, Brendan, I would normally take your head off for you in a situation like this, but it's a little difficult over the phone. Not impossible, just difficult. I just have this thing, that I don't like to get mad over the phone. Except at my suppliers." He laughed again, a casino comedian laughing at his own jokes. "So, seriously, tell me the truth, how are you two doing?"

Maggie and I looked at each other. For a moment we each waited for the other to speak. I could have killed the clowning bastard for triggering the doubts he knew would inevitably be there. "Fine," I said at last. She clutched my hand.

"Can I speak to Hilary? I'd like to speak to someone intelligent," she said.

"I'm sorry, that's impossible right now."

"Why not? Why not, you creep, why can't I speak to my own daughter?"

"Hey. She's in the park with her grandmother at present. It's rather difficult to establish phone communication between here and the park."

"You know, you are a fuck, Michael."

"Hey."

"You got the whole thing under control, right? No problems. You got her and the house. You can afford a lawyer and I can't, and you know I'm not gonna take you to court for custody anyway."

"Yeah, 'cause you're an adulteress, a runaway mother, and a PINS."

"'Person In Need of Supervision,'" she explained, "That's what they label you when you have to go to a group residence. That's me."

"No it isn't," I whispered.

She drew me closer. She rubbed my knuckles anxiously with her thumb. "Well, can I ever see her?" she asked her husband.

"Sure. I'll let you closer than a court would. Court wouldn't let you within ten miles of her; I'll let you within eight."

"Please, Michael . . ."

"I'm kidding. See her whenever. You know where she lives. You got the key."

"Yeah, and if you think that when I'm there to see her, you're gonna get me on the kitchen table, you're making a mistake."

"I'll go with you," I said loudly.

"Way to go, Brendan!" he said. "You got me totally intimidated."

"Don't pay any attention to him," she told me. She gave my hand a squeeze. "Well, okay," she sighed into the phone. "You're gonna do it all by yourself, right? You and Mamma. Got the whole thing down. You're the boss. You can do the job. No problem. Listen, as long as I'm on the phone, do you have any particular questions about how to take care of a two year old? It's not like taking off strips of molding. Anything you'd like to know about her food, her bedtime?"

"No."

"Okay, well, give her her vitamins at night. You fill the dropper up to one point six. She gets a bottle at bedtime, but any other time during the day she has to drink from a cup. In fact she should be going off the bottle, but you can go easy on that, considering what's going on. Not that I would presume to tell you how to do your job. Tell your mother that Hilary still likes the jars of sweet potatoes, but no other baby food; she eats all grown-up food except for that. Okay?"

"Got it," Mike said, and hung up.

"Bastard is glad to get rid of me," she said. She buried her head against my chest, and gripped me so tight her nails made my back bleed.

14

We lived a week at that hotel. We learned all the streets in the dirty chic neighborhoods of lower Manhattan, and for entertainment we read the menus in restaurant windows. One evening we sat on the Westbeth pier and watched a whole long sunset with the sunbathing artists, a really fine sunset, the kind that happens so rarely in New York, that when it does, New Yorkers feel superior to the people in places where such sunsets happen all the time.

As an artist, I was eligible to live in the Westbeth artists' complex, so I went to their office and put my name on the waiting list. The woman who took my application told me the wait might be anywhere from two to five years.

I developed a distressing habit; I forced myself to. Every morning, I made sure that my first waking thought was to try to imagine what Jeff was doing at that very moment. I probably would have done it anyway without a conscious effort, but a conscious effort nailed it down: He's eating his oatmeal; he's upset because a spoonful of it spilled on the table, and he's moaning to Lila to get a damp paper towel . . .

Then I would turn my head and look at Maggie, naked beside me. I would try to keep those two visions in my mind simultaneously, in perfect balance, for as long as I could.

"But you don't imagine what *she's* doing," Maggie said, with a note of sharp satisfaction, when I told her this.

"No. You're right. Thanks for the reminder. I'm not married to him. I'm married to her. And that's where the problem was, that's what I left."

I looked at her. She had a way of staring grimly off to the side after speaking a valuable thought, as if her pride in herself were something she had to keep secret. And yet she must have been rejoicing inside at my statement about my marriage. I put my arm around her; then my hand got restless with affection, and I brushed the short hairs at the back of her scalp, until she *had* to loosen up and laugh abashedly.

"You're pretty good, Ferro," I said. "I'm appreciating your fine qualities all over the place."

"Yeah, I know, I know they're there. Just don't bother me about them, okay?"

"Bother you? It bothers you that I praise—?"

"What time is it?" she asked abruptly, for no reason at all, except to deflect my investigation of her. She drew my left arm toward her, and looked at my watch. Even that mundane action, she performed as if it were a response to a challenge.

If you had told me, a year earlier, that I would leave my wife and child for another woman, I would have said, "No. I can see myself falling in love, being infatuated. I can even see myself leaving home after an argument and escaping with her for a night. But then I'd come to my senses. I'd miss Jeff and Lila terribly and feel overwhelming remorse, and the other woman would probably feel the same way about her family, and we'd affectionately agree to part. Sheepishly, but with the dignity of a return to our responsibilities, we'd go back to Brooklyn, where, for Jeff's sake, Lila would be unable to keep her vow of ostracizing me. It would be a major crisis overcome, and thus a proof of our strength as a family, and even a source of wisdom."

I would have said that, in my ignorance of what love does.

I learned it, that week in Manhattan. Love is havoc. It is primeval chaos. This world was born from it (did you think the love that made this world was *nice*?). Even God fell so in love with this world, He gave up His only son for it.

Love is the destroyer of forms. If it creates new forms, they are only the drab, claylike residue left after it cools. Love itself is an unworkable medium. You can't touch it. You can't reshape it to your will—it will burn you and scar you. And it makes every previous bond seem like the outmoded style of a generation ago.

Try it. Try to handle it. If you can handle it, it's not the real substance, it's a synthetic. Love is a fissionable material. The way to tell you have it is if you start to glow. Its flash will melt your eyes, its firestorm will gut your home. You are gone. You are ashes and you don't know or care.

We lived a week at that hotel . . .

We went to an Indian restaurant on Sixth Street for lunch, and at the next table a young artist-couple were being driven frantic by the way their toddler kept throwing his cutlery to the floor. Maggie and I smirked—how much better *we* would have handled it!—and yet the kid was driving us crazy too, with his babbling, his attempts to leave his seat. How could people be so inconsiderate as to bring an obstreperous child to a restaurant where adults wanted to eat in peace?

We couldn't stand the sight of other people's children, and we fantasized shamelessly about how we would live when we got our kids back.

Maggie was fixated on wresting custody of Hilary from Mike at some future time. I was more "realistic." I used to plan in detail the outings I would take Jeff on after I got visitation rights.

"I think the two of them really get along," I said one day. "Know what I'd like to do with them? Take them camping in the White Mountains. It's so beautiful there. You'd love it, too. We'll buy a tent and a big double sleeping bag, and two kid-size ones:

Smurf sleeping bags, I saw them once in a store."

We were walking past a schoolyard on Horatio Street. All of a sudden I stopped. A small child, a boy, was walking along the inside of the fence, alone. He was three or four. He wore navy blue shorts, a black tee shirt, and had messy hair and a small scab on his forehead. There seemed to be no adult supervising him. A softball game was in progress in the far corner of the schoolyard, and a fly ball sent the center fielder running in our direction. The child didn't even look when the ball hit the fence with a clash of metal. None of the players called out to him in recognition. He walked on, trailing his left hand along the links of the chain fence, making a circuit of the schoolyard perimeter.

He looked at me. He had very dark eyes and a lower lip that protruded with a kind of pendulous indifference. It seemed obvious to me that this little boy had seen more of life—more grief—than I ever had. He turned away from my gaze, and kept walking.

"Who's taking care of him?" I whispered to Maggie.

"None of your business. Someone."

"Are you sure? What if no one is?"

"Someone is. Come on." She pulled me by the hand.

But I stood, watching the child's progress. I knew I looked suspicious—and that in itself seemed to support my belief that this was an abandoned child. If anyone responsible had been supervising him, they would have run right up and put themselves between him and me.

"I think he's lost," I said quietly. "Or his parents ditched him here."

"You're making it up, Brendan. Come on. We'll go to the hotel. You can call Jeff on the phone and feel better."

"Fuck Jeff!" I said suddenly and inexplicably, and I was immediately shocked by my own inadvertent words. "I mean, I don't mean that like it sounded. I'm just saying I'm looking at *this* child now and I'm seriously concerned about his welfare. I'm *not* just projecting my thoughts about Jeff onto him. I mean, my God, look! He's all alone here! Anyone could come up and snatch him into a car or something. What if *I* were the kind of person who did that? I'd be off with him and he'd be missing, forever. Even if he's got a parent or something watching from a window, or in the store across the street, big deal, what good is that? It's much too far away."

The little boy turned the corner of the fence, his hand still trailing along the chain links. It was a bright day; the metal shone, and the light undulated as the child's hand plucked the chain links. He did not look back at us. I stared, mesmerized by dread for him. My mind was filled with disasters I was sure would befall him.

"I love you, Brendan," Maggie said, as a spell to call me back.

It worked. When someone who usually guards her feelings looks up at you with uninhibited admiration and idealization, and you know you are the man who unstopped the hidden fountain that had lain overgrown and blocked for years, it's the all-time charm. I kissed her, delicately at first, then all-out, and we stood tongue-kissing and torso-pawing, me with my back against the chain fence and one foot up on its concrete base, and pulling her toward me.

"Let's go back to the hotel," she said, her voice thick and hushed, and she stroked my chest and kissed the second button of my shirt.

"Maggie, I want to have a full life with you, all right? A new family. Do you want that with me?"

No hesitation, no evasion: "Yes."

"Let's find a place to live. We can't afford Manhattan. Let's look in Brooklyn. Not right near them or anything, but near. You know—for visiting."

"I know."

15

Rawley advanced us enough money to sign a lease on, plus enough beyond that to live for a couple of months. The place we found was in Windsor Terrace, the working class neighborhood just south of Park Slope. Few young professionals had yet moved in here. Our building was a five-story tan brick tenement with black fire escapes, across the street from the parking lot of a shirt factory. No matter how late we stayed up, we could always hear music or arguments from the other apartments. The broad two-way street was treeless and shadeless, and our apartment had a view of a high fence, behind which were a dozen identical shirt-company vans that never seemed to leave the lot. Further down the street, the private homes were of flaking clapboard with shingle roofs, or red brick with flat tar roofs. They looked as if they had been inhabited by the same families for fifty years.

Our building was at the peak of a hill, and down the steep western side was a worse neighborhood, Spanish-speaking and half boarded up. None of our stores lay that way; we hardly ever crossed the street in that direction. The neighborhood we felt we lived in was all to the east of our building, on a gentler slope. It was a neighborhood of Italian pork stores and Irish bars, so similar to Maggie's childhood surroundings in Bay Ridge that when we walked together, the sight of a grandmother peering through a lace curtain, or the calls of teenagers on a streetcorner trying to get acknowledged by older teens in a car, would incite her to angry witticisms, as if she wished to get even with them all. When we walked along the park promenade at dusk, stepping around brown and green and colorless chips of broken bottles, the long-time residents smiled up at us from their lawn chairs and card tables; and their dogs, who were always either German shepherds or long-legged, crewcut brown mutts, treaded their big paws but did not growl.

"Don't worry," I told Maggie, "we'll be able to afford to move. Sooner than we realize, I'll bet. And I bet we get custody of Hilary before long. Mike won't really be able to take care of her. And Jeff will visit us a lot, and I'll visit him. I'm going to make sure he always knows me. Because I couldn't stand it otherwise. I'll be just as much his father as before, just in a different style. In fact I'll be a more typical father this way. I wouldn't take him away from Lila, but that kid is always going to know his father. And if we ever have a new kid"—that made her smile and forget her grudges—"it'll be a combination of Hilary and Jeff, and that's so wonderful. Jeff would be a great older brother . . ."

But we had to begin a new life for real. The first task was to put things in our apartment: things to sit on, to eat with, to wear. I made an appointment with Lila to pick up my clothes and art supplies. We agreed upon a two-hour period on a Saturday morning when she would not be home. She instructed me to let myself in with my old key and to leave it on her desk when I let myself out.

"Would you like me to take my pictures off your walls?" I asked.

"You can leave them. You know, Brendan, you never believed it, but I always liked your work."

"What do you mean I never believed it? How do you know what I believed? You think I'm too neurotic to believe you like my work."

I protested against what I thought she thought I thought; she complained about what she believed to be my disbelief. No wonder it was sometimes too hard for us to utter an unloaded, linear sentence.

Out of necessity, Maggie and I went for the bare look in furniture. Sofas, coffee tables and beds with frames weren't our lifestyle at the moment. We bought a futon mattress to sleep on, and reading lamps to place on the floor beside it. For the living room we bought almost nothing at all. We picked up an inexpensive bridge table for the dining area that would double as my work table. It really wouldn't be too much worse than the drafting table in the alcove in my old bedroom.

Mike came over one day and gave Maggie the second TV from their house, a small color portable that had been considered "hers." He held up one hand when I opened the door for him.

"Don't hit me, Brendan, I'm carrying an electronic instrument." He slid past me with a kind of mock evasive action, his back half-turned. He was shorter than me, and at least ten years older, and he walked with a slight hitch, the left knee not bending fully. But he was wearing a black T shirt with the sleeves pushed up, and his muscles were something to see.

I kept holding the door open so he would leave soon.

"Great place," he said, walking around and inspecting the bare walls and the ancient, buckling linoleum. On his way out, he slapped me three times in the belly. It hurt. "Hey, Brendan, you got any scars yet?"

"What?"

"Scars. You know." He closed his big, black-haired fist and held it under my face. On his forearm were two half-inch scars that looked as if they could have been made with a knife. Smiling, he pointed his chin at Maggie. She bitterly turned her back, and stared out the airshaft window.

"You will," he told me.

As he stepped through the doorway he gave me a playful punch on the upper arm, and I drew in my nostrils so as not to show pain.

"Hey, if you want to fight I'll fight you," I called after him. It echoed through the cool, stone-stepped, graffiti-scrawled stairwell.

"See you guys," he said. I waited a long time, listening to his footsteps descend, before I shut the door behind him. Getting ready for bed that evening, I looked at my arm and saw a yellow and purple bruise.

I went wild painting the walls. After putting down a fresh coat of white, I painted big, childlike illustrations on top of that, in standard latex wall paint, leaving the drips in: an island scene with bright red palm trees and bright green sun in the living room, a crowded restaurant with tray-carrying waiters and cigarette-smoking customers for the kitchen, a night-blue starry ceiling in the bedroom with pine trees and fireflies on the walls, and a rain forest in the bathroom. Maggie shook her head, smiling, the whole time.

"You gonna sign that?" she said.

So I wrote my name in the lower right-hand corner of each room.

The floor of our living room was a linoleum of grime-deepened gray, speckled with eroded gold. Time, temperature, humidity, and inept installation had created a lump which ran the entire length of the linoleum, as if a mole had burrowed parallel to the wall. Maggie called this "the desk." This was where she lay her head when she worked on her new children's book, or studied for the courses in Creative Writing and Computer Science that she had signed up for at Brooklyn College. This was where we put the piles of cards when we played War long into the night, slapping cards onto each other's piles and laughing ourselves silly, for we were both insomniacs. Maggie couldn't get to sleep till one or two. I usually fell asleep before she did, but woke up at three and couldn't get back to sleep for hours. One of us would always be patrolling the apartment, naked and invisible, and in the morning we'd compare notes and realize that we had each been up half the night, unbeknownst to the other.

Each of us had to get used to a new person's ways. Maggie was eating more stir-fried vegetables than she used to, and I was eating more frozen dinners. I changed my news channel for her sake, and she learned to like jazz. Lila and I used to sip cognac at home, but Maggie and I found a café on Eleventh Avenue where they made really good capuccino. It wasn't the chic kind of café you'd find in Manhattan, but a storefront with no sidewalk tables. The decor was photographs of the local Little League teams, and the waitresses were parochial school girls who couldn't work after ten at night. The customers talked loudly about the outrage of double-parking tickets and about the price of the bus to Atlantic City.

Without admitting it to each other, we were trying to fill the hours when we would have been giving our kids their baths and putting them to bed. We made love a lot. We didn't talk about our families much, even when one of us returned from a visit in the park. (Lila refused to let me come to her door, and prohibited me from bringing Jeff to my new place.) We spent a good deal of time, Maggie and I, simply looking at each other with blatant amazed amusement at ending up together. We tested various topics of conversation to see which ones might become "ours," and to try to determine who this other person was. We were still strange presences to each other.

I kept searching for clues to Maggie—I noticed everything she did. If she opened a drawer, I'd think, "She's opening a drawer. Look at the way she does it, not exactly like Lila. What does that mean?" And the elusiveness of its meaning would excite me so that in the middle of her opening that drawer, I would go caress her in order to make sense of her in the most palpable, immediate way.

What upset me most was when she hid from me. I had known all along she was a moody person, but living with her I learned moods I wouldn't have been aware of in a mere friend. Maggie was an expert at hiding—literally. She had the weird talent of being able to find a corner of a room, or a space behind a dresser or a door, and crouch in it, motionless, until suddenly you realized she hadn't been seen or heard for hours. I searched through the apartment, and even though it was a one-bedroom flat with very little furniture, it would take a good five minutes to find her. Sometimes she would still be in the living room where I had been drawing or coloring, and I would miss her on my first circuit, and search the whole rest of the apartment and the fire escape and get all worried and puzzled, only to find her next to the radiator on my return.

She had developed this skill in the group residence, living with twenty other girls, most of whom were thieves, hitters, sickos, perverts, junkies, or some or all of those things. Being small, she needed an unusual defense—the switchblade was only a usual defense—and she had found that the residence, with its dozen dormitory rooms, storage rooms, counseling rooms and offices, offered almost infinite places to hide in. She would hide not only when she felt threatened, but just for practice, the way some kids shoot baskets over and over. One time, she was declared missing from the residence; the police were called, a search made among the neighborhood street people; and after thirty-six hours she emerged from her closet—which had been the first place her roommate had looked. She was quite good at hiding objects, too, and was very useful to her fellow residents in finding nooks and receptacles for small packages they didn't want the social workers to find. But, she assured me, she wasn't as bad as that now.

The physical hiding was at least an interesting novelty, but what really upset me was when she made herself emotionally unavailable. She would be eating with me, watching TV with me, but all of a sudden she would cease saying anything, stare fixedly at her plate, respond to my questions only with a grunt or a shrug, and refuse to tell me what was wrong or even if it had anything to do with me. She wouldn't seem especially angry, she would simply have removed herself from the premises.

At first I took it personally, and racked my brain trying to remember what I might have done to trigger such a reaction. But she told me later that it was not my fault, it was just the way she was. She would be that way with anybody. And so I realized that I was not necessarily the most important character in her personal drama. Strangely, this made me less upset. From then on, when she got that way, I just sat with her and waited, so she would know I was with her. Sometimes I held her hand, sometimes not even that—depending on whether she accepted my touch or went rigid and pulled away—and always, when she came out of it, she gave me a strong hug.

16

"It's him," I said, and held the receiver of our wall telephone out to Maggie.

"What is it?" she said into the phone. I was pleased at the impatience in her voice. "Another one?" She sighed. "She's been having a tantrum every day. What are you doing to her? . . . I'm not accusing you of anything. I'm sorry, forget it. Forget I said anything . . . Okay, I'll tell you what you do. Speak soothingly to her but don't give in to what she asks. It's normal at this age, tantrums are normal, don't worry about it. Just—No, you would not be a bad father to let her cry herself to sleep. If it's only a few minutes or so. Up to a half an hour . . . No, do *not* give her ice cream if she threw out her fruit cocktail. What does she think you are, a dessert tray? Oh, your *date* thinks you should. Well, that's highly interesting news. Oh, your date is *concerned* about Hilary. I see. Let me ask you something, does your date have kids? Oh, so she's *not* the great expert. So maybe she just wants to quiet Hilary down, whether it's good for Hilary to quiet down or not. I mean, since when is quiet your ultimate value? . . . Oh, 'genuine concern.' I see. Well, tell her to keep her pants on for fifteen minutes and Hilary will go to sleep. Tell her, parents always have to wait. But if she follows my advice, she can take her pants off for you in fifteen minutes, a half hour maximum . . . No, I'm not being insulting, I'm saying this sincerely. I'm genuinely concerned about her. Where'd you meet her, what store? I know you never go shopping without shopping for something on the side . . . Oh, she's your client!" Maggie whacked the telephone receiver against the wall.

"Hey, I just painted that!" I said, scurrying up and investigating the gash she had made in the plaster, and the chips of white and of previous tenants' blue and yellow on the floor.

"Shut up, Brendan." She resumed talking into the phone. "She's a widow with three brownstones she wants you to renovate? Well, we're coming up in the world, my my! What is she, fat and bald and sixty years old? Of course not, I would never underestimate you. A tall thirty-five year old redhead. Hey, look what a favor I did you by leaving! And Hilary will inherit three brownstones . . . No, I don't think I'm being premature. I just have the highest opinion of your abilities, that's all. Don't be modest, whatever you want, you get. I know that myself. Just let me ask you one thing—I'm being like a counselor for you now, I want you to feel you can always air your problems to me, and I'll be glad to help with any expertise I can offer. Like if she needs any lessons or anything—so let me ask you, is she good at . . . I'm not vulgar. Who's vulgar? . . . Respect, of course! I respect her like the Pope. Her and the Pope, to me they're in the same breath . . . You too . . . There, you see? Hilary's quieting down. Wonderful. Makes me happy, whatever little help I could give you. Give her a kiss for me. Tell her I'll see her. And if she has any more trouble sleeping, just tell her to count brownstones. Good night, have fun."

17

A woman named Dulcea took care of Jeff in the daytime. She was a homely, triangular-faced black grandmother with an elegant Barbadian accent and hair that stood out in a clump over each ear. She always wore a purple-flowered housedress and brown stockings; she hobbled on stiff hips and bony legs, and made a sandpapery sound as she walked through Lila's apartment in backless slippers, which left flakes of brown vinyl behind her. She vacuumed them up later, as if erasing her trail. Dulcea arrived at eight-thirty in the morning and departed whenever Lila got home. She brought Jeff home from nursery school and, in the morning hours when she was alone in the apartment, she did light housekeeping and heavy romance reading.

And she let me in to see him, which made me a great admirer of hers.

She had looked at me suspiciously through the protective wrought iron latticework of the outer door, that first time I rang the bell. I had walked past the old apartment several afternoons, hoping to catch a glimpse of him through the window and checking to see if he had come home all right from nursery school. But it started to drizzle, and I had a cold.

"So you're the one he's always talkin' about," she said, "when he goes to the big bed and says, 'This is where Daddy sleeps.'"

"He says that?"

"And you know, every time when I make him his afternoon malted, he's tryin' to stop me. He says, 'No, I want Daddy to be makin' my malted.'"

"I make great malteds."

I had taught him to love my favorite foods: chocolate malteds, sausage and pepper heros, and deep-fried scallops. Lila didn't like any of them, she claimed they were men's food. Jeff and I had established a set of vestigial male customs: sword-fighting with paintbrushes, watching the first few minutes of any Western movie that came on the TV. My foods were going to make him grow big and strong. I used to measure his growth in terms of scallop capacity: He's eating six! He's eating eight!

"Does he want a malted now?" I asked. "Let me come in and make him one."

Dulcea sized me up, rotating in her fingers a pale blue hexagonal plastic block. I was miffed at her: they were *my* blocks, I had bought them, it was my job to pick them up and put them away. "She didn't say nothing about letting you in."

"Did she say anything about keeping me out?"

We were already beginning to share a dialect: referring to Lila as "she."

Dulcea kept me at the door just long enough to make me worry. Then she said, "Your hair is getting wet," and, making a sound with her tongue—disapproving of me for getting my hair wet, or of herself for getting soft—she opened the door and turned away. She walked ahead of me into the apartment without looking to see if I followed.

As I stepped into the doorway, Jeff was running into the living room to tell Dulcea something. Even after I had entered, he didn't notice me at first, running in that unseeing way kids have when they're so excited about learning how to form words, how to report an event, that it's a wonder they only run into things once or twice a day.

132

"I'm building a—"

He stopped. He turned white, as if afraid. Then he started running on his path toward Dulcea again, the pink returning to his cheeks in one breath, and just as I was resigning myself to watching him run into her arms, he swiveled in place and grinned at me and said:

"I'm building a very nice building!"

"Well, if it's a very nice building I want to see it." I corrected myself: "Even if it wasn't such a nice one, I'd want to see it, but I'm sure any building you make is a nice one."

We went through the foyer to his room. His floppy moose puppet lolled against the leg of his crib, looking at me. The door of Jeff's closet was an inch ajar as usual, because the threshold was too high. On the wall across from the crib was the super-realist drawing I had done once of a chrome barbell that Lila accused me of not making good use of.

"Hey, that *is* a nice building!" I said when I saw his block construction on the red and blue rug. It was four stories tall, and broad enough to keep from toppling. I sat down and examined the work. I touched the top arch with my fingertip: it held steady. "May I?" I asked, and added a couple more pieces from the discards that were strewn around the rug.

"I'm showing Daddy my building!" Jeff called to Dulcea, who was in the kitchen cutting a carrot for his snack. "I'm showing Daddy my—I'm showing Daddy."

"That's fine, darling," she said, with loud cuts of steel on wood.

The whole afternoon was just fine. We didn't do a thing that was planned beforehand or required special equipment or a specific, distant setting. We kicked a foam rubber soccer ball under Jeff's crib and out again and around the room. Then we drew for a while. Then Jeff, Dulcea, and I all sat at the dinner table eating cheddar cheese slices, sesame crackers, carrot sticks, and apple juice. Jeff was wearing a new shirt that Lila must have bought since the breakup: a green, black, and white rugby shirt that went well with his wavy, light brown hair and broad face.

Jeff was at the garbage truck stage. When he heard the Sanitation Department truck come groaning down the street, he ran to the window in ecstasy, shouting, "Garbage truck! Garbage truck!" I knelt beside him to look out the window. Together we watched the men in olive drab jackets stop in front of each house to empty the cans that the homeowners had set out before going to work that morning. When the truck passed, I pointed at the shadows on the limestone houses across the street, and the sun on their copper-green tile roofs.

"If you come back and look again in a little while, you'll see that the shadow is climbing up, up to the roofs, because the sun is going down."

"Yes, I know," he said.

I looked at him in surprise. "You know that?"

"Yes."

"You know how the sun rises in the east and sets in the west? And as it's setting, the shadows lengthen?"

"Yes."

"Well, did you also know that Copernicus was the one who first discovered that the earth revolves around the sun, rather than vice versa?"

"Yes, I knowed."

I squinted a smile at him and patted his head. It must have been Lila who had taught him to say, "Yes, I know," to everything.

I started visiting him two afternoons a week. More would have been too much; he still needed a nap most afternoons, and I needed to work. But I saw him every weekend too. Altogether, I probably spent as much play time with my son as the average father.

Dulcea greeted me kindly now, and when she opened the door for me, she always called back to Jeff, "Guess who's comin' to visit you, sweetheart?" in the exact same words, so that it became a ritual, and when he heard those words, he came running, wet-lipped with laughter. When I was in the house, Dulcea took up

134

staying in the kitchen, sitting on a blue stepladder and reading, making our snack at a relaxed pace. Every half hour or so, she came in to dust something or pick something up, doubtless as a pretext to check on how I was treating Jeff.

For a couple of hours a couple of times a week, I was again the person who watched Jeff, found activities for him, helped him go to the bathroom, determined when he was sleepy, decided when he deserved a sweet, read stories to him, watched *Sesame Street* with him, showed him pictures by Matisse and Gauguin, and asked him what he had done in nursery school. Dulcea was paid for this work, but I would have paid her to let me do it. I may even have been better on those afternoons than when I had been living with him, because I never saw him as an interruption, and didn't even mind if he practiced his speech skills on me by taking five minutes to ask a question.

On a beautiful November day, I rang the doorbell as always. I was wearing a sweater, tweed jacket, and gloves; it was windy weather, with the usual proportions of clear and overcast sky reversed, so that only a few ovals of brilliant blue shot through the holes in the cloud cover. I waited, looking at the sky and rooftops across the street. I heard the inner door of the apartment open, muffled footsteps come through the hall, then the outer wooden door unlatched. I turned to face the wrought iron protective door, and I heard a gasp from behind it.

Lila's hair was unwashed and her eyes were baggy. She wore a gray sweatshirt, black jeans, and dark purple socks.

"Yes?" she said in fright, as if she was trying to sound officious and knew she wasn't succeeding.

"You're home?"

"Yes, this is my home, why are you here? Jeff's sick." She gave me a suspicious, if marveling look: perhaps I had sensed his illness telepathically and come unbidden to his bedside.

"He's sick? What's wrong with him?" I asked.

"It's nothing, the flu. But he has a high fever and he was crying all morning. I didn't think Dulcea should have to take care of him like that, so I took a sick day to do it."

135

"You missed work? You could have called me and I would have come to take care of him."

"I didn't want to bother you."

"It's no bother. If I hadn't come by, you wouldn't have even let me know he was sick, would you?"

"What about your philosophy that parents worry too much about every little—"

"I wouldn't be worried. I just want to be informed."

"I'm sorry," she said, and it caught me short, I had been so ready to keep exchanging barbs and counting points scored and tallying up resentments. My instinct was to search her reply for sarcasm, or for a kind of superiority-in-humility; but they weren't there.

"I'd like to help," I said. "Would you please let me in?"

Her blond hair drooping and swinging, she unlatched the wrought iron door. I followed her into the apartment. I watched her ass. I wanted to tell her: You look great even when you're haggard.

She led me into the living room with sweeping gestures. "Well, here, as you can see, is the living room. Basically the same as ever. I guess I ought to redecorate, to purge your influence." We caught each other's eye mockingly. She hastily turned away. "There's not much to say. Jeff and I just live here in the usual way. Except that all of life now is routine maintenance. I come home from work; by the time I get him to bed and prepare his next day's stuff, it's time for me to go to bed. Actually it gives me deep satisfaction that I can keep it going. It's just a form of satisfaction without any pleasure."

I stuck my hands in my back pockets, and looked around at the place and the familiar view out the window, and blew out my cheeks.

"This woman I hired, Dulcea," she said, "is a big help. She and he—"

"I know, they get along very well together."

"Oh, he tells you about her on your walks?"

I stood flagrantly mute. She looked at me closely. She nar-

136

rowed her eyes in order to aim at me the full force of her deductive prowess.

"I'm going to fire her!" she said. She sounded doubly betrayed for having just been nice to me. "How many times has she let you in? Once, twice? Once a week? More? Every day? She's been letting you in every day and I haven't known about it?"

"No, not every day." And in a deliberately hesitant, bashful attempt at being disarming, I told her how I used to walk by just to get a glimpse through the window, and how I had wanted to come in out of the drizzle that first time. I made sure to emphasize that Dulcea had been dubious and reluctant. And I described, though not in enough detail to make her envious, the good times Jeff and I had had because of my intrusion. "I should have told you," I said. "And Dulcea should have, but it's a minor fault in her. After all, *you* weren't going to tell me Jeff was sick."

She gave me a familiar look: incredulity that I could be so unfair as to compare my behavior to hers.

I said, "I guess I assumed he would tell you about it himself."

"He didn't." I could see the wheels turning in Lila's head: Jeff was against her, Jeff was being trained by his father to keep secrets from her.

"He's at that age," I said. "Can you get a word out of him about what he does at nursery school?"

"No. According to him, he doesn't go to nursery school. He goes to garbage truck school." She smiled belatedly and minimally, but she did smile.

"Can I see him now?" I asked.

She nodded. She stepped back toward the sofa in order to give me plenty of space to walk by.

Jeff's room was dark, the shades were down. I went to his crib—he wasn't in it. I looked around in alarm. The sound of sniffles guided me to the side of the room. When my eyes adjusted to the dark, I saw Jeff sitting in front of an open dresser drawer, pulling out all his socks and shirts. He had climbed out of his crib—a sign he was ready for a real bed. I made a mental note to discuss this with Lila.

"Hi, sweetheart," I said to him. "What's up?"

He didn't answer at first. He sniffled pathetically, with phlegmy breaths. He was wearing his blue pajamas with a picture of a hound dog riding a motorcycle.

"What are you doing?" I asked.

"I am packing." He snorted back some mucous. I took out my handkerchief and wiped his nose.

"Packing all your clothes?"

"Yes." He picked up four or five pairs of white crew socks, a couple of which fell as he carried them across the room to a bent old shoebox sitting in front of his closet. "This is my suitcase."

"Are you packing like me?" I asked.

"Yes."

I watched him. Solemnly and purposefully, he went back and forth to the shoebox, transferring almost the entire contents of one drawer and getting frustrated trying to fit it all in.

I stopped him. I grabbed him around from behind in a hug. "Okay, you did a good job of packing. Now it's time to rest."

"I am packing!" he screeched, trying to writhe out of my grasp.

"No you're not." He kicked at my shins; I had to quick-step backwards while holding him. "You're sick, Jeff. You have to go to bed." I felt his forehead; it was hot and moist. He was crying. I pressed him to my chest. "Too sick to play today. I'm putting you back in your crib. So you didn't go to nursery school today, huh?"

"Yes I did!" he said, and I lifted him over the crib bars and kissed him.

I stood beside him for a long time, because he was quite agitated at first. I hand-brushed his hair off his forehead, then helped him adjust the positions of his animals. I got him a glass of water and would have held it for him while he drank, but he grabbed it out of my hands. The water calmed him down, though. He lay down, and while worming around in order to wedge himself properly into the corner, he began talking to himself, apparently pretending that he was his nursery school teacher.

"Corinne, where are you going? Give that back to Justin. You can both share. Everyone sit in a circle, we are singing a song. Rachel, you too. Okay, Rachel is sitting out today, but we are singing a song . . ."

And so I got to learn a fair amount about his nursery school.

A few minutes after, Jeff fell asleep. Lila was silent out there. I went to see her.

She was sitting on the sofa with her knees up, her head between them. She lifted her head when she heard me enter the living room, but made no pretense of equanimity.

"Couldn't take raising him anymore, could you?" she said. "Too much of a strain to be around someone like that?"

And before I could answer, she started blinking like mad and holding her hand to her eye in pain. The sight of me had apparently set one of her contact lenses awry, and she had to hold the reddened eye wide open with her fingers, tears streaming down only that one side of her face, while she blinked the lens down from the top of her eyeball and caught it in her palm.

"Okay now?" I asked, as I had during many previous contact lens crises.

She nodded rapidly.

"You know I love him and I always did my best with him," I said. "But *I* have a career too, and I think it was pretty nice of me to take over so much of the child care and housework."

"Nice? You weren't doing us a favor. You were doing your *duty*."

She glared at me with one eye wet, one dry. I had no wish to start defending myself, but she had always considered it a great fault in me whenever I conceded a point to her. She viewed it as a sign of disregard for her that I wouldn't make up some specious self-defense in order to keep the debate going.

"I don't understand," she said. "Even if you love her, didn't you have too much invested in us to throw away? I mean— Excuse me for asking, I'm sure you don't want to favor me with an answer, and I don't even want to know. It's irrelevant to me what you and she have together. I must sound very weak and dependent and contemptible for asking at all—"

139

"No!"

"—but why do you love her more than me?"

The plaintiveness of her question, with the tears still visible on the one side of her face, whether purely from her contact lens or not, not only touched me and took me aback, but irked me like a telegram that arrives too late. So this was the woman who had tried to threaten me into monogamy with ultimatums, who had practically dared me to sleep with another woman by being jealous long before the fact. Jesus, Lila, maybe if you had let on that you might actually feel *sad* if you lost me, rather than just coldly vindictive . . .

"I don't love her more than you," I said. "I love her more recently."

She shook her head to herself.

Not wanting to do either woman the disservice of comparing them, I tried to fall back on tactful banalities. "She's an interesting person, we have a lot in common."

"She's an adolescent!"

"She's twenty-three, and she's been through things that make her more mature than—"

"Oh yeah, don't you love her sordid past? Oh, Brendan. I thought being parents would help *us* grow up. Just an unrealistic idea I had. Which I used to think about, actually, because I mean, to me it justifies parenthood, on an adult level, for more than just the child's benefit. I mean, if you're a parent, you're creating a human being. So you have a responsibility to do a good job. In fact you have a responsibility to try to make that person better than you. I think the first thing a parent ought to do is recognize the weaknesses in himself and vow that he's not going to pass them on to the next generation. If you were an abused child, you vow not to beat your children. It's very hard, of course, but if you always stay conscious of it, you can do it, I really think you can. And everybody has something. If you're a drunk, or an adulterer, or you're fearful or timid or envious or depressive or fat, or a person who couldn't take risks or respect himself or stick to a goal, you have to say to yourself, 'Okay, it stops here. If I really love my child, I'll be able to keep myself from burdening him with my failings.' So the world will have one less example of that kind of failing. And by doing that for your child, you make *yourself* better. It's like the Mafia boss who raises his children to be doctors. I mean, it may involve a certain amount of hypocrisy on his part but it's better than if they became Mafia bosses, isn't it? I think it justifies thinking more highly of him. I think child-raising can be, and ought to be, a kind of healing of oneself, a growing out of one's vices. And I'm so sorry, Brendan, that you couldn't do that."

I stood listening even after she had finished. I replayed the speech in memory, digested it, talked back to it, agreed with it. I thought about the way she had spoken, with that slightly dry-throated breathlessness, those glances at the corner of the ceiling to summon her words, which meant she had resolved not to feel nervous about saying something intelligent. I remembered when she had been afraid to ask a question in art history class, and now she wasn't verbally intimidated by anyone. I was proud of her. I must have helped her in that process somehow, in the years when we were helping each other.

We were still married. There had been years during which we had been very, very married, even more than other married couples we knew. There had been a time when, if our friends started to discuss what a "good marriage" might be, we would go bashfully silent, not wanting to brag that we were it.

Now, standing in the apartment, looking at the red squeeze-bottle of Discwasher fluid next to the turntable, and the Japanese pottery dog on the bookshelf, I was tempted by the old need again: the need for someone wise and strong yet ultimately only soft-strong, and naive-wise, and weaker than oneself; but at least I saw through the need by now.

"That's a beautiful theory you've got, Lila. I hope I can stumble toward one of my own someday."

"Stumble toward it? Is that the male ethic: to have the luxury of stumbling? Are you sure the stumbling isn't more attractive to you than the goal?"

I shrugged. If they don't believe you mean what you say, that's their problem. "You should find some nice guy to take you out."

"I always thought," she said quietly, "that you were the best man I'd ever find. With your sensitivity and your good parenthood and all that. I always thought that compared with you, other men wouldn't be worth going out with. Unfortunately, I still believe it."

I took a step closer to her.

She put up her hand to stop me. "Don't take it as a compliment that you've destroyed my interest in men. I was speaking relatively. If you're a good man, and you loved me, and did this, what would the average man do to me?"

She started to blink as if in pain again. She took a deep breath; she wasn't going to cry for me . . .

Oh, yes she was. She gnawed on her knuckle and cried soundlessly, the pale cheeks red and eyelids swollen, the pupils of the usually calm brown eyes pulsating.

"I know my suffering is very trivial," she said. "It's probably the minimum you can get away with in this world." She took a Kleenex out of the pocket of her black jeans, and blew her nose.

"You ought to at least go to a movie by yourself sometime," I said. "For your own mental health. So you don't burn out. Pay Dulcea a few bucks to stay for the evening."

She nodded. I sat down on the coffee table, catycorner to where she sat on the sofa. She moved her purple-socked feet away.

"You know, he's such a fine boy," she said, as if it were a piece of information I had lacked. "I always hear him calling you on his toy telephone."

"Oh, what does he say?"

"Mostly he listens."

"I'm glad he listens to me for once. What do I tell him on the toy telephone? 'Use your spoon. Use your spoon.'"

We smiled together; then it felt strange to share a smile, and we looked off at different corners of the room.

"To give him up," she said, "you must have totally hated me."

142

"Listen to me: *No.*"

"Then you were just so upset about something—one of your little male things, your work or your self-image or something—that you threw away two people you cared about? And now you're upset about that. Well, so am I."

I bent to pick up the furry blue hippopotamus that was under the coffee table, and placed it beside me, touching my leg. I clasped my hands and tapped my thumbs together, a gesture I make when I am particularly agitated.

"Well, he'll be better in a couple of days," I said. "If you don't want me to come here, I'll understand. Tell Dulcea not to let me in." That seemed to madden her more than anything I had said.

"Maybe I should! Why don't I act like a sane woman and tell her you're never to set foot in here again? Why did *I* let you in today? Why don't I make it hard for you? There are lawyers at my company—why don't I try to limit your rights, why don't I get court orders, why don't I take out divorce papers as fast as possible?"

We stood there, like you wait in the wind from a train that has roared away.

"Well, I better go, so our voices don't wake him up."

"Yes."

We both looked down, and I paced around in a small circle on the corner of fringed blue rug that protruded beyond the coffee table. "Okay then, I'll call you tomorrow to find out how he is. There's no point in your missing another day's work. If he's still sick, will you please—"

"It's all right, you can come," she said.

I nodded a thank you. I took a sideways step toward the front door. Free to move around again, Lila stood up and took the center of the room. I opened the front door and stepped into the outer hall.

"Don't you *ever* take our son to her apartment!" she called out.

"Okay." I thought it was a bit unfair, but I was willing to agree for the time being.

As I left through the front yard, I looked back at the ground-level window, but Lila had shut the light immediately, and it was the time of afternoon you couldn't see in. I imagined what she might be doing in there. She might be wandering aimlessly in the dark, barely seeing the house around her—experiencing it as alien and dismaying rather than familiar. She might be abstractedly, and then intently, massaging her pubic bone, and imagining that it was my hand doing it. She might be sitting on the floor with her head between her knees, trying to be very still.

I watched my shoes as they stepped on white mulberries, on twigs of forsythia, on manhole covers, on chalked radical slogans, on sidewalk and curb and asphalt street, up the slope toward the park. The linden trees on Prospect Park West showered me with yellow leaves as I walked home.

18

The next morning, the phone rang. I ran to the kitchen. "Hello?"

Lila groaned.

"What's the matter?" I asked. "How is he?"

"He's fine. *I'm* sick. I feel terrible. I have a fever and my whole body is aching. It must be some kind of twenty-four hour flu. I can't go to work, and I don't have the strength to take him to nursery school, and I told Dulcea not to come today. I don't want her to get sick."

"It's okay, I'll take him. I told you that."

"Thank you." She groaned again. "Oh, Brendan, I feel miserable."

"I'll be right over. Keep a stiff upper lip."

I rushed into the bedroom to get my outerwear.

"How is Jeff today?" Maggie asked, for she liked him a lot.

"He's fine, all better. I have to take him to nursery school. Now Lila's sick." I blushed and turned to busy myself in the coat closet.

I chose my outfit in a rush, but with care. I chose an old reliable combination Lila had seen me wear many times: Harris tweed jacket over a natural sheep-white sweater, with an Irish tweed cap and pigskin gloves. I adjusted the angle of the cap in the closet mirror until I was satisfied. I dashed away a couple of steps, then dashed back and added my long white scarf.

Maggie looked at me with grim amusement. "You're all set."

"What's the matter, don't I look okay?"

"Fine, if you want to seduce nursery school teachers. Or—"

"Gimme a break. It's November, it's a little chilly, this is what I wear."

She was sitting in bed, naked. She raised her arms and pulled a plain white T-shirt over her head: one of my T-shirts, which fit her very loosely. I watched the stretching and bouncing of muscle and breast, and went over and kissed her. "*Now* I'm all set," I said.

I hurried out so I wouldn't be late for nursery school.

At the Second Street apartment, Lila met me at the wrought iron outer door.

"Get inside, you'll get cold," I said, and gave her a guiding touch on the hipbone as we went in. It was the first time I had touched her since the breakup. She shuffled inside, barefoot, head down, stringy-haired. She was wearing an ankle-length flannel nightgown, white with little blue giraffes all over it, and white lace at the high collar and the cuffs; I remembered suddenly that it had been a gift from me, for her first Mother's Day. Had she had that in mind when she put it on? Or was it just to keep her warm?

I watched her pink feet emerge and disappear behind the white hem of the nightgown as she stepped.

Jeff was running back and forth in the foyer. He had discovered that he could run in a straight line while keeping his head turned and looking somewhere else, and this made him laugh uproariously. He didn't have his shoes on yet, and his shirt wasn't tucked in. When I saw him, I longed to spend the whole day with him, but I called out, "Time to go to school."

"No!" he laughed, and I was glad, even though we couldn't get our wish.

146

"Come on, kid, your father is on your case. Let's get those shoes on."

I chased him into his room and he backed himself against his closet door, giggling, waiting for me to come and bark orders at him in the way he knew so well. But I didn't bark at him. I picked him up, kissed him, and sat him on my lap on the floor to put his shoes and socks on him. Then I brushed his hair and went to the kitchen, where I discovered that Lila hadn't made his lunch yet. She had known she could depend on me. I made him American cheese with mayonnaise, put it in his lunchbox with a cardboard container of apple juice, put his coat on him, and led him quietly by the hand past the open door of Lila's bedroom. She was lying on top of the bedspread, with her pillow on her forehead.

"Going," I said.

"Good-bye."

A two word conversation, just as if we were happily married.

It was a gray but bright day. Most of the leaves were off the trees. On the way to school, I stepped in every pile of leaves at curbside, and kicked brown and multicolored leaves onto parked cars and onto Jeff. He put on bursts of speed in order to be caught by the leaf-wave. But he kept trailing behind to look at himself in side-view mirrors, or to point out letters on hubcaps.

"Come on, come on, you'll be late for school!"

But I didn't really care if we ever got there. The air felt so great in my lungs. There was white woodsmoke coming from a fireplace chimney across the street. A seagull from New York Bay squawked as it flew over the roofs of the brownstones.

Jeff ran up and began kicking through the leaves in imitation of me. There were yellow gingko and plane tree leaves, brown elm, orange maple, and one small, russet leaf variety that I guessed was also a maple. Jeff found a fallen branch of orange maple leaves in one piece; the leaves still had green veins and green centers. He carried it the next two blocks to school to give to his teacher.

We arrived a few minutes late, but several kids were still putting away their coats.

"We missed you yesterday!" the teacher said when she saw Jeff. I knew she would have said the same words in the same way to any kid returning after an absence, and would have sounded equally sincere: I could tell she was a good professional. But being his parent, I imagined that she meant it especially sincerely in Jeff's case: that there was something about him which endeared him even to non-relatives, the absence of which they would genuinely miss. She held Jeff's maple branch aloft to show the class: "Hm, now where shall we put this up for everyone to enjoy?"

We missed you, she had said, after one day.

I walked around the neighborhood and in the park the whole time he was in school.

At twelve-thirty I picked him up and asked the teacher how he was doing. Fine, she said. He had been a little shy with the other children at first, but was getting over it; he was a bit too willing to let things be taken away from him, but that was fairly common and experience would cure it. He was a leader in singing and puzzle-solving, and was liked by all his classmates, and was an enthusiastic painter. In fact he had a ritual which he performed every morning before letting himself join the group: he put on one of the red vinyl smocks that hung from wooden hooks on the wall, and ran to the easel and did an incredibly fast painting—a half-minute painting, in big, thick strokes of a single primary color. She showed me his latest one, hanging from clothespins on a portable laundry rack. I took it with me even though there were still places where the red paint was damp.

The first thing *I* did, when we got out of the school building, was lift him in the air and kiss him on both cheeks.

"What?" he said, grinning apprehensively against the flocked gray sky, his face in shadow.

"I like your work, Old Bean. I like what you've been doing in tempera lately." I turned him this way and that in the air till he laughingly whined to be set down.

We walked home. His home.

"Well, thank you for bringing him back," Lila said, and she ushered him inside and started to close the wrought iron door between us, but I put my hand on the door.

"Wait a second, what's he going to do for the rest of the day? Are you going to take care of him?"

She looked feverishly blank, stringy-haired, defensive.

"I mean you're sick," I said. "You have to rest."

"He'll take a nap."

"I'll put him in for his nap."

"I'm starting to feel better. I don't need you anymore, thanks."

I started walking forward. "You've missed two days of work. I don't want you to miss any more."

"You stay out!" she shouted suddenly. I stopped. Then I think her own vehemence embarrassed her, and she said, "If you want to argue, you picked the wrong day. I'm going to try to sleep."

"I don't want to argue."

She looked at me suspiciously, as if she really did want to challenge me but was too weakened. She turned away. I watched the flannel nightgown, hanging straight on her long torso, quiver as if from air currents as she walked into the bedroom. She closed the door.

Putting Jeff in for his nap took only a few minutes this time—he must have still been fatigued from illness. Afterward, I traveled through the silent apartment as if sightseeing. There were no lights on, and this being a cloudy day, the ground-floor apartment was dark as dusk. White dust particles danced lingeringly in the chute of dim light coming through the living room window. I sat on the sofa, and stared at the covers of business magazines I used to read, even though I had no interest in business.

I leaned my back against my interlocked hands. There was nothing for me to do here. Wait: of course there are things for me to do.

· · ·

First I went to Lila's bedroom. Very carefully and slowly I opened the door. I tiptoed in.

She was asleep, prone, her arms stretched forward so her knuckles touched the warm wall. The sheet was pulled all the way up to the back of her skull. Her breathing was gargly. The curtains were closed.

I looked at Lila's hands, the way they were stretched forward and curled against the wall, the white wall grimed by two oblongs with the oils from her hair and mine. I had been raised as an American boy. An American boy is raised to believe that the significantly desirable parts of a woman's body are her breasts, genitals, legs, ass, and sometimes her face. But when you've been married for a long time, there's another part of your wife's body that's equally beautiful to you. Her hands. Her hands are the part that has touched you most, and done most with you. Her hands look a couple of years older than her face, because of all the things they've done for you or with you, or for your child or with your child.

This sleeping woman, I thought, knows everything about me. She knows the way I cook scrambled eggs: in big clumps, at high heat, with too much butter. She knows which actresses I go for and what kinds of jokes I won't laugh at. She knows almost as much about my high school as if she'd been there with me. When we saw amusing people on the street, she used to anticipate my wisecracks so accurately that I wouldn't even have to voice them: we'd just look at each other and burst out laughing. On vacations, she usually guessed which tourist traps I'd drive past and which ones I'd eccentrically want to see. She knew what I looked like when I sat on the floor reading a story to Jeff, some ridiculous story about rabbits, which she would make fun of me for still enjoying after reading it so many times.

She could tell when I was about to have a bad mood—unless I detected her foreknowledge and decided to surprise her. She knew what I'd been like at twenty. She knew when I'd cried, and when I'd stormed out of our student apartment and slept in the dormitory lounge for two nights. She could doubtless remember the time I'd written a foolish complaint letter to the Sanitation Department and the time I'd heroically gotten the credit card company to remove an unjust charge. She probably had a private, mental ideograph of what my shape looked like under the blanket when she had her contact lenses off and could barely see. She knew how lightly I made a hundred and sixty pounds press on her in the dark. She had been the audience for sentences I had spoken looking at a mountain in the Vermont twilight: dream-talk about the future—about now.

It hadn't happened the way the Vermont mountain had promised.

I covered her properly with the blue comforter and gingerly tiptoed out.

In the kitchen I dialed my own number.

"Hello?" Maggie said.

"Hi," I said in a semi-whisper. "I'm going to take care of Jeff the rest of today. Make his dinner and so forth."

"I know," she said.

"I'll be back probably in the early evening. You can eat without me, or you could wait and we'll have a late dinner."

"One of two choices."

"Yes." There was silence on both ends of the phone. Lila sighed quietly; I wondered if Maggie heard. Lila turned her back to me in sleep, and tucked her hands under the dark blue pillow. "Okay, well, 'bye, okay?"

"Yes," Maggie said.

After I hung up, I cleaned that fucking place.

First the dishes: Jeff's breakfast dishes, his thermos from lunch, two coffee mugs of Lila's, and a couple of plates. I did them by hand so the dishwasher wouldn't wake the nappers, and dried them with the same fringed yellow dishtowel I used to use.

The stainless steel sink looked a little filmy, so I cleaned it with scouring powder and a sponge. "Don't be lazy," I said to myself. "There's a lot more you can do around here."

I shook scouring powder all over the formica counters and the stove and sponged them down. Then I took the cast iron burners off the stove and scrubbed with steel wool the accumulated grease and the black chips of charred food. That left steel wool filings and gray suds on the stove, so I rinsed that off with a fresh sponge I found in a cellophane package under the sink; and when I put the burners back in place, the stove looked as good as new. I sprayed the refrigerator and wiped it with a dry paper towel; then with a damp paper towel I wiped the food stains off the inside of the refrigerator and the crisper. When the refrigerator was done, I replaced Jeff's alphabet magnets on the door.

Repair. Renovate. Restore. Reclaim. Redeem.

Salvage.

I took off my shoes and went in stockinged feet, cleaning from room to room. I scoured the bathroom tub, the toilet bowl, and the sink. I squirted the medicine chest mirror with window cleaner, then decided to mop the floor. And if I was going to mop the bathroom floor, I might as well do the kitchen floor too—in fact I might as well do all the floors in the house. But first you have to sweep to get the hair and dust up; so I did that, and went through the apartment mopping all the uncarpeted rooms. "A mop-up operation," I said to myself in a murmur.

After the mopping, my lower back ached from all the bending and pushing. I stood for a while leaning on the mop handle and feeling good that I'd made so much floor look shiny and clean. Then I went to the living room. Since the vacuum cleaner would have awakened Lila and Jeff, I used an old-fashioned carpet sweeper that we'd bought especially for Jeff's naps. It wasn't very efficient and I had to go over the same areas again and again, but finally I got it to the point where I thought Lila might notice.

I dusted the furniture with spray wax and a clean rag, and straightened the magazines and knicknacks. I wanted to throw out the older magazines, but I thought I'd better leave that to Lila, so I only threw out the garbage that was in the wastebasket under the kitchen sink.

When I opened the apartment door to take out the garbage, I noticed that the hinges creaked. I looked at them, moved the door to and fro, and said to myself, No. You don't have to. It's too much.

What the hell, I thought, I've got nothing better to do. So I got a can of Three-in-One oil from under the kitchen sink and oiled not only the hinges of that door, but every hinge on every door in the apartment.

The lock on the wrought iron outer door was getting loose, so I got a screwdriver and tightened it.

I cleaned the doorjambs where Jeff—or his parents—had left fingermarks.

I cleaned the TV screen and dusted the stereo.

I straightened all my pictures that were hanging on the walls.

Then I went quietly into the bedroom and sat at my old drafting table in the alcove. I tidied up the tabletop, threw some old sketches in the wastebasket, cleared a space to work, and just sat there, my hands spread flat on the pine surface. I closed my eyes for a long time, opened them and stared at the pencil-marked, postcard-decorated wall.

When I had finished, I stood up and walked around the apartment. I looked at my work. The place looked so nice. I had really accomplished something. I had made a tangible, visible change. Everything looked newer and better. The apartment smelled like ammonia and lemon. I sneezed, happily.

I made myself a mug of black coffee and drank it in the kitchen, sitting on the blue stepladder where Dulcea often sat. It was important to keep your place clean. It was a much-maligned important thing. It increased your self-esteem, therefore your esteem for others and theirs for you, and your general ability to handle life. It made life itself seem cleaner and prouder and more worthwhile. I sipped the strong coffee in the slate-gray mug, in the fluorescent light and the light from the small window that faced the backyard.

Soon Jeff awoke, and I played with him until dinnertime. We built a tower out of blocks, then deliberately rammed cars into the tower and toppled it, then built a new tower. We set stuffed animals on the floor and said their lines as they had a tea party. I drew a fox, a coat, and a pencil sharpener—Jeff's requests. We played the xylophone till my ears hurt.

Lila woke up in the middle of our playing. In a circle on the floor were Jeff, a brown bear, a white bear, a monkey, and me.

"Oh, you're still here," she said.

"I'll make him dinner."

"You don't have to."

"I'll make you dinner too."

"I don't want dinner."

"Come on, when you're sick you need protein."

"Do not make my dinner."

"Okay. Sorry . . . Well, look, I'll give him his bath before dinner, that'll take some of the burden off you. You can do what you want as far as dinner."

She looked at me for a rather long time, thinking. "Tonight's a shampoo night. If you want to back out . . ."

"No, that's fine."

I felt a little smug at that, because Jeff always liked my bath-giving better than Lila's. When Lila gave him his shampoo, one or both of them usually ended up yelling protests. But I knew what to say, authoritatively yet patiently, to coax him to keep his head tilted back so he wouldn't get water or suds in his eyes. I knew how to rinse his hair with the washcloth so water wouldn't stream over his face. I know how to do this, I said to myself as I soaped and rinsed him. This is my work.

I presented him to Lila, freshly washed and dried and in a clean pair of pajamas (red with a dog in a fire chief's hat) and with his hair toweled dry and combed. She had been chewing the collar of her nightgown but hastily stopped it.

"Here's the man," I said, and she opened her arms for him and said, "My baby!" as if he had been lost for a day. I watched him cross the space between me and her, with a magnetism that seemed almost not to require any lifting of his feet. She pressed him to her nightgown, inhaling with an eyes-closed smile the clean smell of him, and gave his hair a charming little muss with her hand. She kept her gaze at his level, so as not to show me gratitude.

154

"How are you feeling?" I asked her, with a mixture of belatedness and keen concern.

"I'll get over it," she said.

"Right. I guess I knew that."

19

When I got home, Maggie was lying face-up on the "desk" bump of living room linoleum, with handwritten white pages spread around her. She was wearing an Elvis Presley T shirt with Elvis's lips painted shocking pink, his hair yellow, and his eyelids sparkling with blue and silver glitter. She didn't look at me. Come on, Maggie, I thought. I haven't deserted you. Now don't disappear in front of my eyes. Stay in this world.

"Sorry I took so long," I said.

She didn't respond.

I put my jacket, sweater, scarf, and gloves away. When I returned to the living room, she moaned.

"What's the matter?"

"*Peanut Butter and Jealous.*"

I felt relieved: she wasn't angry at me, at least not primarily. *Peanut Butter and Jealous* was her new children's story, the one Mike had launched down from his window. She had interrupted work on it and had just recently returned to it, but with very little progress.

"I'll never finish it," she said. "I crossed out everything I wrote after that night. It's like my storytelling died there."

"That's ridiculous," I said. I began picking up pages and putting them in order.

"He put a jinx on me. He doesn't want me to do anything now that I left him."

"That would be a great reason to go back to him."

She looked at me as if asking whether I meant it.

"Sure," I said. "He's one of the great creative minds, didn't you know that? He could give you much better advice than I can."

"Leave him alone," she said, like someone guarding a weaker friend against a bully from another neighborhood. It stung me a little but I held my peace.

I turned my back for privacy and began to read her story. It was the second or third time I'd done so, but this time I also read all the abortive endings she had written and crossed out. She was right: they weren't any good.

She seemed totally stuck. She knew she had to get the child characters to overcome the spell of jealousy, and to love each other in the end, but she couldn't think of the specific incidents that would make them. I had tried brainstorming with her before, and had come up with a lot of alternatives that weren't any better than the ones she had crossed out. But for some reason, this time . . .

"Nice Cream!" I said.

She sat up, gradually, suspiciously uncrossing one limb, raising one part of her body at a time. She looked at me for elaboration.

"Nice Cream. They find Nice Cream in the freezer one day," I said. "They're doing all these hostile things to each other, squealing on each other to their parents, excluding each other from their games, but it makes them feel worse. They don't know how to stop, or even that they *want* to stop, because they're just kids. But one summer day they both want ice cream so they find themselves at the freezer together. Then . . . let's see . . . how do we get the Nice Cream in there?"

I paced in a big circle in the bare living room, and I was in the kind of mood where any question could be answered by the time I paced back to the starting point.

"What happens is . . . Yes, I've got it, listen. There isn't enough ice cream left for two. She deliberately takes a gluttonous portion, just to deprive him, even though she doesn't really want that much. So he's crying because he didn't get any ice cream, and meanwhile she has this ball of it melting in her bowl that she just plans to throw out. And she begins to feel guilty. Okay, let's see . . . She wishes she had given him some, but it's too late, it's all melted in her bowl. She sorrowfully opens the freezer to show him that there's no more ice cream. But there *is!* There's this brand-new container in there, and it's labeled not 'Ice Cream' but 'Nice Cream'. And they open it together and taste it and that breaks the jealous spell and so on. There's your ending."

She looked at me. I was grinning, all pumped up with inspiration.

"Shit," she said, and smacked the linoleum with her palm.

"I thought it was good," I said.

"Brendan, it's so much better than I could figure out . . ."

"Oh, come on. It's not."

"It is. I've been working on this for weeks and I didn't come up with a fuckin' thing and you just figure it out like that." She snapped her fingers.

"No, no, no. You're the one who got the initial idea, and it was really good. And *Rhino Yogurt* —"

"Yeah, right. I used to be able to think of things like that. But I only did it once. One and a half times. So something opened up in me at that particular time in my life. Now it's closed. I don't know where it came from, I don't know where it went. Big deal. I'll live with it, right?"

"No, Maggie, you're a very creative —"

"Oh, shit. Who am I to say I can write children's books? I hardly ever read a book before I took a couple of college courses. I have to ask you grammar questions."

"Grammar isn't —"

"Yeah, I know. But I'm trying to say I don't know anything about anything, understand? I don't know what regular writers do, whether they rewrite the same thing fifty times or think it all up at once, or what. I don't know what they do when they're stuck. I don't know how they know they're writers in the first place. I thought up *Rhino Yogurt* one day when I was upset. Maybe it's the only thing like it that I'll ever do. I'm very young; how do I know there isn't something else I'd be better off doing? Maybe a social worker. Maybe open a store. I could never be an executive in an oil company, though, could I?"

"Oh, knock it off."

"She never gets upset about her work, right?"

"Yes she does."

"You should write children's books all by yourself," Maggie said. "You could write them and illustrate them, both. You don't need me."

"You mean I don't need these?" I kissed her eyelids as they fluttered shut in self-defense. "I don't need this?" I strewed kiss-petals on her hair. "Don't need Elvis?" And I kissed her once, lightly, on each little breast.

But there were times when kindness seemed to hurt her. She curled up tight, her head between her knees. And oh, God, had I sensed beforehand that this was such a moment? But you have to do *some*thing.

20

Rawley's prophecies were beginning to come true: my name was becoming known among art directors in Manhattan, and a couple of them had even solicited work from me. The assignment I had the most hopes pinned on was actually a picture of Jeff and me, a pencil drawing for an article on the New Fatherhood in a family magazine. I had work to do on it over Thanksgiving weekend so I was ambivalent about taking time off, but I had been working so much lately, I deserved the break.

Lila and Jeff had flown to her parents' for Thanksgiving, and on the Saturday after the holiday, I went with Maggie to visit Hilary. I still felt a duty to be her bodyguard, though Mike always acted decently when she arrived. He had gotten so used to me that he no longer put on his friendly-sinister act; he just handed Hilary over with barely a syllable, waved a pouting good-bye to her with a child's open-and-shut wave, and walked away—usually barefoot, wearing designer jeans and no shirt, emphasizing the hitch in his step as if to mime desolation. Up his glossy oak staircase into the recesses of his house he went.

I had come to like Hilary; she was a sly one herself, and delighted in sneaking up on me and pelting me with grass or twigs when I was staring at the sky and thinking. We liked to run races in Prospect Park, and I had recently bought her her first pair of roller skates (which we kept at our apartment, at Mike's request).

It was getting into cold weather. On the little traffic circle at Sixteenth Street, the sidewalk vendor had sold most of her pumpkins and Indian corn, and was replacing them with Christmas wreaths and ornaments. Maggie was wearing a nubby purple and blue sweater under her jacket, and I had on my knee-length gray tweed coat. We clutched close for the whole quarter-mile. After we rang Mike's doorbell, she gave me two squeezes of the hand, which gave her courage.

"Please come in," he said when he opened the door for us. He stroked his black-haired sternum up and down with his fingernails.

"Hilary," Maggie called out as we walked in. She did a parody of her own Italian inflections: "Eh, you. Eh, kid, whereda fuckareyuh?" She looked slowly to the left, then to the right.

There were two middle aged people sitting on the living room sofa, with Hilary between them. When Maggie saw them, she froze for a second, then turned about-face and began to walk out of the house.

"Hey!" Mike said. "Maggie, honey!" He ran up beside her and caught her by the elbow. I moved close. Pure rage shot through me when he called her "Honey"; I had to think away the white flashes in my head. Mike took his hand off her when he saw me approach, but he circled around so that he was between Maggie and the door. "A little tolerance. A little charity, what do you say, good feeling. It's almost Christmas time, you know?"

"You motherfuckin' son of a bitch," she said.

"I knew you'd respond like that. So I understand, and it's okay, no one's blaming anyone. We'll get past the cursing and ugliness and try to get together as people and find something valuable for the season. Come on." He stretched his hand toward Maggie's elbow; she jerked away, but turned in the direction he wanted her to. "Sit, have some coffee and cookies, talk. That's all I'm askin'."

It was the first time I had ever seen Maggie submit to another person's will. Though she did it with sulky reluctance, she walked into the living room and around to the front of the sofa. The woman stood up, and gave the man a poke so that he stood up too. He was a very small man, no more than five foot four, and bony, with a fragile rectangular face, a snub nose bent to one side, and sparse gray hair combed straight across in separate rows. His eyes focused on the sleeves of his brown and green checked sport jacket, which exposed too much white shirt cuff. The woman was a trifle shorter than her husband, neatly outfitted in a brown shirtdress, and looked like Maggie, but twenty years older.

Maggie stretched her arms out to Hilary. "Come here, baby." Hilary looked at the old people on both sides of her, and didn't move. "I said come *here!*" She stretched across with her knee on the coffee table and grabbed Hilary by the hand, practically yanking her, the way you would if your child was about to be run over by a bus. She took Hilary to the far end of the room and pressed Hilary's face against her leg as if to shield her sight. Maggie herself had to look at the wall while addressing them.

"Did you come here by yourselves or did he invite you?"

Mike rushed up. "It was a surprise. It was my idea. It's my fault if you think it's bad, but I think if you let it happen, if you try to overcome the past and everything—"

Maggie screamed—no word, just a scream. Then she seemed to remember Hilary, and bent down to see if the child had been upset, which she had been. Hilary was looking up, scared and uncomprehending. Maggie kissed her and murmured comfort.

"Margaret," the woman said. "Your father and I . . ." She stopped, as if choked by memory and hope. "Tell her," she told the little man.

"Mags," he said.

Maggie acted like he wasn't there. Although by this point she could bear to look at her mother.

"I'm only going to ask you one question," the older woman said. "Do you see any alcoholic beverages on this table?" She took Maggie's refusal to respond as a response. "That's because we don't drink. Do you hear what I just said? Your father and I don't drink anymore. Now—" She had a brassy, didactic voice, like a New York City schoolteacher. "Now I want you to think about what that means. Don't you think it might mean we've become slightly different people from what we were? Don't you think it might mean we've struggled very hard to overcome our difficulties? I can't tell you that we're perfect people, Margaret. If you'll excuse me for saying so, maybe you'll think about it and realize you're not a completely perfect person either. No one is. I'm not saying anything about you, but we're trying to change. With His help." She gave a crediting glance upward. "Nothing is possible without His help and a lot of other people's help. The list is too long even to mention, the people that have given so much to make us what we are, that we're so grateful for. Now I can't promise you, darling, that we'll be perfect tomorrow either. We only talk about today. We used to talk about the future, how we'd change in the future, but that was long ago. You can talk and talk about tomorrow, and all it does is, it turns today into yesterday, and then where are you? Maybe someday we'll be able to talk about the past, but not now. Now all we want to deal with is now. You see, darling, we *have* changed."

"We don't drink," the little man said. "A short beer in the hot weather, what harm is that?"

His wife parched him with a look.

"Let's go to the park," Maggie said to me. "Or take car service into the city, show Hilary the museums. Please?" she said in the tone of a child entreating its parent.

"Please, Maggie," Mike said. "Plenty of time for your museums. Right, Brendan? The museums are open all day, right?" I didn't answer him. "Look, Maggie, I knew when I did this you'd throw a fit. You can't say I did it to get you back or nothin'." He and I glared at each other. "I did it 'cause I thought Hilary ought to know her grandparents, that's all."

"That's right," the older woman said. "If you're not ready to make your peace with us, we accept that as your present opinion, which we hope you'll change in times to come, even though, very frankly, we don't have so much time left." She looked all of forty-eight or -nine to me, and she probably looked older than her age because of wear and tear. "But we'd like to know our grand-child—this dear who's hiding from Grandma!" she said with a sudden, ferocious smile and a loudly thrown kiss. Hilary peeked out from behind Maggie's leg, giggled, and ducked back as if to shield herself before the kiss could hit her. "Smartie! Tell Mamma to let us see you!"

"People change," Mike said. "Life's a surprise, Maggie. Gotta open yourself up to it."

"We don't drink no more," the little man said, turning his hand palm-up at beltside like a racing tout asking for his share of the winnings.

"I called your Dad up at his office," Mike said. "I told him the situation."

"We were very concerned," the older woman said.

"I take responsibility," Mike said. "I invited them here. I knew it might cause trouble, but like I said, I figured I'd give it a shot. You never know what good can come out of trouble. Because who can really say the true story of who did what to who?"

I turned to him. "What?"

"It was so long ago. Who knows what really happened?"

"Come over here," I said. I walked to the far end of the living room and into the kitchen, looking back to make sure Mike followed me. He walked in on the balls of his feet, good-naturedly wary. I indicated the refrigerator, like a spot on a police line-up. I put my hands in the back pockets of my cor-duroys. I spoke in a very low voice. "Are you saying her father didn't rape her?"

"Shh." He put his finger to his lips. "The guy's right out there, have some discretion. Don't get me wrong. I believe Maggie. You gotta believe her or she'll slice you," he laughed. "But rape is a very extreme kind of word. A father on his daughter, and the guy's a respectable person, not a scumbag? I've talked to the guy. He's a quiet little guy. I can believe he got drunk, I can believe he don't hold his liquor well. But do you believe . . . ? I mean, reason it out. It was many years ago. Memory changes things. She had grudges against him from before. Everybody's got his own version of what happens, you know? She says one thing, the two old bastards each say something different. I can't believe one without calling the other two liars. I don't like to call anyone a liar, that's all I'm saying. For Christ's sake, I could lift the guy with one hand!"

"Yeah, but we're not saying he raped *you*." I walked out of the kitchen in disgust.

"Don't abandon your family," the woman was saying to Maggie.

"Specially your daughter," the man was saying. "A girl needs two parents."

I went up to Maggie and gave her a hug of belief and protection and belonging. She was trembling from her parents' assault. I felt the flesh of her back grow calm beneath my hands, and I was glad her parents and husband were watching.

"Let's go," I said.

"Great idea."

We each took one of Hilary's hands. I saw Maggie's mother raise her eyebrows in Mike's direction. Mike shrugged tolerantly.

"I'm sorry we didn't have a chance to be introduced," Maggie's mother called out to me as we headed for the front door.

"Don't torment yourself about it," I said.

21

The rest of the day went well. We called a car service to take us to the Guggenheim. Hilary loved the spiral ramp, and I picked her up so she could look over the railing to the coin fountain and the tops of people's heads six stories below. She even looked at a painting or two. She even let *me* look at a painting or two. After the museum, we walked down Fifth Avenue for a while, and as Park Slopers always do, we compared Central Park with Prospect—the topography, the greenery, the promenades—and concluded that Prospect was the greater masterpiece. Hilary sat between us in the yellow cab going home, and I put my arm around the two of them as we went over the Brooklyn Bridge, the lights on the suspension cables lit up in the streaked autumn twilight. We told the cabbie to stop at Mike's house, and I lifted out the sleeping child and handed her silently to her father.

Maggie and I bought a pie at Smiling Pizza on Eighth Avenue, and ate it there with cans of cherry soda, and listened to a beat cop talking to the counterman about the football playoffs, and to two teenagers in black leather jackets catechizing each other about the plot of *The Terminator*. We went home, brought the TV into the bedroom, watched the middle of some movie for a few minutes as we lay on our futon, then turned the sound off and fucked in the TV light. God it was good. Just before we fell asleep I commented that it was only ten-thirty: the earliest either of us had gotten to sleep in a long time.

In the middle of a dream I heard a scream, and realized it was coming from real life. Maggie had screamed, and now screamed again. I leaned over and looked. She was asleep; something had terrified her in her sleep. She woke up, but looked as if she didn't know where she was.

"Maggie." I put a hand on her shoulder, and shook it a little. "Wake up, you had a nightmare. It's okay, it's over."

She reached one hand under the futon mattress, and pulled it out again, and the hand swung above both our heads in a fast arc and came down toward me, and in the light from the TV and from the street I saw the short glinting line of metal and the white handle, at the exact moment it plunged into my right hand.

I screamed.

It woke Maggie at last. She shook her head, found herself standing up. She groped for my hand; I pulled it away in pain, but she had already felt the blood.

"Oh, shit, I thought you were someone else," she said.

I moaned with pain and frustration, holding my own fingers, shaking out my hand and spraying blood all over the place, and keeping the knife, which I had pulled out myself. I had never been stabbed before. It hurt a surprising amount.

"Oh God," she said, in contrition rather than squeamishness. "Come here, come with me. Get off the futon, you're getting blood all over the place." She gripped me by the wrist and pulled me, with crisis strength, into the bathroom, where she stuck my hand under running cold water, wrapped a lot of toilet paper from a new roll around the wound, and had me apply pressure with my free hand.

"I'm so sorry," she said.

I smiled. "Yeah, you already said that." The pain was becoming duller and less frightening. "I hope I can get away without going to the emergency room."

"How is it?"

I lifted my hand off the toilet paper bandage. The center was soaked with dark blood, but the stain was drying around the edges and didn't look as if it was spreading very far. Slowly and with a certain amount of nausea, I peeled the paper away to take a look. It was a short and moderately deep incision, still bleeding but not profusely—the blade must have missed the veins—and the seams of skin were already trying to close.

"I don't know, looks not too bad. Let's give it some more time."

Maggie made a new bandage, and this one became less soaked. I sat on the toilet seat, sagging back against the tank, shutting my eyes and falling into a shiny half-sleep, and wishing that nothing bad ever happened. One little cut in your skin and you feel like the world is crumbling around you, and you're on the streets with the homeless, and you're unloved and untaught, hunted, hungry.

"I wonder when I had my last tetanus shot," I said. "A couple of years ago, I think. Yeah, I stepped on a tack while stretching a canvas." I looked at the wound again. "I don't know, Maggie, it's still bleeding pretty good."

Maggie was sitting on the edge of the bathtub, where it was near the sink. She had washed the knife, dried it with toilet paper, and closed it. Now she held it in her fist, so that only the protruding ends were visible. She was naked, and the knife looked like some kind of esoteric jewelry. A primitive talisman.

"You always sleep with that thing?" I asked.

"I can't get to sleep without it. I try sometimes—I get insomnia. I get insomnia with it too, sometimes, but . . ."

"It's okay." A twinge of pain went through me at those words, as if my body were censuring me for allowing liberties to be taken with it. It hurt especially when I tried to open and shut my hand, so I stopped doing that. "I think I'm going to have to go to the emergency room, though. This thing isn't closing up." I peeked under the bandage: blood, and pink dermis a good inch deep, and even something I thought might be a tendon.

So I slowly stood up, and cradled my hand as much of the time

168

as possible while getting my clothes on. Maggie and I got our coats on, went downstairs, and walked half a mile to the hospital. The armed guard sitting at a table in front hassled us about insurance as if representing some kind of totalitarian state. There was the usual three hour wait while all the more serious cases were taken care of, and finally, when I thought I was becoming a serious case myself by almost bleeding to death, I heard my last name being called through a throbbing field of light and was given into the hands of two residents and an earnest intern who very commendably wanted to learn the right way to stitch a knife wound: "Is it this way? No? This way?"

It required seven stitches that took fourteen attempts. I went home with a big white bandage wrapped around my hand, with a crosspiece covering my entire thumb and slanting down to my wrist. We returned to our blood-stained futon. It was three a.m.

22

W̲e removed the big bandage the next day, and I snipped my own stitches out, ahead of schedule. Even after they were out, I felt a tightness across my hand, and it hurt to grip anything, but I sort of got a kick out of working in pain—it made me feel like Monet strapping his brushes to his hands to do the waterlilies. I finished the pencil drawing of Jeff and me, and the art director was quite pleased with it and gave me the assignment for a parent-and-child calendar that the magazine was going to publish. It would keep me solvent for six months. That evening I took Maggie to Raintree's, on the corner of Ninth Street and Prospect Park West, and celebrated with champagne and a terrific poached salmon, but she didn't even try to pretend to share my joy. She flaked off pieces of rosy fish and pushed them around on her plate, twirled a sprig of parsley lackadaisically in her fingers, and whenever I asked her a question, I had to repeat it before I could drag her up from her fog. She kept saying, "I'm ruining your big celebration, now you hate me," and I kept saying, "No, no," but she seemed intent on believing it.

She was plunging into a bad time. I kept telling her not to feel guilty about stabbing me. "A mere case of mistaken identity, it could have happened to anyone." But she insisted that she *didn't* feel guilty. "So what are you so depressed about?" I asked. She couldn't answer.

The next day she said: "Okay, now repeat what you want me to do with *Peanut Butter and Jealous.*" So I explained it a second time. But she gave up trying as soon as she started, and threw the pen across the room and announced that she was too stupid and uneducated to write those stories anymore and that I would have to dictate it to her, word for word. Which I did, when it became clear that that was really the only way the project would get done. When she typed it up to send to her publisher, she at first wanted to list me as co-author as well as illustrator, but I told her, "Fuck you," and retyped the title page with her as sole author. I held it up in front of her, thinking the sight of her name would make her proud. "There. All right?"

"Whatever you want, Brendan. You got the brains; if you want to call me the author, I'm the author."

"Oh, that's bullshit, Maggie. Even if you're feeling bad about things, you should never start to think you aren't smart. You have no right to; it's totally unrealistic."

"Whatever you say. I'm a whiz kid."

She went to the bedroom to lie down.

I had to do all the work of submitting the manuscript: putting it into a padded envelope, addressing it, taking it to the post office. I sort of resented having that chore imposed on me, but I figured it was a kind of errand of mercy, a response to a temporary need. Once *Peanut Butter and Jealous* was out of her sight, she seemed to relax a little—at least she laughed at one or two of my jokes at dinner. She spent most of the evening sitting against the living room wall, her knees up and bare arms dangling over them. She seemed to be observing the diminishing light in the airshaft window.

The next morning, she shook me awake urgently. It was only seven-thirty.

"What, did you have a nightmare?" I asked.

"Brendan, I'm gonna have to go back."

"No?" I said, which I knew was a garbled answer as I was making it.

"I gotta be Hilary's mother. I can't make her turn out the same as me. Listen," she said, stroking my arm, "if I stayed with you, I'd leave you someday anyway, but probably for something worse."

"No," I said, reduced to monosyllables. "Stay?"

I felt sick. My stomach was going in circles, and my legs and arms felt as if they were separated from my body by an inch of space. I was astonished at how immediately and absolutely your whole state of being can change, but even my astonishment was blanketed in a pins-and-needles numbness.

I must have looked pretty stricken, for she stepped back to look at my face and give me an encouraging, false smile. "I'm happy about this decision. It's the first time I ever went back to anything. And you helped me."

I rubbed my face. It felt like mere skin on top of bone in an arbitrary form.

"You'll get Lila to take you back," she said. "That's what you really want."

"No. I—"

There was silence, as if I had interrupted myself.

"We're just people who go," she said. "There are people who stay, and people who go, and we're people who go."

"No! I'm a person who stays!" Hadn't I left only one person, one time? Hadn't I stayed with her a long time before that, and I wanted to stay with Maggie now? In fact I had wanted very much to show that I had improved myself: that I would not abandon a second woman.

"We stay long enough so it would hurt them if we left," she said. "Then we go."

I did not truly believe that about myself, but it was convincing enough to silence me momentarily. I covered my eyes and rubbed them. All at once the right logic seemed very simple: she and I loved each other, therefore we should stay together. But the retort was obvious: she loved Hilary too.

"What do you think?" she asked. "Think I should go?"

"I don't want you to go."

"But do you think I should?"

"You're asking me?"

"You're the person I ask important things."

"You're asking a lot," I said. But it was good to have a lot asked of me.

We were sitting up naked in bed. I turned to the wall, and after an interval I faced her again and asked: "Are you going back for *him*?"

She shook her head. "It's Hilary. It's just Hilary."

"Because if bringing your parents over actually worked—"

She shook her head more vehemently, then said: "But I can't do the things I thought I wanted to do with you. Be your artistic partner and everything."

"You can! Just wait! Be patient, I'll help you."

"Got no patience."

"I'll help you get some."

"I won't let you." She shifted herself down on the mattress as if to evade me and cling to me at once: she pulled me down beside her, so that we lay embracing in separate states of mind, me staring at the ceiling. "Let me tell you something. When I was in the group residence, I used to try to imagine some perfect guy I would fall in love with and have a happy family with, etcetera. But I always caught myself and said, 'Uh-uh. That's not what you're gonna do.' And I realized what my real goal was. It was to find someone like that and then leave him. Leave him wondering why."

"No. You're just telling yourself that."

"Know what else? It had to be a nice man. A bad man, it wouldn't bother him enough."

"Maggie, don't do that to me."

"Who said you're a nice man?"

I shook my head and laughed.

She pressed closer to me, her head up against my throat, her words buzzing my collarbone. "I saw this story on the news once.

About this little boy whose father set him on fire. Threw whiskey on him, lit a match, boom, that's it. I'm sure the kid asked him the wrong question when he wasn't in the mood or something like that, and who knows, he probably had money problems or something, something preying on his mind the kid couldn't possibly know about. The news showed the boy all in bandages—head, arms, his whole body. And he's smiling in his hospital bed. What a courageous little boy he is, and so on—they love to say that on the news. The kid will be a monster for the rest of his life, and his father did it. And I was thinking, When that kid was on fire, screaming, who do you think he was screaming for? Kid sees flames running up and down him; father already knows, I bet, that he's done the most horrible thing anyone could ever possibly do. All he wanted was a quiet drink and now he made his kid a monster. Father is screaming too, I guarantee it. Trying to roll the kid around, but it doesn't work. Who do you think the kid was screaming for?"

I didn't answer. I knew the answer.

"I bet any amount of money," she said, "he was screaming, 'Daddy! Daddy!'"

I nodded, staring at the ceiling.

"He wanted Daddy to save him," she said. "Daddy was the one who could help. Daddy knows right from wrong. Daddy can punish you, or take away a punishment. The kid must have thought he did something terrible, for Daddy to punish him like that. He's gonna spend the whole rest of his life, the whole rest of his life wondering how to make Daddy love him instead of punishing him. Believe me."

I gave Maggie many gentle pats and kisses. I stroked her shoulderblade and ran my hand over her short hair. The light from the digital clock tinted the walls green, where I had painted a forest. The windows were full of gray cloud light.

"I'm here, Maggie."

"I'm going for Hilary's sake."

I kissed her face. "Don't go today."

"No. But I have to tomorrow. Or I'll never get to leave you."

23

All that day, we made love. There was nothing but love in that bedroom. We didn't allow anything else in. Between orgasms, we lay sweatily coupled, talking quietly. We thanked each other and said how happy we hoped each other would be. We told each other the things we liked about each other: some that we had said often before, and other things that we had never said. It surprised me that Maggie liked my voice and the way I talk back sardonically to commercials. I told her I loved her little tits. We let the radio play all night.

At about noon I woke up and turned the radio off, then sat on the edge of the bed and watched Maggie sleep. She stirred, turned one way and another, gradually stretched. Her fist tapped me in the leg as she stretched, and I caught it and kissed it.

The shades were up; the day was bright and cold; on the bed were thick slabs of sunlight that forced you to squint. I watched Maggie's bare chest move, and her blanketed legs. As she always did when waking, she shook her head from side to side and made a complaining sound.

"Are you really leaving today?" I asked.

She squeezed my hand.

We ate an afternon breakfast in a luncheonette across the street from a red brick Catholic church on a hilltop. It was a school day, and children in gray and green plaid uniforms were swarming at the streetcorners, textbooks in their arms. Delivery trucks were double and triple-parked in front of the stores. There was a constant uproar of truck engines revving, children laughing and gossiping, the luncheonette grill sizzling, workingmen calling out food orders. At the counter and the tables a gas meter reader, a potato chip route man, and three tar-handed members of a pot-hole repair crew were having hero sandwiches. Maggie and I had French toast with maple syrup, and thick coffee.

"Can I take just one suitcase today, and come back for other stuff later?" she asked.

"If you'd like me to, I'll help bring stuff over. Or Mike can come over and help."

"I haven't told him I'm coming yet."

"What? Gonna surprise him?" I looked down and stirred my black coffee. "What about his brownstone widow? Is he gonna give up three brownstones?"

Maggie smiled. "She's no competition. I know how to get things."

"Yeah," I said. We grinned at each other for a long time.

"Well, make him cook a meal sometimes," I said.

"Yeah, he should be doing that by now."

We stayed in the luncheonette long after we finished our food.

"Maggie," I said, "I just want you to know that I don't consider you a mistake. On my part, I mean—living with you and everything."

She looked down silently. Did it mean that *she* considered living with *me* a mistake? Or that she thought I ought to consider her a mistake? Or was she simply touched by my statement and bashful about returning the compliment? I don't know.

I paid the check and we walked around the neighborhood. We stopped at the window of a hardware store and looked at venetian blinds. I looked at our reflection in the window, standing side by side.

A couple of hours later, her suitcase was packed. It was green and made of textured vinyl. It stood upright next to the slanting steel pole of the police lock braced against our front door. Through the barred kitchen window, which faced the airshaft, we heard a man and woman talking in a soap opera, and a third voice, a woman, saying, "Goddamn these fuckin' new contraptions. I can't get this open. I can't get it open."

Maggie was wearing a knee-length, big-shouldered, charcoal gray overcoat that she'd bought in a thrift shop; it was unbuttoned, over a white T shirt, pegged black pants, and white anklets. She knocked the inner edges of her fists together, swinging them like two pendulums.

"Well," she said.

"Should I call car service for you?"

"Don't be silly. I'll walk."

"Let me carry the suitcase for you. I'll walk you there."

"No."

We went downstairs. A beautiful day. I walked her a couple of blocks to the traffic circle in the south corner of Prospect Park West. We looked ahead at the park on our right, the blocks and blocks of three-story buildings on our left.

"Can I still be your illustrator?" I asked.

"If I ever need one."

"I'm still your friend," I told her.

She nodded.

"Kiss?" I asked.

I had anticipated it would be a soft, brief, letting-go kind of kiss, but it was much heavier than that. I worked hard at memorizing that kiss.

When I ungripped her, I said: "Gonna be fine."

"Maybe, I hope."

"You can always come back to me."

She picked up her suitcase.

"I'm proud of you, Ferro," I said.

She stood there with the suitcase. She held it posed in front of her, both hands on the handle.

"Maggie, don't pay any attention to what I'm going to say now. But—please don't leave me? I don't want you to go. I want to live with you. I want to see you every day. Please . . . I had to say that. Don't pay any attention to it, don't let it bother you."

She put the suitcase down, threw her arms around me, and buried her head against me. We stood in that position until it got ridiculous. Then she left.

24

I worked—I had a regular hot streak, and I became successful. According to Rawley, I had joined the ranks of illustra-
tors who had stable markets: who were known well enough
to art directors so that someone would always be offering an
assignment of some kind. In certain seasons I might even have
the dangerous luxury of being able to turn work down. I could
count on a predictable base income, enough to pay my rent in
Windsor Terrace anyway, and special assignments, good luck, or
personal growth might take me well past that base at times. My
style was becoming a trademark, a commodity, with sales value; I
was becoming known for doing a certain kind of thing well, and
when an art director wanted that particular kind of thing in his
magazine or on his record cover, he would now say—if he was on
top of things, if he knew his field—"I want Brendan Beame."

Without my planning it, I was becoming a specialist in illustrating a distinct subject: I was becoming The Master of
Parents and Children. I found it very unsettling. If I had had my
choice, I wouldn't be concentrating so heavily on drawing and
painting Jeff, or other children who, in my hands, invariably
developed a family resemblance to Jeff. That subject didn't take
me out of myself the way my art used to. When I was portraying

him I always became extra-conscious of the fact that I was sitting at a small formica bridge table in a room facing an airshaft, with a lumpy, gold-speckled gray linoleum on the floor, and a steel pole braced against the front door in the glass-cupboarded kitchen, three-quarters of a mile from his home. I would rather be illustrating the Canadian Rockies or the African savannah. What bothered me most was that whenever I put my hand to this subject, praise and money came rushing in, while when I put my hand to some other subject which I thought I was handling equally well or better, the reaction was so-so.

"Oh, those children's faces!" the art director gushed when I showed her February of the parent-and-child calendar, and the spot illustration for Presidents' Day. The art director was a forty year old twice-divorced childless brunette. The children, huddled around maple sugar cooling in the snow, were only part of the picture—she didn't mention the snow-covered pines, or the distant farm rendered hazily yet with great skill, or the grownup couple ice-dancing on a frozen reflection of the sky. Ah, what the hell—she paid me.

I visited Jeff a lot, not only in my paternal role but also to sketch him for the calendar. He wouldn't sit still as a model, of course, and I spent my share of time running after him with a pad and pencil in my hands, pleading, "Wait, wait, just let me get that side for ten more seconds!" "No, I don't *want* to," he would say, and a laughing chase would ensue, usually ending up with my giving the pad to him so that he could sketch me and crumple the pages in the process. From that, I got the idea for the calendar cover: a small boy at an easel in his father's studio, painting his father as a stick figure in red: circle face, circle eyes, and a big crescent smile.

Maggie hadn't called me, and I wanted to give her time to get resettled without my intruding. I walked around her part of the neighborhood a lot in hopes of accidentally bumping into her, but I never did.

I felt like a person with two painful illnesses, each one preventing the doctors from treating the other. Since leaving Lila, I had gone around with a chronic ache of regret, which I knew would be with me always. But at least I had known Lila for many years and had thousands of memories of her and had done good things with her which would outlast our union. With Maggie, the pain was that I had just started living with her, getting used to her ways. I had just begun to see past my fantasy of her, to the individual who served it, and then she had stopped me. After leaving Lila I became prey to sudden spells of going around numb with shock. That hadn't diminished. But after Maggie left, I cried more. I went into the shower and banged my head against the tile walls. It was as if one of my organs had been ripped out of my torso and I wasn't even sure which one.

My anesthetic was Jamieson's Irish Whiskey. I started drinking it at a jam-packed Irish bar on Windsor Place, and the next day I bought a bottle for my apartment; but I didn't want to drink alone, so I went back to that bar, night after night. It was a saloon in which everyone was so exclusively intent on getting drunk that there was barely any conversation, except for the shouted names of I.R.A. men who had died on hunger strikes, or of New York politicians deserving of death, or for curses—identical except for intonation—when a sports bet was won or lost. The bar and the walls were of good oak but there was absolutely no decor and there were only six bottles on the shelf below the mirror. No one ever ordered a mixed drink; no woman, not even a hooker, ever sat in the front room. I sat and watched the bartender wipe beer glasses, pretending to be watching whatever was on TV. At eleven I went home, not drunk, just tired enough to sleep. It wasn't even winter yet, just the bad end of autumn.

25

I got a phone call from Lila in mid-December.

"Hello?" she said after I answered, as if she couldn't quite place my voice. When she remembered that she was the one who had made the call, she said: "I'm going to have to ask you a question."

"Yes."

She cleared her throat slightly. I heard muffled talking pass by in the background, in the hall outside her office: a sound familiar from many afternoon phone conversations over the years. "Well," she said, in a lowered, confidential voice which made me feel she was almost ready to be my friend again, "This guy asked me out."

I stopped breathing. I couldn't see anything beyond the buttons on my wall phone.

"Dulcea had agreed to babysit," she was saying, "but then her husband slipped his disc. I mean, she agreed to do it anyway, but I'm not going to make her when he has a slipped disc."

"I'll do it," I said. "I'll be glad to babysit."

"Oh, thank you, Brendan!"

Those words were so sweet to hear, they made me uncomfortable.

"So where are you going?" I asked.

"I don't know exactly." She sounded excited at sharing the news of her adventure. "Dinner and a movie, I guess, or a jazz club, or all three. This guy Roy, at work, asked me."

"Roy?" I said.

"Don't make fun."

"I'm not making fun."

"I think Roy is a nice name," she said. "It's simple and strong, and unfashionable enough to come back into fashion."

"It means king. If you lose track of him in the movie theater you can go down the aisles waving a dog biscuit and shouting, 'Here, Roy! Here, Roy!'"

"That's very juvenile of you."

In the past I would have responded with more raillery, but her comment now had a sobering effect.

"You think you can invalidate a human being just by saying his name in a certain tone," she said. "Is that how you used to say, 'Lila?'"

"Come on, I was just trying to lighten things up. You sounded a little tense. You don't have to start getting angry in your office—you don't need that. I'm really glad you're going out, you should go out more. Tell me about it."

"I was going down to Xeroxing, he was going up—to see *me*! We talked about Vermont a little—he goes skiing there—and, I don't know, a few other things, and just before he had to leave for a meeting, he asked me for a date! Do you think I shouldn't have said yes on such short notice? Should I have put him off for a week or so, to show him how much in demand I am?"

She sounded like a college freshman again. I imagined that she had slipped her shoes off under her desk, and was sitting cross-legged—her favorite pose—swiveling, bending the cord in and out.

"No, you did right," I said. "No point in not being honest. Well, when do you need me? I can be there any time."

I didn't get much work done the rest of that day.

. . .

I got to Jeff and Lila's house at five-thirty, and Dulcea commended me for being early; she usually didn't leave until at least six.

"Now, you be good tonight for your Daddy," she told Jeff, shaking her finger at him and smiling. She was more old-fashioned, stricter, than the way I wanted my son raised, but he giggled at her finger-shaking in a comradely and not disrespectful manner. You could tell they had practiced their teamwork.

"Tonight is his shampoo night," she told me, as she put her brown slippers into a yellow plastic shopping bag and stepped into club-heeled black shoes. "You getting your hair washed tonight, young man."

"No!" he laughed.

"Yes! That hair of yours, it's getting so dirty, pretty soon you know what's going to happen? A big green parrot is going to make his nest in your hair. He'll wave to his parrot wife and tell her, 'Look at this. Jeff's hair is so dirty it makes a wonderful nest.'"

"I want them!" he laughed, and she flicked her wrist at him. She put on a charcoal gray knit hat with a stiff brim, then buttoned her brown topcoat over her black cardigan. It was very odd: as soon as she got her outerwear on and peered out the unshuttered top pane of the window, squinting one eye into the lamplight for the possibility of snow, and hobbled arthritically toward the door I held open for her, she seemed to have left our social world completely and entered another. A figure in blacks and grays and browns except for the bright yellow of her plastic bag, she set her mouth grimly and tucked her chin in guarded thought, and gave a small grunt of pain as she hoisted herself up the two steps to street level. She didn't look back at us or say good-bye. He was the third white child she had taken care of. Yet I'm sure she loved him.

Even though Jeff had protested against the shampoo, he was fine about it when the actual time came. In fact, he was so well-behaved all evening, it was as if I were a real babysitter and not his parent. He hadn't seen me in the evening in a long time, and he spent the first hour showing me his toys, as if I had never seen them before. Running back and forth from his room to the living room, he pantingly brought me one toy at a time. "This is Koala, he isn't a bear. This is He-Man. This is He-Man's shield. This is He-Man's axe."

We spent much of the evening manipulating the He-Man doll's arms and legs and trying to rebuckle his armor, which he shed at every opportunity. A fantastically muscled, loinclothed blond, He-Man fought for right, had vowed never to kill, and ended every television episode with a psychologically impeccable moral for youngsters.

"He-Man is having a tea party," Jeff announced, and placed the figurine on the floor in front of a cracked, cornflower blue demitasse cup which I recognized from our cupboards. Lila must have given it to him recently. "He-Man, would you like tea or coffee?

'Tea.'"

Jeff nodded at He-Man's wise choice. He pushed the cup toward the doll, then ran to his toy box and got a green pail, a dice cup from some discarded word game, and a small dump truck with a blue bin, and said, "Sit down, Daddy." I sat down crosslegged, and he set the dice cup in front of me and poured imaginary tea into it from the bin of the dumptruck. "Do you want sugar?" he asked.

"Yes, please."

"No, you can't," he said. "Sugar is bad."

"Oh, come on, please?"

"No. How is your tea, He-Man?"

"I want sugar," I said. "Come on, it's a special occasion."

"No!" he said, with a hint of a shriek. "I gave you your tea, now drink it!"

"Okay, okay." I sipped from the dice cup. "Very good tea, Jeff."

"Yes, it is." He hadn't drunk any from his green pail, however.

"Why don't you taste yours?" I said. "It's good tea."

"Yes," he said. "I will." He picked up the dump truck and

poured some more into each of our drinking vessels without taking any himself. "Do you want more tea, He-Man?" he asked belatedly.

He-Man apparently said yes.

A couple of hours later, sitting in the living room by myself, sipping non-imaginary apple cider, I heard Jeff talking happily to He-Man about my visit, in the past tense: "Daddy came and stayed with me when it was dark out and Mommy left. Mommy is coming back though and Daddy is going. You and I and Daddy had tea . . ."

Lila came home early! It wasn't even eleven o'clock.

She came in laughing to herself. Her trenchcoat was open. She brushed her blond hair off her face but it fell right back. She kicked off one shoe in an arc that made her put her hand to her mouth when the shoe crashed into the record cabinet. She stepped rockily out of the other shoe, slipped off her trenchcoat and heaped it on the floor in front of her, and stepped on the heap as she walked forward. Then she gave an odd sigh, in which I thought I heard equal parts of rue and merriment, and knelt on the rug and rested her head on the cool wood of the coffee table.

"I won't offer you a drink," I said. "They might take my license away."

"Caffeine!" she moaned.

I went to the kitchen and made her a mug of instant coffee. When I set it down before her on the coffee table, she gave a thank-you look, not quite to me, but aimed somewhere between me and the mug, as if I could catch it if I wanted to. I sat on the sofa and watched her wave steam impatiently away from the mug, pucker her lips to drink the liquid and then back off because it was still too hot, try again and slurp some up and wipe the dribbles off her mouth with her fingers and lick the fingers, and snatch her arm away when her white cuff threatened to dip into the coffee.

"Roy have to go home early?" I asked.

"Oh, Brendan, you were right," she laughed, and looked away as soon as she saw how good that made me feel. "We went out to eat. He began telling me how boring it is in the legal department. Well, it *is* boring! It was boring all through dinner. Apparently his job consists of sitting in his office, evening after evening, waiting for our quarterly reports to come back from the printer—so he can *proofread* them."

"My God!"

"Yes, such things happen. But the thing is, if it was so fucking boring, how come he couldn't talk about anything else? 'My job is so boring,' he would say—in this self-effacing way? As if it was actually very high-powered and he was too modest to say so? And whenever I tried to put in something of, shall we say, a little broader scope, he would get this condescending, *approving* tone in his voice. Like, 'Yes, it's okay for women to talk about that.' Like, at one point I couldn't help myself and I started talking about my child."

Our child. But I didn't bother to correct Lila. And she didn't seem to notice the slip.

"I mean," she said, "it's uncool. You're supposed to avoid the subject around single adults. It's in poor taste. But I weakened: I mentioned something about the fact that when Jeff began going to nursery school—you know—I felt more separation anxiety than he did."

"I hadn't known that."

She looked down. "Yes. A couple of times I was late for work because I would sit on the stoop across the street from his school."

"I'm sorry, I wish I'd known."

"That's all right, it's okay now. Anyway," she said, "I described this to him, how I felt about Jeff going away, going to school, and Roy sort of, I don't know—snickered, I think. I mean, I couldn't prove in a court of law he was snickering. And I'm sure he didn't know he was—I'm certain, Brendan, I'm so certain he doesn't know *anything* about his own existence. He would have been shocked if I accused him of the dreaded crime of snickering at

187

his date. But he was. And he said—back to my point, I know you always hate when I stray from my point—"

"No, no."

"—but he said he was *amazed* at how well I juggled the *responsibilities* of career and parenthood. Apparently this is why he was attracted to me: I can juggle. But you know? He was condescending to me for bringing up family life when he had *real* things to talk about, like which investment banks are underwriting our latest stock issue. He thought I would receive it as the highest possible compliment, that I can juggle my child's life on an equal basis with that sort of thing. Not aware in the slightest that raising a family isn't just a 'responsibility' equivalent to working in an office. It's not just another institution that you owe a block of time to; it's your *life* . . . Oh," she said, putting her head in her hands, "I guess what he said wasn't so bad, was it?"

"No," I laughed. "You do juggle your responsibilities pretty well."

"Oh, Brendan, am I an idiot? Did I spurn him for no reason?"

I was glad she did. "The poor guy's sitting home now, thinking, 'What did I do wrong? I've got this big salary and I can't get to first base.'"

She was laughing in a tearful voice. "He *was* a bore, though. It was terrible! I was a terrible date. I'm so out of practice. I hardly knew what to say to him. And I was so nervous, and I took everything the wrong way . . ."

"You're fine," I said, trying to imagine what it would be like to go on a first date with her if I had just met her. Would I, like her, like Roy, be too nervous to make a good spontaneous impression, and would our evening be a bust, leaving us with no desire ever to see each other again? "What did you say to him, anyway?"

"I don't know, I just tried to pass the time relatively painlessly. I suppose I made a couple of witticisms."

"Oh, no, you gave him witticisms on the first date? Lila, they're not ready for that. He's sitting home thinking, 'I'm a nice guy, why was she making fun of me?'"

"I'm an idiot!" she laughed, with transparent insincerity. "He got the world's worst date!"

"You lost Roy—the nicest man in Legal."

"Well, better now than after five years of marriage."

We got quiet.

"I've been talking to you as if you were a regular person, haven't I?" she said.

"Yes. Do you not want to?"

"I thought I didn't." She sat up straight, on the floor beside the coffee table, and tucked her legs under her and smoothed the skirt. "Well, consider it your pay for babysitting."

"If you're not going out with Roy anymore, I guess I won't be babysitting again."

"Oh, I'll be going out," she said.

She waited for, and I think savored, my involuntary look of dismay. "Probably not with Roy," she said, "although I was so abrupt with him, maybe he does deserve another chance." She mused about it, looking up at the ceiling. "No, not Roy, but I have to start getting some dating practice. And I'll probably be asked. There are a lot of hard-up men in a company like mine."

"They're not hard up if they can get a date with you."

She smiled at me. Shyly she whisked the knee of her gray wool suit skirt. Perhaps she'd been fishing for the compliment, but I didn't mind giving it to her.

"So you're going to bestow yourself on those undeserving cads?"

"No. I'm just not going to let them make me a hermit."

I nodded. Then I thought of a question I wanted to ask her. I moistened my lips and took a deep breath.

"Look, let's say some guy asked you for a date. And you found out that he used to have a wife and kid, but he jilted them for another woman. Since then, he broke up with the second one, not because he keeps jilting one woman after another, but the woman left him, for, you know, non-incriminating reasons. He's living alone now, he's starting a new life, he hopes he's matured. Naturally you'd have to be cautious with him, make sure he

189

wasn't going to use you and was really a better person now. But if he asked you for a date, would you automatically say no?"

She turned very serious. "No, I wouldn't."

"Would you go out to dinner with me some time?"

She shook her head, and it sank me. She shook her head with her eyes closed.

"You're not that guy," she said. "You're not somebody who hurt someone else and wants to do better with me. You're the one who hurt *me*. You can be a new man for someone else, but not for me. We're having a friendly conversation. But I don't want to touch you sexually again, I don't want to be in the same bed with you. It would be déja vu, it would be spooky and . . . regressive. You seem to feel that we grow by having these disasters—leaving Person A, who is limited to Phase A in our lives, and joining up with Person B, who represents Phase B. I don't. I feel that we grow by preventing disaster."

I nodded. Premature. Maybe I was premature. Shouldn't have asked her for a date so soon; maybe if I coddled her along for a few months there'd be a better response. What were a few months, for a prize like this?

"I *have* thought about this on my own, Brendan, and I've realized it's true: I might be sentimentally tempted to go back to you, but it would be self-denying and stagnant. And I would be rewarding you for what you did to me."

"Well," I nodded slowly, "at least you've thought about it. That means it isn't unthinkable."

She refrained from replying.

26

I called her up a couple of days later and asked her if she
wanted me to help her buy a Christmas tree, but she said no.
There was an outdoor Christmas tree display a block away,
right outside the pizzeria, and she would pay a couple of neighborhood kids to carry the twine-wrapped tree to her apartment
while she oversaw Jeff. Well then, I asked, did she need any help
decorating it? No, but thanks for asking. Okay, I told her, I would
come over and view her handiwork when the decorations were
up.

I had always thought that my artistic eye was needed to make
our tree beautiful, but when I stopped by to deliver Jeff's presents, I saw that Lila was quite up to the job. The trimmings were
all white: white light bulbs, white-gowned open-mouthed blond
angels, white unicorns, and lambs in matchstick mangers.

I had bought Jeff an armful of presents with my newfound
discretionary income. I had also bought a small gift for Lila:
some makeup in a brand I knew she liked, nothing special. I
didn't call it to her attention. I slipped my presents stealthily
under her tree, and left after only a brief, cordial conversation.

On Christmas morning I waited till almost noon, to give Jeff
and Lila time for their private gift-opening ceremony. Then I

walked over. When Lila answered the doorbell, she seemed surprised and happy to see me. She had always loved Christmas: she was one of those small-town Protestant girls who get wacko about gingerbread houses and stocking stuffers and poinsettias and caroling. From outside the ground-level window, I had seen the living room littered with tumbleweeds of colored paper, and I could see a corner of the white-lighted tree, and Jeff sitting solemnly in the center of the room, ignoring everything except the mallets and keys of the new xylophone I had bought him.

"Merry Christmas," I said to Lila, and hurried past so she wouldn't have to fear I would try to kiss her. I walked into the living room, acting as if—and perhaps believing that—Jeff was the person I most wanted to see. I opened my arms as he looked up.

"Daddy, look what you gave me for a present!"

"I know!"

He stood up and handed me the xylophone with its varicolored keys. Then he glanced around the floor and picked up all the other presents that had come from me. "Look, you gave me this—"

"Easel," I supplied the word.

"This easel, and this—"

"It's a watercolor set. We'll open it later."

"Watercolor set. We'll open it later. And this camera—this is only a toy, not real—and this sweater. That was very *generous* of you, Daddy."

"Thanks, Pal." I tousled his hair for conveying Lila's word choice in such a precocious manner.

She told him: "Why don't you show Daddy what *you* bought *him* for Christmas?"

She and I looked at each other. Jeff appeared eager and a little confused, as if he wanted to remember what he had bought but couldn't.

"It's under the tree," she said. Jeff brightened: he remembered now.

"Daddy, I bought you a present that you will really like!"

192

He darted under the balsam fir, grimacing as he pushed a branch away from his face. Green needles fell with a whisk-broom sound onto his brown hair and red sleeve and the floor, and a strand of lights dropped from its branch to a hanging position in midair. Jeff reached behind the tree for a small, flat package I hadn't noticed.

"Merry Christmas," he said as he gave me the package wrapped in dark blue paper with a silver bell pattern and a silver ribbon.

I was so impressed by how polite and mature he was, it took me a couple of extra seconds before I started to open it. I could tell before opening it that it was a book. I tore off the wrapping paper. It was an edition of Gauguin's letters. Lila knew I had always treasured his letters.

"Thank you, I really like it!" I said to Jeff, which made him giggle with pleasure because I had repeated his words. I looked at Lila. "Thank you."

She gave me the slightest nod. "I was going to make some cocoa. Jeff, do you want any?"

"Cocoa?" he said. "Uh, cocoa . . . ?" As kids sometimes do about precisely the things you'd think they'd go wildest about, he took an eon to decide, as if it were a trick question.

"Will you please give me an answer? Will you *please*?" she said, with a stamp of her foot and a querulous shout that was louder, I think, for being aimed at more than just him. She turned her back and began walking toward the kitchen.

"Mommy, yes, yes, I, I want cocoa!"

She stopped, and nodded. She started walking away again. Then at last, when she was almost into the foyer, she stopped again, and without turning toward me, asked: "Do you want cocoa too?"

"Yes," I said.

A couple of days after Christmas, she called and asked if I would babysit again.

"Roy?" I asked.

"No, Forrest. He's from Houston headquarters, but he's in town for the holidays. He wants to see a Broadway show with me." She laughed—she and I had always ridiculed Broadway shows. "The company gets great seats."

"Forrest? The guy is named after a biome."

"Oh, shut up," she laughed sternly. "He's a nice forty-year old man."

"You're going for older men! That's why you didn't like me: I should have been older."

"A little wiser would have sufficed."

The night of the babysitting was cold and clear; you could actually see stars above Prospect Park. I wore a blue oxford shirt, cream colored sweater vest, pressed flannel pants instead of jeans, and black loafers instead of running shoes. Lila raised her eyebrows when she saw how nattily I was got up. She herself looked great. She was wearing a calf-length purple dress and dangling, crescent-shaped purple earrings. She had had her hair trimmed; it was the same style as before, but more neatly shaped, and lighter blond. She paced hectically as we waited for the cab to drive up.

"You know where everything—Give him his vitamins at bed-time. Ice cream only if he finishes his dinner." She counted off the instructions on her long, pale fingers. Her nails were painted a darkish mauve. I watched her dress swirl as she paced.

"I know," I told her. "Calm down. He'll like you."

"Okay," she said in a tone which seemed to mean she valued my support. She spread a hand on her breast, and took deep breaths as she paced.

I thought: What if his cab doesn't come—he's stood her up—he got drunk and picked up some prostitute on the way. Or no, he's not a bad guy, just a nitwit. He forgot her address and phone number and now he has no way of getting to her. I'll take her out. I'm dressed well enough for most places, and maybe one of my old ties is still in her closet somewhere, if we looked. Yes, we'll look into the dark closet together, and our bodies will touch, and despite herself she will find herself kissing me amid the swaying dresses . . . The horn of the taxicab honked outside.

"Oh!" Lila said, and practically jumped out of her shoes. She turned to me, wide-eyed, almost afraid. I placed my hand lightly on her shoulder, to steady her, and it worked.

"Have a good time." I smiled, and she said, "Thank you!" and gave me a kiss on the cheek just as she was turning to leave. *That* startled us both, and she scurried out of the apartment with only one arm in her trenchcoat sleeves. Maybe she had kissed me reflexively out of the habit of former times; or maybe she was consciously trying to get used to me as a brotherly friend; or maybe the arrival of the cab had aroused a flustered desire and she had merely kissed the nearest person at hand. I pondered the possibilities.

27

I waited for Lila to come home.

I watched various TV series till eleven. I was going to turn off the set then, but I decided to watch the news, and then a rerun of *Saturday Night Live.* I turned it off halfway: I expected Lila to open the front door at any moment, and comedy in such a circumstance made me nervous. But by the time the show would have ended, she hadn't come, and I was looking at my ghost's reflection in the blank screen.

At one in the morning, I fixed myself a ham sandwich and a glass of milk, and started making regular trips to the window to look through the slats of the shutter. My sandwich was on the coffee table, and I established an orbital route, taking one bite each time I reached that point, then finishing my circuit with a peek through the window.

When the sandwich was all gone, I started reading a paper-back copy of *The Diaries of Virginia Woolf* from Lila's bookcase. Then I switched to her old Management textbook, thinking it might give me more insight into her mind. Then I looked at her appointment book. "Forrest—7." That's all it said for tonight. Couldn't she have written anything a little more revealing? Given me a break? I kept looking at the single word and number.

I tapped the book against the shutter. I tapped my fingers against his name. I decided I hated Virginia Woolf.

It's two in the morning, do you know where your ex-wife is?

Okay, well, maybe they've stopped for a last drink. I kept checking the window. There was no one out, no lights on across the street. What if I needed help? Don't any of these neighbors care? No, they just sleep. Do they think I believe their lives are smooth?

She'll lurch into the apartment distraught, half drunk, clothes mussed—"Brendan, he tried to rape me!"—I'll calm her down, heat a cup of milk for her, put her to bed, sleep on the sofa, and stay here tomorrow and the next day and the next.

I went into the bedroom and lay on our bed. There were still two pillows on it, but they were piled atop each other in the middle. I separated them and arranged them side by side, and lay down on my half of the bed. The scents of Lila's hair and perfume were on my pillow—I could tell it was mine because it was flatter, Lila was fanatical about keeping her pillow fluffed. I took the pillow out from under my head and put it on my face and inhaled.

Same old Tohaku pine trees in the reproduction on the wall.

I turned the clock radio on, and looked at the ceiling while staticky jazz played. We used to put this station on as background to Sunday breakfasts, though less after Jeff was born. I said to myself: I'm going to wait up for her, no matter how long it takes. If she comes in at four she'll find me lying here with the light on, contentedly snapping my fingers to McCoy Tyner. I won't be angry at her for keeping me up so late. I have no right to be jealous. If that fucking forest returns with her, that Birnam Wood, he'll find me the soul of sweetness and enlightenment. I'll carve my initials in his trunk.

I waited for a news report on the radio: "This just in, the body of a Brooklyn woman has been found slashed and sexually assaulted . . ." I glanced at the bedside phone—it looked the way a phone looks just before a voice inside it identifies itself as a police detective with bad news.

It was three o'clock. It was three-ten. It was three-sixteen.

I sat at my old drafting table. Lila had finally removed my art stuff from it; it was now bare except for a portable accordion file containing bank statements, expense receipts, and bill stubs. That bitch, I'm going to take this home to work on, I thought. It's my table, I deserve a good drafting table. I kept it here because . . . Didn't I keep it here because I thought I would be coming back someday? So that it would have been extra work to lug the table to Windsor Terrace just to turn around and bring it back here? Hadn't I been planning—with varying degrees of consciousness, hiding the plan from myself as I went along—to spend gradually more and more time here, so that I would not only babysit for Jeff but occasionally stop by for brunch on a weekend, and perhaps linger to do some recreational drawing, a portrait of mother and son perhaps, which they would cherish, their esteem for the portrait inevitably transferring itself to the artist?

Fuck it. I am not coming back here. I know that now. Oh well. One has to accept these losses as part of the process of maturing. Give up one's fond illusions. Yes, that's all it was, eight years of illusion. Your task now is to identify reality. And your self-interest. Where does it lie?

I slapped the drafting table rhythmically with both hands. Here, here is my self-interest. Work, and nothing else.

I got up and went to the bathroom, theorizing that my shitting would, by the laws of cosmic irony, coincide with the exact moment of her opening the front door. But the cosmos was always a step more ironic: the front door remained shut.

I considered turning off the bedroom light and going to sleep. But I decided to shame her by showing that I was ever on duty. Besides, a light would help guide her once she came home. After a long evening with her contact lenses in, her eyes would be stinging from fatigue; she would be cranky, complaining that she could hardly see; she would burst right past me, claiming that she couldn't answer me until she got her lenses out. I would listen, fascinated, to the running water. Then, when she returned to the living room with her glasses on, she would tell me how Forrest had had the gall to think he could sleep with her on their first date, and how she had spent the whole long horrible night trying to fend him off.

By this time at night, the babysitter is allowed to sleep. If Lila's shocked to find her husband sleeping in her bed, it's her own fault for staying out so late.

I yawned and closed my eyes.

But in the morning, when I woke up in my clothes on top of her navy blue bedspread, she still wasn't there.

28

"Mommy, I want French toast," Jeff said, trotting into the room with the slithery sound of footed pajamas; but he stopped. I was there instead, haltingly lowering my legs to the floor. He only missed one beat; after all, it was natural for his father to be there.

"Mommy went out," I said. "She'll be home soon."

"She'll visit me a lot."

"No, I mean she'll really be home."

I got him dressed, washed, and fed, and she still did not arrive. We watched the Smurfs for half an hour, and by that time I was disgusted. I snapped at Jeff for asking me a question during a promo for a football game I wasn't even interested in. I decided to take him for a walk—spend a long time exploring the park with him, teaching him a little about nature and a lot about light, color, angle of vision, and when Lila got home she would be worried at finding us gone. But then I remembered I didn't have the goddamn key anymore, and I didn't know where she had put it.

Jeff watched cartoons all morning, and I, sitting beside him on the floor, jerked my head toward the window for the passing footsteps of neighbors, parked-car owners, meter maids, delivery boys, apartment hunters, dog walkers, basketball dribblers, pizza eaters, quarrelers, whistlers, coughers, spitters, and my ex-land-lords—a dentist and his former hygienist. They virtually hopped downstairs in their bright down coats, buoyant as moon explorers from the effects of property ownership, then spent half an hour crouched at the wrought iron gate like archeologists at a ruined temple, conferring as they wiggled the latch up and down and dabbed with reverent fingertips at the flaking metal.

It was noon when I saw her walk into view from right to left, letting the crouching dentist swing the gate open for her, and stopping to exchange pleasantries about metal restoration and its relationship to crowns and fillings. Then she crossed the front yard and peeked into the ground-level window, shielding against the glare with a cupped hand. When she saw us sitting there peacefully, she knocked on the glass, smiled, and waved.

"Hi!" she said when she entered the apartment. She was looking from one of us to the other, not just as if the sight of her family filled her with happiness, but as if in her present state the sight of anything at all would do the very same thing—as if a glimpse of the dust on the tops of our bookshelves would cause her to well up with tender affection for the whole universe. She didn't seem to know what to do with her feet. She turned from left to right and back again, with a kind of dance step, although she had never danced during the entire time I had known her, and she gave a little bounce on her black high heels. I believe that if she had been alone, or if Jeff had been her only audience, she might very possibly have stepped out of her shoes and started pirouetting around the room. Ah, shit, despite everything it was good to see her happy.

"It's awfully decent of you to drop by," I said.

She was folding her trenchcoat over the arm of the sofa and smoothing the sleeves of her purple dress. The dress looked a bit rumpled, but Lila herself was freshly bathed and shampooed. She wasn't wearing any makeup, since she hadn't taken any with her, but she had always looked even better without makeup.

"Are you mad at me for not calling?"

She slept with him, I said to myself. She took off all her clothes and let him put his penis inside her. My wife did that.

I waved off her apology. "Forget it. Why should I be mad?"

"I don't know." She blushed happily and looked away. She'd been saying "I don't know" lately.

She had the right to sleep with him. That was what made me mad: that she had the *right* to, because of me.

"So it went well?" I laughed.

"Well." She laughed and nodded, her blond hair swaying alongside her ears.

I stepped close to her and patted her on the shoulder. She grasped for my hand—but she didn't quite take it, she brushed my wrist with a pressureless, ephemeral touch, then went to put her coat in the closet.

"Mommy, we're watching cartoons," Jeff invited. When she didn't answer, but continued toward her closet, you could see the distress on his face: should he keep watching TV or follow his mother and watch her change her clothes? He stood up and left his place on the floor vacant. By the intricate laws of family romance, I immediately sat down on that warm spot even though I had had no particular desire to sit down before.

Jeff was soon standing so close to her that her pantyhose flopped against his side when she took them off. She pulled the bedroom door half-shut when she noticed me looking at her. Jeff meanwhile was not only right there, but was dallying, asking her what coat hangers were for and why he could see himself in the doorknob. He asked her so many questions that she finally had to say, "Please just let me get dressed and we can watch cartoons. Why don't you go back and watch cartoons and wait for me?"

"Don't start with me! I'm talking to you!" he replied, and Lila and I, from our separate positions, exchanged laughs of amazement. The way they throw your own expressions back at you . . .

When they came back to the living room, I stood and gave Jeff his old place on the floor. But he didn't look at the TV screen very much: he looked up at us.

"So you like Forrest," I said quietly. She and I glanced now and then at some show about superheroes, a kind of individual the nursery school disliked its students' modeling themselves after.

"Brendan, he's such a nice guy. He's forty-two."

"Decrepit."

"Come on." She smiled out of courtesy, but with a lip curl that said she didn't want me to joke about him at all. "He's very nice. He's my friend."

When a woman says, "He's my friend," in that tone of voice, you know it's all over. "Okay," I said, "tell me about him."

"I *am* telling you about him."

And I thought to myself: She probably wants to talk about him all the time, twenty-four hours a day. She's undoubtedly been thinking of him without a stop from the moment she left his hotel room this morning: thinking his name, seeing his face, and remembering over and over the same few idiotic quips and gestures that at dinner had made her think, *Yes, him* . . . Thinking about him so much it was a surprise to her that she knew how to get into a cab and give her address and get out at home. Repeating his name to herself, just his name, for no matter where she is, whether in a meeting or on the subway or walking home with a bag of groceries, all she has to do is repeat his name to herself and she's somewhere else, she's launched into the sky by a jubilant yearning. She wants to think his name all the time. I know. I've felt like that.

"He's forty-two," she repeated defiantly. "In fact you'll be self-satisfied to know he does have a little gray hair. But most of it is brown. He's very nice."

"You said that. Tell me something concrete."

She glared at me as if to say something concrete about him would be somehow to cheapen him: to reduce him to a level comprehensible by me. "He grew up in Huntsville, Alabama, but he's lived in Houston for fifteen years. He's also lived in Bahrain, and he speaks Arabic, with a Southern accent he says." She laughed at this drollery, and looked at me as if she expected me to join in. I did not. "Actually he hardly has any Southern accent, though—a nice one, not a thick one."

"Of course."

"Oh, cut it out! He's a Vice-President in Operations, he has two kids. He's divorced, his ex-wife has the kids."

So he was the guy she would date knowing he had jilted a previous woman.

"And he's in New York for Christmas." She shrugged blithely at my refusal to be thunderstruck by this miracle. "He's here because his ex-wife took the kids to their grandparents'. He's been to New York a number of times before, of course,"—my God, the guy was sophisticated!—"but never more than a couple of days at a time. I've been telling him how nice New York is at Christmas, and he wants me to sort of take him to all these New York places this week. He wants to see the usual museums and Chinatown and Lincoln Center. I thought I'd also take him to the various downtown neighborhoods and the Public, or perhaps the Hudson Guild—do you happen to know what they're playing?—and up to the Cloisters if they have some nice music, and—what else? Perhaps some club?"

"How about the Café Carlyle? We always talked about going there."

"Yes, great idea! Thank you! Oh, Brendan, he's so nice. He asked me a lot about myself, and he listened. He was impressed that I was an Art History major, he didn't think it was frivolous. He likes Abstract Expressionism and he was very interested when I criticized it for being the art form of corporations. We didn't talk about petroleum once the whole night, though obviously we both could have if we wanted to. He's interested in sailing, and collecting Shaker furniture; he hates people who try to make a virtue out of vulgarity; and there's a statue of his great-grandfather, who was a Confederate hero, in some town in Virginia, I forget, some famous stand or charge or something."

"Okay, okay," I said. I was afraid I was about to get depressed.

"Mom," Jeff said, with a suddenly remarkably mature voice, "I'm trying to watch cartoons, *please*?"

"Yes, in a minute," she said hurriedly, as if there was something she just had to say first, as a matter of life and death. "It's amazing. He has a very responsible, high-paying job, but he's not arrogant like people in New York are."

"No?"

"No. He doesn't make you feel that his job is what's important about him."

"The statue of his great-grandfather is."

"I'm saying," she said with a wonderful show of patience, "he doesn't equate his job with himself, as if there's nothing else worthwhile about him, i.e., that you better give him all sorts of fake homage or he'll take his worthlessness out on you. He's a confident, capable man who knows he can do his job well and still have plenty of room for his life. Of course he works hard too."

"Yes, yes, yes!" I moaned, spinning in place.

"You're a jerk," she said. "Yes, I think the Café Carlyle would be perfect. He'll like it, don't you think?"

Five times, between Christmas and New Year's, I stayed with Jeff at night while Lila went out with Forrest. I did it to be with Jeff. The fifth time was New Year's Eve; I sat in Lila's apartment and watched the ball drop down from the Allied Chemical Tower. Lila and I had always scoffed at New Year's revelry in the past, saying it was for people who never went out the rest of the year. Now she and Forrest sat enchanted among streamers while a tuxedoed singer-pianist with a voice like ground diamonds nearly threw himself off his bench pounding out accelerated Cole Porter.

It was the third New Year's Eve of Jeff's life, but to him the difference between one day and the next was whether it was raining or snowing or clear.

Lila slept in Forrest's hotel room again that night. A couple of times that week, she had returned from her dates at reasonable hours, but she always looked pleased with the evening, and gave no hint of the disenchantment I was scrutinizing her for. Forrest was apparently some sort of contemporary chevalier, and understood her need to see her child when she awakened. The scheming son of a bitch.

29

I usually said a few friendly words to Sharyn, the receptionist in Rawley's office, on my way in and out, and if I had a long wait we sometimes had a conversation which combined innocuous information about Jeff with sordid whispers about Rawley's sex life.

Sharyn was a tall, green-eyed high school graduate with permed blond hair, who commuted in on the Staten Island Ferry every day. Her features were a bit mismatched—eyes narrowly set, but too much space between nose and chin—but she was attractive in the way most ordinary-looking women are, and she was fun when she rolled her eyes at clients who called on the phone. I assumed she sometimes rolled her eyes at me, too, when I called up to nag Rawley about something, but that's a normal part of this business; underneath, I suspected her liking for me was genuine.

I rested my portfolio beside her desk, and felt the odd, pleasant sensation that I would like to stay and talk with her and learn all about her.

"What's that?" I asked, pointing to a stuffed animal on her desk: a small, tan, long-haired kind of mole.

"That's my woozle," she said.

"Your what?" We both laughed.

"My woozle. Don't you know a woozle when you see one? He's from *Winnie the Pooh*."

"Oh, my son hasn't gotten to that one yet." I rocked my portfolio on my metatarsals. I was pretty sure she knew I had left my wife, Sharyn and Rawley being the gossips they were. "Your woozle keeps you company, then?"

"Yes, it gets lonely here," she laughed.

It sounded not just like an airily expressed truth, but like something she had specifically formulated for me to understand and act on. I was a little rusty, so it took me several seconds to alert myself: Hey, you're supposed to ask her out to dinner. When I did, she simply and immediately said, "Sure." I felt a giddy pleasure, beyond the usual satisfaction of having an invitation accepted by a woman. I also felt the pleasure that comes when you exercise a skill for the first time in years, and find that it returns to you right away: a few short words bubble up from your fantasy life and make something happen in the real world. In other words, I got more out of the asking than out of the date.

We went to a Spanish restaurant on Greenwich Avenue—a good restaurant, but possibly it was a mistake to choose a place so close to Rawley's office. Perhaps Sharyn had eaten lunch there with Rawley, and was jaded with it in a way I wasn't. The surroundings led us to talk too much about work; and then we both, I think, felt the sinkingness of getting off on the wrong foot with a person, of helplessly hearing everything said or not said make it worse, of realizing together that you make each other tense and apprehensive, and of this realization being the only thing you have in common.

We split a bottle of white rioja. Waiting for the food, we asked each other rote questions about our backgrounds, and smiled guiltily at the fact that each other's presence did not spark us to easy, spontaneous talk.

"How's your paella?" I asked, after we had each had a couple of bites of our dishes.

"Eh. Your snapper looks better."

"Your paella looks better to me. Hey, why don't we switch?"

She shook her head almost in disbelief, as if I had asked her to gobble her food directly from the plate like an animal.

"Really," I said. "You like my dish better, I like your dish better. Why don't we just switch? Then we'll both enjoy our dinner more."

"No." She took a forkful of yellow rice and chicken as if staking her claim to it. "Are you serious? Switch plates?"

"Sure, what's wrong?"

She seemed to think about it; then she set her jaw. "No." Quickly she got down a couple more forkfuls, but that was the last she ate of it.

I thought: She won't exchange plates? That's taboo in her view of life? Communication between us is impossible.

Lila and I used to share our dishes almost automatically. If Lila had a quirk like not wanting to share food, she would at least laugh about it—at least in my current retrospective view of Lila. But Sharyn seriously believed that your portion in life was yours, for good or ill, and you didn't have the right to try to exchange it.

I thought it was incredibly petty and uptight of her to make such a big thing out of simple sharing, and no doubt she thought exactly the same of me.

We actually did see a movie after dinner—I guess we both wanted to see the plan through, rather than declaring the night a total disaster—but neither of us so much as rested our elbows on the seat arm between us. Afterward, Sharyn thanked me and said she had to go, because the ferry could keep you waiting a long time at night. I offered to accompany her on the ferry, and she declined. Which disappointed me, because I hadn't ridden the ferry in a long time and I had a sudden yen to and also I felt a duty to protect Sharyn during the trip. She declined a second time. After we said goodnight, I walked around Battery Park, which was full of junkies and drunks but had a rim of tourists at the county-fair-bright boat dock, and I got on the next boat by myself.

I saw her at Rawley's office a few days later and we were

perfectly nice to each other in our former style, making trivial, impersonal jokes, and it was remarkable how much more relaxed she appeared when our friendship was kept at that level.

Rawley asked me about our experience, for he had heard about it from her, and wanted to compare our versions. And I told him how amazed I was that millions of energetic, bright, young unmarried Americans pursue this unrewarding, frustrating, nerve-wracking, ego-twisting activity week after week after week, that it's their major recreation, the center of their social lives and of their workplace daydreams.

"You mean there's some other way to live?" he said. "I hadn't realized."

I told him I thought his sarcasm was getting a little thick.

30

Then I got a phone call.

"Lemme speak to her, Brendan."

"What? Mike?"

"Come on, lemme speak to her."

"Who? Maggie? She's not here. Did she go somewhere and tell you she'd be here? Is she—"

"Brendan, I got no time for this bullshit. Put her on the phone, I won't ask you no questions, I just want to get things settled."

"She's not here." She left him! She's coming back to me! "Tell me what—"

"All right, if that's the way you want to play," he said, and hung up.

Five minutes later I heard him running up the stairs of my building. I opened the door of my apartment and stood in the doorway, not belligerently, but attentive and curious.

She left him, she'll be calling me up soon, or ringing my doorbell in person! She doesn't want to live with him anymore, she wants to live with me!

He didn't slow down, but pushed me out of the way with a single hard shove and stalked through my kitchen into the living room.

"What the fuck do you think you're doing?" I said, hitching back my shoulders and straightening my posture.

He turned, and came slowly toward me. I closed my fists and semi-crouched into a karate stance. He snorted a laugh. I began to circle slowly to the right, at kicking distance, keeping one fist up to guard my face and the other pressed to my solar plexus. I had it all worked out. If he approached closer and seemed about to strike, I would kick him without warning, swiftly and viciously, in the kneecap of his left leg, the hobbled one. I would rapidly follow this with a kick or two to the right kneecap, so that both his legs would be out of commission; in fact the kneecaps might be broken at that point. Without pausing to let him recover, I would finish him off with—depending on his general condition, the position of his head, and the direction of his glance—either an uppercut to the chin, an elbow to the cheekbone, or a fake jab followed by a kick in the balls. He would be falling at that point; if he needed an extra impetus, I could take him down with one arm hooked around his neck and one foot tripping him. When he was on the ground, I would stand behind his head with my shoe poised to swing into his temple, and I would shout, "Freeze! Don't move, motherfucker! Now slowly, very slowly, crawl toward the door, and if you do anything else I'll fucking kill you. Because I don't care." I would allow him to crawl out of my apartment on his back, like a helpless turtle. I would slam the door after him, and worry for a few weeks that he was going to ambush me and retaliate, but he wouldn't.

That was my plan.

What actually happened was that he countered my stance with one of his own, a more conventional, technically faulty, street-style boxing stance, big fists held low and hypnotically circling, leaving his derisive, hungry smile temptingly exposed. He bobbed on his toes from side to side and leaned forward, while my back was straight, my weight on my rear leg, and I shuffled carefully and solemnly in one direction with long, flat-footed steps.

He feinted a couple of jabs; I moved back slightly. Then, when

211

I was expecting him to keep feinting and feeling me out a while longer, he came in like a bull charging at my belly, and I felt a rush of fear which had not been accounted for in my original plan. I gave him the kick to the kneecap, and it seemed to sting him, but it did not halt him in his course, and the momentum of my own kick set me off balance. Hastily I kicked at the other kneecap, but the kick was mis-aimed and grazed the side of his leg painlessly, and by that time he was practically on me, his smile replaced by an expression of businesslike ferocity. He punched me one time in the solar plexus. As I collapsed, with a blossoming of light in my visual field and a grunt from the nerve-pain in my chest, I wondered why my right fist had not been covering that spot as it was supposed to.

He trotted backwards to the airshaft corner of the living room, as if the room were a boxing ring. But when I stood up, catching my breath and recovering my normal vision, and raised my fists again (making sure to keep them tight and properly placed), he held up a hand in a pacifying gesture.

"Wait a second," he said. "Take this, it'll make it more even."

He took something metal out of his hip pocket, and slid it across the floor to me. It stopped at the lump in the linoleum, and spun a time or two before the head pointed at me. It was a six-inch adjustable wrench.

I looked at it for a good ten seconds, which in a fight is a long time. Then I kicked it back to him. He picked it up, and replaced it in his hip pocket. Then he wiped his palms on his pants legs, and walked toward the center of the room with his hands open at his sides.

"Golden Gloves junior welterweight division, 1962," he said. "United States Marine Corps, Hué, 1966."

I put my hands down and glowered at him from the corner.

Apparently paying me no further attention, he strode into the bedroom, calling, "Maggie! Maggie, get the fuck out here, will you please?"

After a short breather, I followed him. I stopped rubbing my chest when I entered the room, but he didn't look back. He was looking in the closet, under the bed, under the *mattress,* on the fire escape. He unlocked and opened my bedroom window, crept out onto the fire escape, and looked at the fire escapes above and below mine. He leaned out over the fire escape railing and looked this way and that down the street. He came inside again, closed and relocked the window, and went to search the bathroom. My bathtub was the old fashioned, footed kind, and he not only looked in the tub but under it. I half expected him to look inside the medicine cabinet. He went back to the living room, searched it very thoroughly even though it had practically no furniture and was a small room with no hidden nooks, then searched the kitchen, including behind the refrigerator, be-tween the refrigerator and the stove, inside all the cupboards, and the space between the top of the cupboards and the ceiling.

"Wha'd you do, tell her I was coming so she split?"

I spoke calmly and severely: "She is not here. She has not been here. I have not seen her since she went back to you. I thought she was happy to be back with Hilary, and you and she were getting along fine. She never called me. I didn't want to call her because I didn't want to intrude on you guys. Now what the fuck are you talking about? Did she say she was going to me? Because I had no idea she was going to do that. Were you having prob-lems, did she threaten to leave you? Is she missing? Or did she just go down to the store and you got nervous and started imagining things? And then you call me up and harass me and assault me in my own home and act paranoid, like I'm hiding her or something? You fucking asshole, what do you think you're doing, barging in on someone and beating him up in his own home? Do you think that's going to gain you anything? It gains you that I realize what a fucking dipshit you are. And undoubt-edly Maggie realizes it too, I'll tell you that. Can't express your-self in words, so you start swinging? And you think you're hot shit 'cause you know how to strip away plaster, or how to restore crown molding in the latest middle-class pseudo-gentry style for rich peasants? Let me tell you, you're a fucking jackass, even if you make a million dollars. Maggie's an artist, and that's worth more than any amount of money, and she knows you have no conception of that, and I happen to know she hates you for it. So don't be surprised if she can't take being with you anymore. Bringing her parents in to make her feel guilty, that was fucking great, wasn't it? Really a loving, considerate gesture. Yeah, it worked, and so what. Now she's gone anyway. You don't have the simple faith in her to believe what she said about her father. Well, I do, and she knows it. If you'd had that from the beginning, instead of treating her as a pet and thinking you could get the better of her because you're a man and you're strong, maybe she would have actually loved you and stayed with you. Instead of using you, which is what she did all along, and very successfully, and she laughs at you for it. And let me tell you, shithead, that if Maggie wanted to come back to me she would do it openly. We didn't hide from you the first time, and we wouldn't do it now. So this searching for her is bullshit, and you're bullshit, and I don't know whether you know you're bullshit or not, and I don't know which is worse. But you aren't worthy of her. So punch me in the face. Kick me in the balls. I'll still be worthy of her and you won't be."

He took everything I dished out. He tried to parry with his actor smile, but it fell short this time, he couldn't sustain it. The fact was, he looked pale and worn out. He was wearing a white T shirt, but had forgotten to keep his stomach muscles tightened, so that it seemed merely like the undershirt of a burly man with a paunch, rather than the skin-tight garb of a weight lifter. With an almost lost expression, he took in my living room. I had painted over the primitive scenes I had done when Maggie lived with me, and the walls were freshly white. I had some new posters in glass frames: for a William Steig retrospective in Connecticut, a Kandinsky exhibition in France.

"She left," he said. "I don't know exactly when. Sometime last night, 'cause when I woke up, she wasn't there. I looked all around for her at home. I called her parents, they don't know nothing, anything. I took Hilary to nursery school—"

"Wait, Maggie left without Hilary?"

"Uh-huh."

"Then she'll be back. She wouldn't desert Hilary."

He looked at me. I realized that I had very little idea of what went on between them, in their own house.

We were both walking back and forth now, on separate tracks so to speak. Every time one of us caught himself mirroring the other's gestures—scuffing the linoleum, rubbing a fist in a palm—he immediately shifted to a different gesture.

We were speaking quietly now, but I was not speaking as calmly as when I had excoriated him. A tremor periodically came into my voice, and I stopped and swallowed so it would go away.

"Okay, tell me," I said.

"I'm tellin' you. She's gone. Maybe she'll come back tonight, but I doubt it. I think she ran away. I went to work this morning, we're doin' one of these beautiful neo-Romanesque homes on Montgomery Place, with the bronze pilasters and everything; but I left my foreman in charge and went looking for her. I didn't find any clues. She didn't leave no note. She didn't take Hilary, thank God. I want to spare the baby that kind of experience."

"Okay," I said. "I think you're right: she ran away. The question is where, why, for how long?" I stopped, in his path, and asked him point-blank: "Why?"

He stopped just short of ramming me with his chest. I could smell a trace of wine on his breath. "Things were going good, Brendan. You can fuck yourself if you don't believe me."

"Yeah. Look." I paced, to get away from him. "What are your ideas as to where she might have gone?"

He shook his head. "I called her parents, they hadn't heard from her. I called the school. They don't take attendance there, I guess; they didn't know if she came to class or what. I think what happened, she just realized she wasn't suited for married life. Even though I treated her well, she in her own mind would rather be miserable. And even though *I* think she was a good mother, she panicked and told herself Hilary would be better off without her. Because of her problems. I think she went to some specific person that we don't know. But if that's what, I can find her."

I looked at him in stunned alarm. Was there another lover besides me? If so, had Maggie known him all along, or had she just met him recently? Was that the real reason she had left me?

I rubbed the knife scar on the back of my hand. If she had wanted to come back to me, she would have done it. On the other hand, if she were fleeing to someone else, she would have done that openly too. Unless it were someone whose existence she wanted to conceal. Or maybe she was sitting across the street behind a tire of one of the shirt-company vans, waiting for Mike to leave before she came upstairs for our reunion.

I shook my head. "Maggie could hide from you in the same room. Now she's got the whole world."

He didn't want to believe it. "She gotta be with someone, and I bet it's near here. I'm not necessarily sayin' a man. A woman friend, maybe. Like who's that one, before, who killed herself?"

"Bonnie."

"'Cause I don't think Maggie would travel alone very far. She's brave, but she was afraid of living alone."

"People change." I thought for a while. A truck went by outside. In the hall my neighbor's door opened, footsteps sounded down the stairs and a woman's voice shrieked, "You whore! I won't forget this. I won't forget what you called me."

Then I realized that Mike's bullying act was his way of asking for help in finding Maggie. And for me, to help him would be to show him up.

"Okay," I said, "did she take any money?"

"A thousand dollars out of the account. No checks, just cash. Also she left her Mastercard in the bureau drawer."

"Shit." She didn't want to be traced by her purchases, and she was planning to find another source of money by the time the thousand dollars ran out. "Okay, look. There are people we can contact. Her publisher—she's got to give him her address if she wants to keep collecting royalties. I'll call him, actually—he's my publisher too. Then there's the group residence she lived at when she was a kid. Locate all the social workers who knew her. If they changed jobs, find out where they are now. Ask them who her friends were at the place; locate the friends."

"The plant store," he said. "Who knows, she might be with Mrs. McNichol, that's the owner. Or she might of heard from Maggie, or at any rate she might know, I don't know, some friend or co-worker or something from when Maggie worked there. Then her parents, ask about childhood friends—if those fuckin' parents of hers ever noticed."

I looked at him in surprise, and we laughed. So he wasn't as thrilled with her parents as he had seemed.

"Also talk to Hilary's nursery school teachers," I said. "Ask them if Maggie was especially friendly with any of the other kids' parents. Or just ask which are Hilary's best friends, then ask their parents."

"Right, right, those educated assholes, that's what she'd want to hang out with."

I smirked. "Okay, can we think of anything else? How about the foster parents? Though apparently they weren't very—"

"It's okay, we contact them. One thing you gotta learn, Brendan—everything. You want to get something, you gotta do *everything* to get it, not just a little of this and a little of that and 'Okay, we showed that we tried, now let's sit and eat cannoli.'"

Kiss my ass, I thought, but I didn't add it to the discussion. All right, fucker, watch this. "The rock band she lived with on Avenue B. Did she ever tell you what happened to them? Did they ever make it, did she follow their careers?"

He shook his head. "I don't know."

"You can also go interview the Public Defender who represented her. And for that matter, the judge. Some of the records might be closed, because she was a juvenile, but you never know. Her parents ought to have some papers with the lawyer's and judge's names on them. Also, her college professors might not take *attendance*"—I felt entitled to a little superior irony—"but if you describe her to them, they might point out which students she sat with. They might know if she had any friends we don't know about."

"I thought of that, Brendan, I just forgot to mention it." He smiled.

217

"I'm sure you did. Okay, now, listen, how about the police? Or are you thinking at all of hiring a private detective?"

"Gotta call the police. Not that I expect them to do anything. But in case they find a body or something." We looked at each other, then averted our eyes. "As far as a detective, I can do the legwork myself—"

"I'll split it with you."

"—but I got a business to run. You got something to do too, you got your drawings to do, right? It takes more than, let's say, a week, two weeks, we delegate it to a professional."

He had to go back to Montgomery Place, he said, to make sure his mother was on time to pick up Hilary at school. Hands in pockets, he headed for the door.

Our preliminary investigation turned up one childhood friend and two former social workers of Maggie's, none of whom had heard from her in years. I also discovered the classmate who sat with her in Introduction to Poetry, a black woman who was pregnant with her first child. But she had no idea Maggie was missing; she just assumed she had stopped coming to class. She told me she had never heard Maggie express a desire to leave Mike, much less Hilary. She said, in fact, that Maggie had shown her a wallet snapshot of Hilary and had glowed about the girl's development, that much of their conversation had been about child-raising, and that Maggie had seemed almost wildly positive about its joys and overeager to play the role of prenatal mentor.

Later that week, Maggie's editor called me. He had received a handwritten letter from her, on plain white tablet paper, instructing him to deposit all her earnings from *Rhino Yogurt* and *Peanut Butter and Jealous* directly into a trust account she had established for Hilary at a bank around the corner from the publishing company. She asked Mike to give Hilary a kiss for her, and said she would explain things to Hilary as best she could when the child grew up.

"That means she's gonna come back!" Mike said. "I knew it."

Knowing Maggie, I was afraid her note meant she didn't intend to explain things until Hilary was eighteen or older, and that she had no intention of returning before then. But I didn't share this interpretation with Mike.

The letter was postmarked with the same zip code as the publisher and the bank, a midtown Manhattan post office serving virtually no residential customers. Mike rushed uptown and badgered the bank officer into showing him her application; but it listed Eleventh Street in Brooklyn as her address, Mike as her next of kin, and her editor as the non-relative to be contacted in case of emergency. All we learned from it was how cagey she was.

A week later, Mike hired a private detective who had a reputation for finding missing persons. Mike refused my offer to pay part of the expenses, but he did invite me to periodic briefings. The detective was a six-foot-six, bald, ex-St. John's basketball player with huge, freckled hands, and staring blue eyes with spiky lashes—someone who couldn't have made himself inconspicuous in a crowd if his life depended on it. He borrowed a photograph of Maggie from the family album and put it in his wallet after writing her name and some relevant statistics on the back. I asked him whether we ought to circulate photographs of her throughout Manhattan and Brooklyn, but he said it might only drive her further underground. He directed all his answers, no matter which of us asked the question, at Mike.

"Don't worry, Mr. Ferro, nobody hides from me."

I began to like the idea of a five foot, ninety-five pound woman teaching him a lesson.

31

J eff had his third birthday. In some ways the transition from two to three is the most crucial of a person's life. At the beginning, he has a vocabulary so small you could list all the words, and he can only say one of them at a time; at the end, he's discoursing and debating with adults, asking questions that test their wits and their pedagogy. At the beginning, he scarcely knows what to do when another child sits beside him and grabs one of his building blocks; at the end, he's asking to visit his friends' houses. At the beginning, he follows you into the bathroom, and gets in the way of your legs when you take out the garbage—he's afraid of not being in the same room with you; at the end, he runs all over the house waving a rubber magic sword, and only notices you when he finds it expedient to turn you into a red and green striped battle cat. At the beginning, you worry that any mistake in discipline might misshape his future personality; at the end, he already has a personality which you don't have any power to change. And sometimes he calls you "Mr. Beame" in a Barbados accent, because his nanny does, and sometimes you hug him harder for that than when he didn't know you had a name besides Daddy.

I helped Lila make his birthday party—this year it was a real party, all the kids from his nursery school class were invited. I thought I recognized a couple of the kids and their parents from the old days in the playground, but the children had been much smaller and less individualized then, and so much had happened in between. I stood at the opposite end of the apartment from Lila, serving cheese and crackers and nuts and wine and coffee to the parents, and asking them what they thought of the nursery school. Lila supervised the kids' playing: they were still too young for organized games like "Pin the Tail on the Donkey," so she had just lined up all Jeff's toys, moved the living room furniture out of the way, and let them loose. She served the cake and ice cream, I took photos.

Jeff, like all birthday children that age, seemed troubled by the festivities. He spent most of his time kicking wrapping paper instead of playing with his new toys—he kicked it more frequently after I told him not to.

My presents to Jeff were a doctor kit and a copy of *Mother Goose* with the classic Frederick Richardson illustrations. And one present which I put on his bed but didn't open: a first edition of *Rhino Yogurt*. It had just been published; the copy was in mint condition, new smelling and glossy, the pages making a cracking sound when you first separated them. On the cover was my pen-and-ink drawing of the yogurt factory, with four white-coated, bespectacled rhinoceroses overseeing the vats, and the homeless girl crouched in the corner watching. The cover said: "Story by Maggie Ferro. Illustrations by Brendan Beame."

All the guests had left. Jeff was carrying his toys into his room one by one, making a separate trip for even the smallest model car or warrior. "What's that purple monster's name?" I asked him as he carried out a rubber thumb-puppet with sharp teeth, red-rimmed eyes and wagging antennae.

"Mr. Monster," he drawled tartly, pleased that the name which had been unguessable to me had been obvious to him.

Lila and I engaged in that most universal of parental activities: suppressing laughter behind his back. If he so much as suspected us of thinking him cute, he would scold us mercilessly.

Late afternoon sunlight came in the windows and made the center section of the sofa too bright to sit on. Lila and I sat on opposite sides of it. The shutters were open; the day was clear, the limestone buildings across the street appeared in high relief, but soft-textured and rose-tinted, in the shadow. The horizontal lines of the roofs were thin and black, slightly wavering, and brightened the blue sky above them like lines done in ink by a good draftsman.

"How are you doing?" I asked.

"Pretty good," she said.

"I've been lonely," I said.

"Me too."

We had eaten cake and ice cream and felt a post-sugar letdown; we were thirsty and wished we had the strength to get up and make a cup of coffee.

We were both feeling depleted after the party and the year it represented. We felt as if we couldn't budge ourselves, as if we were sunk into the cushions of the sofa by the sheer weight of the air.

I tapped my foot against the edge of the coffee table. I turned to Lila. She was wearing a calf-length blue denim skirt with magenta blouse and socks.

"I've been running up terrible long-distance bills," she said.

"What?"

"Calling Forrest. "He calls me a lot too, of course. It's been so hard, having to get to know each other over the phone. But he's good on the phone: not inhibited, but not falsely loquacious."

"I knew he would be." I slid lower on the sofa, my knees bending higher above the coffee table.

"He did fly up last weekend."

She must have seen the surprise on my face.

"I had Dulcea babysit," she explained. "I didn't want to bother you."

"Goddamn it, Lila, I told you it's no bother."

"But aren't you busy finishing up that calendar or something?" I didn't like that "or something"; I didn't like her slighting my work.

"Yeah, but I told you I would *always* make time to babysit for him, and I meant it. Don't you believe what I say? You see, this has been the problem all along . . . Oh, shit, forget it, I don't want to argue. I don't mind if you see Forrest; I'm not about to get jealous. Why you felt you couldn't call me—"

"I called Dulcea because she needed the money." But I knew from many previous cases that while her stated reason was technically valid, it was only an excuse. "I'm sorry, Brendan," she added, which was less usual. "I should have called you. It would have been a chance for you and Jeff to be together."

"Oh, we're together a lot."

She didn't reply to that. She stared down through the butcher block table. "Brendan?" she said finally.

"Yeah?"

"I applied for a transfer to Houston headquarters."

"Houston?"

Because what can you do but buy time with a question?

"Forrest and I want to be near each other. I'm sure the transfer will go through: Forrest is calling people he knows."

"Oh."

"If you object—"

"I can't object."

"You could. In fact Forrest is very concerned about your reaction. Sympathetically concerned, I mean."

The fucking son of a bitch. And she falls for it.

"If you really objected," she went on, "you could probably get a court order against my taking Jeff out of the state. After all, I'd be taking your son away from you. And we're not even divorced yet. Forrest doesn't want to hurt you."

"That's awfully sporting of him." I got up and walked around. I raked my hair. I can really rake my hair when the situation calls for it. It ends up looking like the aftermath of electroshock. I walked in a big, frenzied loop. "No. If you want to be with this man, I want you to be with him. I deprived you of myself; I can't deprive you of him too. I'll visit Jeff no matter where you are, don't worry. You won't escape me. I'm gonna see that kid. Not as often as now, of course, but it'll be good. I'll save my money for plane fare. Better than spending it on dates. You can send him to New York sometimes, too, you know."

"I know."

She sat forward on the edge of the sofa, and rested her head on her closed knees, and folded her arms around her head.

"What's the matter?" I asked.

She shook her head in that position.

Then Jeff came in, which brought Lila upright for reasons of decorum, of exerting a good influence. I looked carefully at her eyes, but I couldn't tell whether she had been crying or whether her face was merely red from being pressed against her knees.

"Daddy, I'm having trouble opening—"

"Later," I said.

"But I'm having—"

"Later!" I shouted, and he ran off, scared, looking back at me over his shoulder.

32

T HEN there was a time which seemed to pass at the same rate as any other time, except that when it was over, I was shocked at how little of it there had been, and that there was no more of it to spare.

Lila's transfer came through quickly; the Houston office was thrilled to get her. Her new job would train her in broader aspects of oil company operations than the traffic management she had done previously; with this broadening, she would be able to rise higher than if she had stayed in New York. If she ever did return East at a later stage in her career, it would probably be to policy-making responsibilities and a Manhattan apartment, a company driver, and private schools for Jeff.

The company—that is, her boyfriend—was handling the move for her. Her boyfriend—that is, his secretary—had found a furnished house for her to rent. Lila told me they had decided to live apart for six months, after which they would determine whether they still wanted to try living together. Not that they had any doubts at present, but they were adult enough to know they might discover incompatibilities, irritations, surprises, during six months of steady dating.

"I'm impressed by your plan," I said, sounding more facetious than I really was. The truth was, I was impressed.

I increased my visits to Jeff to three, then four, then five times a week. I painted only in the evenings during this period, and I postponed work on all new assignments till after the move. I rang Lila's doorbell at nine in the morning every Saturday, and she let me keep Jeff, even let him sleep in my apartment, till Sunday brunch. We weren't sure it was beneficial to increase his contact with me before suddenly depriving him of it, but what was the choice?

I helped her sort her belongings. She was leaving most of the furniture behind: the move was an opportunity to finally get rid of the studenty old pieces—the pine dresser, the loose-legged rocking chair—that we had carried from one dwelling place to another for years. She gave me the drafting table, the end tables, and the pictures off the walls, except for two she liked that I had painted a long time ago, not as an assignment, just because I had wanted to paint them.

Her employer was paying the moving company to pack her things, but there were a few fragile items she wanted to pack herself. At least that was the reason she gave for inviting me over to help. Together we disassembled the stereo and put the components in their styrofoam boxes. There were also the camera and its attachments, and a little box of necklaces and earrings and brooches accumulated from girlhood on and the sterling silver flatware.

"That's yours," she told me. "Your parents gave it to us as a wedding present."

"Keep it."

"You know how much a set of sterling silver flatware costs nowadays? I think you should keep it, it's yours."

"Keep it!" I snarled, with the sudden, throat-constricting kind of anger you feel toward someone who is not letting you be good to them. "What do I want with silver flatware? Sell it and put it in Jeff's account."

"Okay, I'll do something with it," she said. "I won't do anything without consulting you."

226

"Consult me."

I wiped my forehead with my arm, and hurried away to Jeff's room to dig out other hidden possessions. Lila went through the apartment with a roll of packing tape around her wrist like a bracelet, and a scissors clenched between her teeth like a pirate's dagger, the sleeves of her gray sweatsuit pushed up past her elbows. I turned around when she walked in. Her hairline was damp, her face shiny. I went up close to her and peered down at the parting of her hair: the roots were turning brown.

"I'm late for my coloring, I've had so much to do."

"I've never seen your real hair color."

I stared at it, but she walked out from under my eyes.

Each day, the apartment looked barer and messier. There were scraps of old newspaper and strands of twine on the parquet floor. The rug was gone from under the coffee table: taken to be cleaned and stored. There was almost no food left in the refrigerator or cupboards. The last couple of dinners were Chinese food out of white cardboard containers, which we ate by candlelight because she had given our old lamps to the Salvation Army.

"Dad, would you please buy this Chinese food more oftener?" Jeff said. "I want to have this for dinner every day."

"Well, I don't know if I can do that."

"Why not, Dad? Please, I like this Chinese food. I'm sure it has a lot of protein."

"Yes, it does."

"Then we will eat it for dinner every day," he decreed.

"We're having it now, and it's good. So eat it. *With* your spoon and fork."

Then one day Lila called me up and said, "Today's the day." Which I had known already, of course. But not really known.

It was the finest height-of-May morning you could ever hope

to see. The sky was that deep shade of blue you sometimes get in New York on clear days because of the way sulfur dioxide refracts the sunlight. It was the kind of day when your natural urge is to go deep in the woods, and rest on the grass as long as you like, and eat sandwiches that you brought from home, and never see a building or a vehicle. Lila was fretting about the timing of the move, and about whether I would oversee the movers in case they were late and she had to go to the airport.

"I want to check in early so we can get seats together"—so she and Jeff could get seats together, that is—"and you can never tell about the traffic to Kennedy. If the movers aren't finished by noon, you'll have to stay."

"They'll be finished by noon. You don't have much stuff to load. I'm sure they want to get started as soon as possible also."

"I just hope they finish before I have to leave for the airport."

I wondered if that meant she didn't trust me to oversee them, or if, on the other hand, it meant she wanted me to be able to go to the airport with her.

"I'll be there," I said.

The moment I hung up, I had a mild hallucination, a kind of experience I had been having more frequently during this period of stress, and most commonly when talking on the phone. I heard Lila call my name from inside the receiver after I had already put it on the hook. She called out to tell me one last thing she had forgotten: a final note to the conversation which she simply had to add despite the opposition of physical laws. You're crazy, I told myself, and picked up the phone. It was just as I expected: a dial tone.

A huge, dark green moving van with yellow lettering was parked in front of Lila's house; the whole remainder of that side of the street was vacant because of alternate-side parking rules. The truck was much too big for Lila's possessions, but the big moving companies take several families' things in one haul. One family might be going to Atlanta, another to New Orleans, then the truck would head west along the Gulf Coast to Houston.

Through the open side doors of the van, I saw the other families' belongings, neatly piled from floor to ceiling and strapped with olive green safety belts. Why were they moving? Would their kids feel lonely and bewildered when they disembarked in some strange neighborhood and were watched in the unloading process by kids they didn't know? Was the family that owned these boxes—so many of them, piled and strapped at the front of the van!—were they happy, and heading for a bigger, finer dwelling place with bouncy anticipation, while the family that owned those others, adjacent to them on the right hand side, was unhappy, being transferred to a town they didn't want to live in, from a New York they hated to leave? Who did they work for, what did they hope for, what did they face?

I went into the apartment, stepping out of the way of two black men who were carrying the sofa up the loading ramp. From the living room window, which Lila had left dusty, I watched them up-end the sofa onto a dolly and push it, showing me its beige gauze underside. All the doors and gates of the apartment were open; anyone could have wandered in but there was nothing to steal. With its rugs and furniture removed, the place had become an echo chamber.

"Hello," I called, and it sounded like a tunnel.

On the floor, which we had thought so well polished, there were dulled and scratched patches where furniture legs had stood. On the walls, there were holes from picture-hanging nails, and all the forgotten damage left by habits and mistakes: the gray place on the doorjamb at the height Jeff could reach to grip; the permanently food-stained area next to where his high chair had been; the corner where I had knocked a chip of plaster off with a surprise frisbee throw to Lila on the very first day we moved in, because I was happy to have so much space after our Manhattan studio. In the corner of the living room, packed to bulging, were two dark blue canvas on-board bags with stickers saying, "DO NOT MOVE."

I heard Jeff's footsteps, not running, but hurrying as kids' feet always do, trying to keep up with adult commands and with the urgings of their own minds, which are so much more capable than their bodies. The empty apartment amplified the scrape of a zipper being dragged along the floor, and the slither of a sleeve licking the wood. He came into the living room with his baseball jacket trailing: it had baseball-shaped patches all over it, one for each major-league team. The first insignia that caught my eye was that of the Houston Astros. I had never paid it the slightest attention before.

"Pick your jacket up!" Lila called after him from the foyer.

"I'm pretecting it from the movers!"

"You don't have to drag it along the floor to protect it. That's making it dirty."

"I'm *pretecting* it," he said, exasperated that she didn't understand the word as well as he. He looked at me, and put on, as he usually did nowadays when he saw me, an unsurprised, matter-of-fact expression. "Mom, Dad's here."

"Hi, would you please tell this boy not to get his jacket dirty?"

She came through the foyer doorway. She, unlike Jeff, showed surprise—as if, when speaking to me just now, she hadn't really believed I was there, but had merely been answering a daydream out loud. Then she tried to conceal her expression and continue forward as if unconcerned and having nothing on her mind, but she was never really very good at that.

She was a little breathless from many crossings of the apartment, and from the idea of moving. She was wearing baggy gray pants, a dusky purple blouse, and pale pink lipstick. Her hair had been colored at last.

"It's almost ready," she said. "Just the linen closet and the paperwork."

"See, they were fast after all."

The truck driver came out of the shadows of the foyer, making pencil marks on some forms clipped to a clipboard. The two laborers walked in again, and walked out carrying two brooms, the carpet sweeper, the dustpan, and the orange vacuum cleaner, its hose wrapped around one guy's waist and its head knocking into the other guy's legs. Lila and the driver, a short, wiry man with a black mustache and a tattoo, checked over the yellow and pink and white copies of the inventory sheet in the light from the living room window, a light which, I noted for professional reasons, seemed stronger for falling into a bare room.

Jeff and I sat against the wall, *pretecting* the canvas traveling bags. I stretched my legs out straight, he stretched his legs out straight. I drew my legs in, he drew his legs in. I laughed at his good comic timing. He laughed too, even harder.

"Hey, listen to this," I told him. I called out, "Hello!" and it echoed through the apartment even better than the tunnel I often took him through in Prospect Park.

"Hello!" he shouted out, and laughed at his echo, and heard his echo laughing too and laughed at that.

"Hello!" I called out louder, in my deepest register.

"Hello!" he called out, in a child's imitation of a man's deepest register.

I got up, and pulled him up too. "Let's do an experiment. We'll see how it sounds in different rooms."

We ran, our shoes echoing, through the foyer. "Hello!" I called.

"Hello!" Jeff said, running and laughing.

His room. "Hello!" I said, turning this way and that.

"Hello!" he said, turning this way and that also. Good echo there.

The kitchen. "Hello!" Not such a great echo, in a narrow, ceramic-tiled room with bulging cupboards.

"Hello! . . . Can I have something to eat?" Jeff said.

"I don't think there's any food left." I opened the refrigerator; it was empty. "Hello!" I shouted into it, and hooked my fingers over the cold metal shelves. "No, you'll have to wait till the airport."

"Oh, but Dad—"

"You'll have to wait till the airport. Look, it's empty. Do you see any food? What am I supposed to do, magically make food appear?"

231

He looked up at me silently. After a while he said, "No."

"Just say hello into it."

"Hello!" he shouted into the refrigerator, and laughed, and we stuck our faces in, and grinned as we imitated each other touching our noses and cheeks to the metal shelves.

33

Traffic was light on the Belt Parkway to Kennedy. The car service got us there well ahead of time, and we had an hour in which to do nothing but wait.

Jeff was amazed by the place. We must have shown him every store and convenience in the terminal: the gift shop, the snack bar, the liquor bar (which he insisted on seeing, because we told him it was just for grown-ups), the shoeshine stand, the male and female symbols and wheelchair symbols on the bathroom doors, the TV sets attached to the chairs in the waiting area, the bank of storage lockers in the side concourse.

I held his hand, and when we came to passageways that weren't too crowded, I let him go so he could walk ahead by himself like a big shot. It felt strangely typical to be a father introducing his son to the noisy, busy, important airport with its masculine connotations of flight and of big machines.

Lila and I walked side by side, separated by a few feet of corridor. We didn't talk much. Whenever I glanced at her, hoping to share a smile at how cute whatever Jeff was doing was, I got discouraged if she didn't happen to smile at me at the same time. And the times she did happen to glance at me and share a smile, it cancelled itself out by calling forth confused, antagonistic thoughts. She's thinking about Forrest, I thought; she doesn't want me intruding into her mental space.

We walked down a bright corridor with a white, perforated ceiling. "Gee, I haven't been in an airport in a long time," I said.

"Mm," in what I'm pretty sure was a kind, generous tone: she appreciated the fact that I was trying to make conversation. But she looked very abstracted, and flicked her fingernails as she walked, and scuffed her toe once on the blue carpet so that she stumbled forward, and my hand shot out to grab her. She steadied herself without assistance and I withdrew my hand before touching her.

We got in line at the boarding gate, to check in.

It was a quiet, orderly line populated mostly by businessmen, some of them wearing cream colored cowboy hats. A little way behind us, a girl Jeff's age was waiting with her parents, and Jeff, ever the ladies' man, stepped out beside the line and blatantly stared at her. She was a cute girl with light blond curls cut short. In her arms she held a black Cabbage Patch doll. Perhaps she preferred a black doll, perhaps the store in her neighborhood had run out of white ones. The girl was wearing a white dress and a yellow cardigan, and so was the doll, which she clutched tighter when she saw Jeff coveting it.

Apparently his method of initiating play was to stand immobile and stare at the intended playmate for a long time. Then, with an almost inaudible gurgle in his throat, like some sort of ocelot or cheetah, he darted forward—and stroked the doll's cardigan. The girl twisted away and began to cry.

"*Ask* her first, Jeff," I said. "Then maybe she'll let you touch it."

"Leslie, let the little boy see your doll. Don't be selfish," her mother said.

You could practically see, in Jeff's expression, the process by which a human being learns to play along in order to get what he wants. "May I see your doll, please?" he said.

"Yes, you may." Leslie held the doll out to him in two hands. Her parents and his parents all smiled at each other with incandescent pride.

234

It took no time for Jeff and Leslie to get deep into play. "She's wet," Leslie said, "she needs a diaper."

"No, she's not wet," Jeff said.

"If you make her get a rash . . ." Leslie warned.

Jeff was stunned by the accusation. "There is no rash. What rash?"

Leslie's mother, a thirty-fivish short-haired blond in a checked shirtdress and gold hoop earrings, gave us a tanned, creased smile. "How old is your boy?"

"Three. How old is she?"

"Three last November."

"Oh, he was just three in March."

So that they must have thought: Ah, Leslie's older, you can tell she's more mature; and we thought, Ah, Jeff's younger but he seems just as mature as she, even though girls are supposedly more advanced. We nodded and smiled, rival mystics who had bumped into each other in an airport and were sharing and withholding their gnostic secrets in the midst of the uninitiated crowd.

"Going to Houston on business?" the father asked me, though I was wearing my denim jacket.

"No." And Lila and I, with a quick glance, decided what we *weren't* going to share with these people. We focussed our attention on Jeff, as if we were too intent on caring for him to be very good conversationalists.

Leslie's father had a single ticket showing in triplicate in the inner pocket of his gray suit. "It's just me getting on board this thing. The family came to see me off. I can't get rid of them."

"Well, you're going to be away for a whole week, dear," his wife said, and they smiled like two people who want to kill each other.

Lila and I took a couple of not-really-imperceptible steps toward the left side of the line, and stretched forward for a better view of what the ticket agents were doing at the counter.

"Yes she does, she pooped!" Leslie said.

"I don't smell it," Jeff said. "Oh, well, I'll take a look. There, no poop."

"There *is* poop!" Leslie said.

"Ah, the trials of the imagination," Leslie's mother said, and flashed me a look that stated clearly that she wanted me to know she was an intelligent, well-educated person with a complex sensibility. A distress signal, in other words; it's a goddamn distress signal that they send you, but this ship was steaming past her.

"Come on," Lila said, as our turn came at the head of the line.

She got the boarding passes. On the white-bordered blue departure board behind the counter, the time of the Houston flight was listed, with a notation: "ON TIME."

We sort of drifted to the far end of the counter, and leaned against it. We looked at Jeff, but it was one of those times when you're sure your child isn't going to get into any trouble for a few minutes, and he's too absorbed in play to notice you, and you grant yourself the leisure of gazing through him, using him as a kind of blandly pleasant visual stimulus, equivalent to a TV show, to stimulate alpha waves, to make you feel restful.

"I hope you have a good life in Texas," I said.

"Thank you."

"I hope it works out with Forrest. If it turns out that he's better than me, then I guess you gained by my leaving you."

She laughed cynically.

"I wasn't trying to justify myself," I said. "Or to get you to forgive me. Just showing you a way to think about it to feel better."

"Thanks for trying."

She turned her back to me, and watched her own fingers travel the edge of the counter. The passenger behind us, a plump, balding man in a blue suit, flung his brown attaché case onto the counter, and I gave a start and moved away from him, toward Lila.

Suddenly she said: "You'll come to see him, won't you?"

"Of course."

"You really will? It's important to him; please say you will."

"I will! I've said this—"

236

"It's expensive."

"I *will*! It's the same old thing. You won't trust me to. How many times do you have to be reassured?"

"I'm sorry. I'm not doubting your word. If it's too expensive I'll help you with the fare."

"I'll manage somehow," I said sarcastically, thinking, Don't you know by now that your doubts can be self-fulfilling? If you doubt I'll visit, it could make me decide not to visit, out of spite. Just to prove I am what you think I am. Hurting you by condemning you to your own false perceptions.

If we had still been a couple, we could have had a nice argument on the subject. Including making up after the argument, with hands and lips and loins.

"Hey, Jeff, want to take a walk around the airport with me?" I asked. "Want to go see some airplanes?" Jeff was standing alone now, looking abandoned: Leslie, reminded by the needs of her Cabbage Patch doll, had announced that she had to go to the bathroom too, and her mother had led her down the hall, leaving the father to scratch his nose and read the fine print on the red side of his ticket. "Come on, we can watch the airplanes taking off."

"Where are you going?" Lila asked in alarm.

"Just for a little walk. He'll be sitting in the plane for hours; he needs a chance to use his legs."

Jeff looked at me with disquiet. I could almost see the phrase, *Sitting in the plane for hours*, sinking into his mind and forming a picture that must scarcely resemble a real plane ride. *For hours:* did he have any accurate idea of how long an hour was? Two Mr. Rogers episodes, or one Sesame Street; but did he notice the time when he watched those shows? *Sitting in the plane:* did he imagine it as some dark box, more like a pet carrier than a passenger fuselage, where he would be shaken cruelly and wouldn't be able to see or talk to his mother or stand up or get anything to eat? To comfort himself, was he telling himself: *Probably the people on the plane will be nice to children. Probably they'll have toys?*

237

"But they're going to board in fifteen minutes," Lila said.

I gave her a look.

"What?" she said, but her embarrassment was visible.

"You think I'm going to kidnap him? You think I'll take him home and leave you at the airport?"

"No, I don't think that at all. I don't think any such thing. Why do you make things up like that? And then you accuse me of them and act as if I've accused you?"

I stared at her. "Why, why, why. Come on, Jeff, let's go." I held out my hand. "I'll bring him back well before takeoff."

We didn't say much. We stopped at a stainless steel water fountain and I picked Jeff up so he could drink. He turned the knob all by himself and lowered his mouth very close to the faucet—which makes me nervous because of germs—and I wiped the water off his chin with my clean handkerchief. On our walk we saw a very old, tiny woman with white hair being pushed by a young black man in a porter's cap, and I explained what wheelchairs were for. We saw a couple of stewardesses pass by— tall, calfless, long-striding in unison, in navy blue uniforms and pinned-up hair—and Jeff stopped like any male primitive and turned to stare at them clicking by. We stood against the wall to watch people walk through the metal-detector doorway, and their purses and bags slide through the rubber flaps above the conveyor belt and emerge on the other side of the machine. Jeff himself loved to walk through the metal detector, but I only let him do it twice. We stopped to gawk at a ticket counter where a crowd of people with big suitcases was pressing forward and shouting imprecations at the agents. We saw a young woman with a light brown braid and a fifty-pound backpack lean against the wall, shrug the pack to the floor, and close her eyes. We saw a man at a phone booth cover his eyes and not say anything for a long time, and put more coins in the slot and still not say anything. We saw a pair of pilots walk by, so straight-backed and fine in their dark blue uniforms with white-chevroned sleeves, and their caps with silver wing insignia, that you hoped they wouldn't see the man covering his eyes as he listened to the phone, or the woman drooping against the wall and mouth-breathing, for fear that they would be weakened by these people's weakness, or else merely scorn it.

"Those are the pilots," I said. "They're the men who fly the planes."

"Oh." He didn't sound as awed as I'd hoped; yet it may have been more the product of incomprehension than of apathy. I squatted down next to him, to be at his height, and from there a place like an airport really did look threatening and overpowering and mysterious.

We went to watch the airplanes. We found a big window at the end of the hall, looking out on a strip of runway between the hangars of two different airlines; a handful of other watchers were there, mostly solitary men, and they let the small boy and his father get in front, right up against the glass, for the best view. Squatting beside him again, I stretched my arm out to point out the sights. We saw planes taking off, planes landing, planes taxiing, men with flashlights and headphones and padded blue jackets waving them to their gates. Planes being refueled, planes being catered, planes being loaded with baggage, wings being crawled over, underbellies being inspected, patted, rubbed, loved, by miniscule-looking men. The planes on the right-hand side were red and white, the ones on the left-hand side were blue and white. We saw them rise nose-up into the air. We heard the jet noise. We imagined we were on them; we imagined we could stretch our hands out a little further and grab them out of the air and bring them back.

I made a mental note to scour the library and bookstore to find out what children's books had already been published on the subject of airports, particularly fathers and children at airports.

"Why are there so many planes?" Jeff asked.

"Well, they're going to all different places. Some might be going to Chicago, some might be going to Washington or Boston or Toronto, or Paris . . ."

"And some are going to Houston," he said, with the solemn diction of a child who has learned a difficult fact.

"Yes. I mean, one of them will be going to Houston."

"Because people have to move to Houston."

"Yeah."

I wondered what it looked like in his mind: people, as a species, hordes, planesful of them, all getting up on the same May morning and moving to a never-before-seen city?

I stood up.

"Pick me up," Jeff said, and I did.

"You will root for the Astros," I said. "And the Oilers and the Rockets. You will eat, I predict, my son, a certain amount of chili and of Gulf shrimp."

"Oh," he said, with an uncertain little laugh, as if trying to please me.

"It'll be hotter in Texas, did you know that?"

"No."

"Yes. But you'll have air conditioning all over the place."

"Oh."

"You'll probably see more horses in Texas than in New York, although you did see some mounted police here once, and some horses on the bridle path. Remember?"

"No."

I shook my head in despair. "Oh well. You know, you might learn to ride a horse someday, down there. Maybe Forrest will teach you and Mommy. Do you know Forrest, Mommy's friend?"

He put his arms around my neck and put his face against my cheek.

"Forrest's nice," I said.

"Oh."

"And I'll visit you in Texas. I've always wanted to go to Texas, and I'm so glad I have the chance now."

"Oh."

I put my hand lightly on the crown of his head. I cleared my throat. Another airplane was taking off. I watched it, and in emulation of me, Jeff perked his head up and watched it.

240

Then I began telling him things I was sure he wouldn't understand except in the dimmest way.

"You'll probably be a Texan. You'll talk with a Texas accent.
You'll grow up in some way I won't have control over. But I'm not
worried about your ultimate development."

"Oh."

"Listen. You will pass any test life gives you. You will, okay?
Your father is telling this to you now. If you ever have some hard
thing to do and you don't know if you can do it or not? First of all,
I want you to know that everyone feels like that, even the people
who can do it. Everyone wonders if they can make it or not. So
when you ever find yourself in that situation, I want you to
remember this. Your father, your father knows you can make it."

"Oh."

"Look," I said, "I don't know why I did it. Sometimes I think,
what if I planned the whole thing as a kind of trick to get your
mother jealous so she'd appreciate me more, but it got out of
hand? But that can't be it. That's not the real reason."

"Oh," he said. And the fact that he didn't understand was
making it easier and easier to confess to him.

"I think there were stresses—I *know* there were stresses and
strains and discontents on both sides, and even when we fought
we didn't really resolve anything. Your mother and I would fight
about something and then act as if that cleared the air, as if
fighting purged the system. But it didn't purge the stresses; they
built up, and finally I had to point them out in a really drastic way.
We were getting tired of each other, and I cut the knot in a way
that took all the blame on myself."

"Oh."

A plane which had been parked in front of us on the runway
resumed taxiing. For professional purposes, I tried to memorize
how the sun-gleam on its wings changed as it moved.

"I mean, everybody has discontents. Maybe ours were about
average. Who knows? An outsider may have said that we had a
good marriage. But if people have a good marriage, why do they
feel this compulsion to test it, and doubt it, and risk it, push it to

241

the breaking point? Why would they do that if there weren't a lot of hostility which they weren't getting out in other ways?"

"I don't know," he said. Just like his old man.

I set him on the floor so I could think. Jeff was obviously a little puzzled at having this done to him, but he didn't say anything. I stared out the big window but didn't focus my eyes. Jeff wiggled his blue jeans by the pockets to make them settle more comfortably.

"Here's what it is. I felt . . . I felt that I was being left behind. There were three of us and I felt like I was the one that mattered least. She was going so far ahead with her job, and she was a terrific mother at the same time. And even you, when you were born . . ."

I cleared my throat. I looked down at him. Good, he was looking at the planes.

". . . I mean, it was the greatest thing in my life, but also, I have to tell you this, let's face it, the younger generation comes along and that's it. One thinks, 'My replacement is here, time for me to step aside.' I'd had my turn at the front of life and now it was your turn. And I was so idealistic, you see—I wanted to give you everything that was in me—but sometimes I felt like I was emptying myself out in the process. As if everything I did or learned from then on could only have value to the extent I could transmit it to you. Not from how it affected my own life. When you were one month old—you don't remember—"

"I remember," he said, just like his mother, and I laughed.

"Okay. Well, anyway, when you were one month old you used to look at my paintings on the wall, incessantly. I was so proud! I thought, 'This kid is going to absorb design and color in the deepest centers of his brain, he can become a better artist than me, like Picasso with *his* father.' But I wonder, was Picasso's father always so pleased with his role? 'Okay, kid, here are the brushes, here are the paints, what do I do now, stare at the wall?' It was such a great accomplishment for you just to *look* at my paintings, it seemed like no accomplishment at all that I had painted them. You were *it*, Jeff, you were so wonderful and alert and taking everything in and everything was new for you. And I wanted to be that way too. When you fall in love—you'll find out—that's what you feel like. You are, let me tell you, when you fall in love, man, you're at the front of life."

"Oh."

I put my arm around his shoulder, and it made me feel better. Perhaps because I had been rambling, I tried to concentrate solely on Jeff at that moment: I tried not to see anything beyond the little circumference of blue carpeted floor in which we stood. And at that moment it seemed to me that nurturing a child was always, everywhere, the right thing for me to be doing. For Brendan Beame, this particular, atypical but normal, man. In the midst of makeshift and disastrous adulthood, I could be instantly healed by attending to someone from whom I could not expect gratitude. I was a parent, someone who had crossed the great border in life: between being one of the receivers and one of the givers.

And I had the sudden, despairing urge to tell Jeff everything I knew about life, to pour my whole brain into his, not so I would be left empty, but so I would have made a copy of what I knew. I wished that in one lecture I could arm him for childhood and adolescence, for junior high school cliques and high school sex, for college drugs and post-college panic. I wished I could give him a store of knowledge that would put him ahead of all other kids and make up for what was being taken away from him. I wished I could fill his head with wise aphorisms and directives that would lie buried in his unconscious until, when needed in a crisis, they would pop up with unfailing effectiveness from he knew not where. A copy of my notes, in case the original got lost.

"You know, there are a lot of things I wish someone had told me when I was a child."

"Oh—but Dad?"

"Yes?" I crouched closer to his ear, hands just above my knees like a third base coach.

"Dad, why do engines make noise?"

I laughed. I looked up. There were still people around us: a flat-faced man in a hip-length, iridescent raincoat; a ticket agent with short, neutral-colored hair, doing absolutely nothing at the unused counter near the window; a mechanic outside turning his back to the wind and clutching his headset as his pants legs flapped like flags. We weren't in another world. People had probably overheard me. The hell with them, maybe they learned something.

"Engines make noise because they have moving parts. Anything that moves, makes sound. Because the movement makes waves in the air, and the waves travel to our ears." I moved my hand up and down near his ear so he could feel the vibration and laugh. "And we hear them."

"Oh." He looked completely confused.

"Don't worry, you don't have to understand that yet."

"I will understand it tomorrow."

"That's the way. Come on, time to go back to Mommy."

"I was getting frantic!"

And I admit she had reason to. The boarding had begun a few minutes earlier than I had anticipated. Half of the passengers were already on the plane; the rest were strung in line in front of the window, filing through the door to the loading ramp. Two stewardesses stood at the door, collecting boarding passes. Only a few small clusters of people remained in the seats of the waiting area, saying good-bye to companions. Lila was patting herself worriedly with folded arms.

"What's the matter?" I said. "I have a wristwatch, I know what time it is."

She extended her hand downward for Jeff to hold.

"Are we going?" he said. Then he turned to his friend Leslie, whose father had already boarded the plane. "Did you change the baby's diaper?" He went up to the little girl and stroked the black doll's hair, and murmured something to it which I couldn't hear. "Can I hold her?" he asked Leslie.

Lila glanced at the door of the loading ramp.

"Let him play for a minute," I said. Just one more minute!

244

Lila and I looked at each other. The sounds of the airport streamed over us. A loudspeaker summoned a Mr. Wexler: would Mr. Wexler please pick up a red paging phone? A check-in agent walked up and whispered something in a stewardess's ear; the stewardess laughed and pushed him away. Four business-men, each trying to walk faster than the others, blew through the corridor like thunderclouds that don't rain, saying, "The seminar last Tuesday . . . Did you remember to bring that thing . . . ? Bob, when you have a minute I'd like your opinion on something . . ."

The stewardesses, one blond and one brunette, smiled at some of the passengers who surrendered their boarding passes, but gave others vacant looks, as if suddenly preoccupied.

Even through the thick windows the whine of jet engines was loud. The sky was blue, the planes were shiny.

"Well, this is a surprise," I said to Lila. "I'm surprised we ended up here."

"Yes."

She had beautiful, straight, blond hair, a thin, oval face with brown eyes and dimpled cheeks. She looked great in business suits or in sweatclothes or in baggy gray or plum-colored pants.

"What do you think you'll do if it doesn't work out with Forrest? I mean, I think it will, but—"

"I'm not making plans that far ahead," she said. "That's an-other thing I've learned. Plans are for work, not for life."

"Well, it's connected to your work, because you would then have to choose whether to stay in Houston or come back to New York."

"I can't discuss that now, Brendan. You know, those aren't the only two places in the world, either. A career like mine has a fair amount of mobility. I used to expect that I would be an art history teacher, an academic nomad, seeing the world by going from one college town to another. But now, if I want to, I can check out L. A., London, Paris, Bahrain."

"Tulsa," I added, and she laughed.

"Come on, honey, it's time to go," she told Jeff. The last few people in line were shuffling through the loading door. Jeff was holding the black Cabbage Patch doll tightly to his chest, tucking his chin into its scalp. "Time to give Leslie back her doll. You made a nice friend, now it's time to say good-bye. The plane won't wait for us, you know. We have to get on or it'll leave without us."

Jeff looked around in a panic. He looked at me. "No!"

"Jeff, please, we have to go," Lila said.

"No, we have to stay!"

Lila—gently enough, though with a parent's forcefulness—took the doll by the arm and began to tug it away from Jeff, and he screamed, a sobbing scream. He looked at me for help. I ran up to him, knelt down beside him. He was crying louder than I had ever heard him cry. The stewardesses were staring, and exchanging inaudible comments. Pedestrians passing by in the concourse slowed their steps to see what was going on.

I hugged Jeff close, with the doll between us.

"The baby needs me," he said.

"I know, sweetheart."

"The baby loves me. It wants me to stay."

"Yes, my big boy, I know. But you know, it's really Leslie's doll."

He leaned his head on my shoulder, and sobbed anew, but with a sweeter, more easy-breathing melody this time, not with the harsh bawling of his first protest. The shoulder of my denim jacket got a little wet. I rubbed his back so he would stop trembling.

I closed my eyes and put my face against his baseball jacket.

"You have to give me my doll back," Leslie said, in a surprisingly patient voice.

"I'm just starting to know you," I whispered in his ear.

I stood up. The blond-haired stewardess was walking toward us, to remind us that all passengers had to board the plane, and possibly to offer help. I didn't want her to come near; I didn't want to hear her voice.

"Okay, Jeff, it's really time to go," I said, in a tone that he knew, my tender-but-serious tone.

He gave it one more try. "I will take the baby with me!" But you could tell he already knew the answer.

I shook my head. Make-believe was over.

"Here is your doll," he said to Leslie.

"Thank you," she said.

"You're welcome."

Leslie's mother came and put her arm around her, and looked at me. I looked away. "Come on, dear," I heard her say. I turned and saw the woman in the shirtdress and the girl in the yellow cardigan and the black doll in the yellow cardigan walk out of the waiting area and down the corridor.

Lila led Jeff to the boarding door and showed the brunette stewardess their boarding passes. The stewardess, smiling down at Jeff, took his free hand to help him over the threshold. Escorted onto the ramp by two women, he forgot to look back at me.

"Lila!" I called out.

She stopped instantly, on the threshold. She turned around and waited for me to run up to her. The stewardess gave a little frown which erased itself in the very act of showing itself, as if appearance and disappearance were part of a single unified gesture, and she walked with Jeff deeper into the loading ramp.

"When you talk to him about me," I said to Lila, "would you try not to say bad things about me? For his sake, not for mine. I mean, you can think all the bad things about me you want, but a boy should—"

"It's okay, I—" and she had to stop speaking. In fright, she glanced at the blond stewardess, who was openly eavesdropping. Lila turned and ran up the ramp to Jeff, and took his hand again, and at the end of the ramp they turned out of sight into the plane.

34

W̲e haven't found a trace of Maggie so far. The basketball player gives Mike these sales talks—"Don't
worry, Mr. Ferro, there was a girl last year that the
parents had given up hope, and I found her alive and well
working for a pimp on Forty-Second Street"—but the fact is he
doesn't have a clue. Because Maggie doesn't want to leave him
any. If she wanted to leave clues, she would do so. I have a lot of
faith in her.

I worry, of course, that she will die or drift into some ruinous,
sleazy environment and become a person I wouldn't recognize,
too disconnected to feel her own sadness. But actually I think
that's the less likely outcome. For one thing, if she were dead we
would find her—her body, that is—her skills at hiding having
died with her. And she already has a decade of experience at
surviving ruinous environments intact: singularly changed, but
blossoming.

I think we will hear from her, but not soon. We'll hear from her
after she has become the next thing she must become. Because
she may be unequalled at hiding, but she is not the kind of person
who leaves this earth unknown. I expect to read her name, a few
years from now, in a book or newspaper, or see her picture in a

magazine. Maybe she'll be writing for adults—her autobiography, perhaps, or some quirky, fictionalized autobiography where reality and imagination entwine with each other and beget something one-of-a-kind, mercurial, splendid. Or maybe she'll surface as the manager, girlfriend, and brainpower behind some rock group that takes the world by storm. More likely, I think, she'll become an activist, agitating for the rights of abused children or single parents, or for peace. Or a prosecuting attorney, the kind that gets her name in the papers for putting rapists away with a vengeance; or a lawyer in private practice, earning renown in the most difficult and controversial child custody suits. It'll take her a little extra time to get her diploma, because she can't transfer her Brooklyn College credits without leading us straight to her; but it would be just like Maggie to repeat a year of college to keep her pursuers away.

I imagine many futures for Maggie. And I think about my role in her life, and realize how small it was. What was it, a little more than a year? To me it was a year of unprecedented turmoil and dislocation; but those experiences were probably fairly easy for her, compared to what she went through as a teenager and what she may go through from now on.

I'd most like to hear from her through a simple phone call. I keep imagining what I'll say to her. What's the matter, Maggie, you have to take revenge on all men, and that's why you discarded Mike twice, and me? What's the matter, you have to ensure that you'll always be miserable in life, so you throw your loved ones away? You have to run away from everything good you ever find? Or were you using me from the start because you found out somehow I was an illustrator, and you needed one for your children's book?

No—her explanation would be much different from those. My interpretations of her are just clever constructions. They're not Maggie as she senses herself. She didn't experience this through my interpretations. She acted spontaneously—expecting and desiring and hoping, and having expectations smashed, and shaping new expectations out of them, but not merely scheming.

I've finished doing the pictures for *Peanut Butter and Jealous,* and have started a new children's book after that one: writing as well as illustrating it. It's called *Dozens of Cousins.* It's about a big family with lots of kids, and they love each other so much that when they grow up, they don't want to move out; they all keep living in one house together. When the kids in turn have kids, all those first cousins still want to live together, so they build a neighborhood of houses in one place and all live there. When *they* have kids, in turn, all those second cousins still love each other and want to live together, so they have to start a new town just for all those relatives. Then *their* kids, the third cousins, still love each other and want to live together, and by this time there are so many of them that they have to found a whole new country. Pretty soon there are so many cousins, all loving each other and wanting to live together, that they fill a whole new world.

It's a utopia with a sneaky, subversive countertheme: if all people are kin, and we ought to love each other, then all human love is incest.

I'm going to start setting all my children's books in Texas, so that I can deduct the cost of travel as a business expense.

I work a lot at night now, a time when I rarely used to work. I've collected all the airline schedules on my drafting table, and during breaks I read the timetables and draw multicolored squares around the flights to Houston, and elaborate these simple outlines with curlicues, exclamation points, animal heads, boats, planes, little Biblically dressed people—creating the *Book of Kells* of airline timetables. I also have a travel guide to Houston, which I've been reading in order to study up on parks and attractions to take Jeff to. Reading these materials puts me in an agitated but clear frame of mind, which is very beneficial when I get back to my inks or paints or pencils for an energetic, concentrated stint.

I have no distractions or restrictions now. I needn't fear that my light will wake anyone, I can cook a snack at two in the morning and clatter the pots and pans, I can even leave the apartment and go up to the roof to look at the sky. Even in the daytime, my work is never interrupted by someone asking me to put his shoes on for him after he has just asked me to take off his shoes. There is no playground sand on my bedsheets. At mealtimes, there are no milk spills or cookie crumbs or bite-sized squares of ketchup-smeared bologna to wipe up.

Often, in the middle of the night, when I'm working or just sleepless, I fight with myself over whether I ought to pick up the phone and call Lila's number and have a long, intense, haranguing, re-charming, and ultimately forgiving talk; but in the nick of time I realize that this is an essentially hostile impulse despite its passionate feel. There are proper times for me to speak to her—daytime or early evening, in conjunction with plans or news about Jeff—and we've made use of those times. We've spoken on the phone.

"So how are you doing down there?"

"Oh, fine, fine."

And Jeff likes his new nursery school, and is at the "why?" stage of development—which, she assures me, I'm lucky not to be subjected to—and has found a friend on his block, and loves the hot summer.

After these conversations, I get upset that she's been cool and false and distant with me; but she hasn't been cool and false and distant, just routinely cordial and unrevealing, the way she might be with any office acquaintance. I used to be the person to whom she showed tones of voice, gestures, friskiness, fears, silliness, intensity, anger, that she didn't show to anyone else: I was the cherished audience for the exhibition of her free soul. Now a different man serves that purpose, and I'm grouped with everyone else.

I have the telephone numbers of new women, too. People give me the numbers of single or divorced women who like the arts. Rawley and my other contacts slip me these pieces of paper; even

Sharyn does, as if our date had somehow turned into a positive recommendation. And sometimes I see interesting women in stores or art galleries and I start a conversation and I ask them out.

I'm a socializing single man. I'm looking. They're looking. Invariably, eating dinner with one of these new women, each of us is looking past the other, at some apparition standing behind the chair. In bed, on top of her, I'm trying to plunge through into the arms and breasts and cunt of the apparition behind her; and her arms and legs are wrapped not around me but around the apparition sharing my place.

I fantasize that Lila and Forrest don't get along. Lila is lonely, disappointed. She wants to go back to New York. She still won't let me stay in her house when I visit Houston; I sleep in a motel.

In fact—yes, get this fantasy right—I rent a furnished apartment, where I can draw and do research and linger. Arising early in the morning while it's still cool, I stay in shape by jogging in a nearby park in the dawning Texas sun. And there's a pretty blonde, in a ponytail and bright blue shorts, whom I pass on the jogging trail almost every day. She's absorbed in Walkman music, but after crossing paths so often, we start to nod to each other, then smile, then say "Hi." She has a cute Texas accent, and speaks too loud because she's got earphones on. One morning I see her, in a gray scoop-necked tee shirt with the white of a bra strap showing and big oblongs of sweat going from her breasts to her waistband, as she takes a drink from a public water fountain, the earphones relaxing around her neck. "Hi!" I call out, trotting up behind her. She is glad to see me. She waits for me to take my drink. Our chins are both dripping water, which we laughingly dab on our bare arms. I ask her where she's going next, and she says "Just home"; and after no more than ten seconds of mutual verbal circling, she invites me to stop at her place for breakfast after my shower. Her name is Joal; she's a graduate student and loves museums. Meanwhile Lila is secretly longing for me to try to reconcile, so she can escape this Southwest frying pan; but I'm saying, "Gee, you know, I like Texas after all, and I don't really have to be in New York. I can just mail my stuff to Rawley. Why don't I move here and be close to Jeff? Have you met Joal? We're going to be living together . . ."

Even the apparition has an apparition behind her.

In most American families, the father is just propaganda issued by the mother. "Your father says . . . Your father is . . . Your father's going to . . . Just wait till your father comes . . . Your father and I want you to . . . Your father's tired, your father's angry, your father works hard, your father didn't mean it, your father meant, your father loves you children very much, don't bother your father . . ."

My son Jeff—well, we're physically separated now—but that kid knows me. I'm imprinted on him, goddamn it. I formed him at the earliest age. I was with him night and day. I made him. I'm on his case. He won't forget me. He can't get away from me that easily. I don't believe I'll always be physically separated from him—although it's part of the natural course of things that children do part from their parents as they get older. Even if Lila and I had stayed together, Jeff would be starting to grow more independent of us very soon.

But I'll be a clear image in his mind, at the times when he needs an inner voice to push him on or to help him solve a problem. If he gets homesick at summer camp someday, I believe he will write me as many letters as he writes his mother. If he ever runs away from home, he will have a place to run to. When he takes his first vacation from college, I believe he will visit me. And when he brings home the woman he wants to live with, I will take them out to the chic-est restaurant in town.

And his own shadow will be cast in my shape, and when he's a teenager he'll have to wrench me off his back so he can cast his own shadow in his own shape, and finally, when he's a man, he'll re-approach me, cautiously, grudgingly, then speeding up when he sees that *his* shadow falls on *me,* and he'll hug me for that.

You fear losing yourself to your son, and then you fear losing your son, and then you fear losing yourself if you *don't* lose yourself to your son.

But, finally, I don't think it's so terrible for a son to have as an example a father who did something hazardous and free, and suffered the consequences, and got back up again.

Lila would undoubtedly have some dry, pithy rejoinder to all this, and I would acknowledge her rightness, but then I would try to explain to her that despite it, I have to see things this way and go about things this way: that knowing the right answer from Step One is not necessarily the most fruitful procedure in this life, that stumbling and roaring through the vines and thorns may make you a wiser and truer person, that doing things your own stubborn way, even if it takes longer, is bound to enrich you, and that if you don't find the clearing at the beginning, you may hack one out of the underbrush for yourself anyway, just as useable. And she would shake her head briskly and say, No, that may sound fine but when people really act on it, it creates nothing but unhappiness.

I ran into Mike in the park the other day.

It was a sunny but humid August weekend and I was going for a walk. The temperature was in the mid-eighties and Prospect Park was full of families cooking barbecue: mostly black and Hispanic families, also some white ones. Poor families from more remote neighborhoods had loaded their grills and charcoal briquettes and lighter fluid and soda bottles and beer cans and corn on the cob and hamburger meat and rolls and relish and potato chips into shopping carts and pushed them all the way up the slope, past the high ground of the gentry, for the ancient pleasure of eating on grass. Balloons and streamers were hung from tree to tree to mark off each particular family's knoll or hollow. Flames licked up beside wooden picnic tables; huge metal radios played conga drum and sax. The warm breeze smelled like charcoal smoke and lighter fluid. I was walking through the long meadow, trying to stay clear of frisbees and softballs and an Irish setter, when I heard him call, "Hey, Brendan!"

Mike had stopped giving me weekly briefings with the detective, and so he was especially genial this time.

We approached each other, squinting, giving tense, one-cornered smiles, throwing back our shoulders and tightening our bellies. "How are you doing?" After a moment's hesitation we shook hands. There was a hint of wine on his breath. "Hi, Hilary," I said, and Hilary made a face and ran to wrap herself around her father's leg from behind.

"Oo, ow," he laughed, and gently pried her off his bad leg. "Go to Gina, honey, she'll play with you. I want to talk to Brendan for a second. Gina . . . ?" he called to the delicate-looking redhead who was ambling behind. He wig-wagged his finger to indicate that she should play with Hilary. Hilary, kicking the grass like an angry baseball manager, stalked back to Gina, and Gina said, "What should we play?" But they ended up just standing together on a dark green, clovered patch, backing away from bees.

"Throw me like a pizza!" Hilary said to Gina.

"No, I can't do that, your father can do that, ask him later."

"She's nice," Mike said to me in an undertone that was meant for Gina to hear. She turned away, trying to look as if she hadn't heard it. Then in an undertone Gina *wasn't* supposed to hear, he told me: "I'm thinking of firing this detective. He's not getting anywhere. Keeps telling me he's making progress, but I haven't seen one concrete thing. If she wants to come back, she'll come back. I mean, I'm a very successful businessman, but I'm not gonna keep paying his expenses for the rest of my life."

I nodded, and ground the toe of my running shoe into the sand of the meadow's central strip. "I think you're right." I looked up at the sun, then down at a troop of brown ants crawling over the sand grains and the white pebbles and the black chunks of obsidian.

"Anyway"—he gave a big, theatrical shrug—"I got a new lady now, you know what I mean, I'm putting divorce papers through. You got yours yet?"

"It's in the works."

"Yeah, you see what I mean. I feel for Maggie, you know? I

255

hope for the best for her, I consider her as a wonderful person."

"Yes."

"Here, let me introduce you. Gina!" He waved her over. "Come here, this is my friend Brendan, we know each other from—"

"From the war," I said.

"From school," he laughed. "Brendan, Gina. Gina started out as a client of mine, but she keeps up the way she's goin', I'm gonna have to start working for her for free."

We all laughed. Gina seemed shy about it. "Hi," I said.

"Nice to meet you," she said. We shook hands. So this was the brownstone widow. Maggie, who of course had not seen her either, had given me a different impression: of someone big and loud and busty, a saloon hostess type with dyed copper hair. Gina, instead, was another slightly built one, though taller than Maggie and willowier, her light red hair verging on blond, with freckles across her small nose, and blue eyes that darted self-protectively toward the distractions of every clover flower, every starling, every spinning maple seed. She wore a man-tailored white shirt with the sleeves rolled up and the tails out and sharp collarbone points visible in the neck opening, and faded blue jeans, and sandals that showed slim, pretty feet.

"I want Gina to throw me like a pizza," Hilary said.

Gina tried to smile. "I'm new at this."

"It's okay, it's okay," Mike said. And he bent down to Hilary and said in a mock-scolding voice: "Who throws you like a pizza? Huh? Who?"

Hilary giggled.

"Who throws you? Come here, I want to throw you," he said, and swooped down to grab her. Giggling, she twisted away from his grasp, but ran in circles so that he was sure to catch her very soon. He got her under the arms and lifted her up to his face, his big, hard hands covering most of her torso. "What are you today, pepperoni?"

"No, green pepper."

"Okay, my green pepper, I'm gonna make pizza out of you."

And he tossed her into the air, higher than I would have dared to toss a child, and I glanced at Gina and saw her bite her lip as she tried to smile un-nervously. He caught Hilary, and said, "Up you go, you lump of dough!" which made her laugh a lot as he tossed her again, and he caught her again with no problem. It was a game they had practiced, and he threw her and caught her, threw her and caught her, and I looked up at the little girl shadowed against the blue sky, with the white vapor trail of a jet plane behind her and the sounds of ballplayers around us, her arms spread wide to fly, laughing with fear and delight as she fell into the grasp of her father.